The Cadillac Cowboy

The Cadillac Cowboy

A Novel By

Michael Collins

DONALD I. FINE, INC.

New York

To Brian and Bina
friends, colleagues, poker players

Prologue

Ralph Baliol was the sixteenth Ralph to be born into the Baliol dynasty on this side of the Atlantic, the son of railroad tycoon John Marshall Baliol's old age and fifth wife.

The Baliols were an ancient family. They began back in the tenth century in the part of France that became Normandy, when a freebooting Viking chief who sailed up the Seine with Rolf the Ganger to besiege Paris couldn't resist a French lady too proud to be seduced and too important for the Viking to even think about the usual rape. Of course, the Viking thought about rape anyway, but after a serious man-to-man talk with Duke Rolf himself, who needed the good will and muscle of the French lady's father, the Viking decided he had really always wanted to marry the lady after all.

The marriage ended a few years later when the Viking found a more pliant French lady who could be seduced or raped. His wife sent for her brothers to kill the Viking and his new lady in bed with battleaxes. But this ill-fated marriage had lasted long enough to leave an heir, one of whose descendants helped conquer England with Duke William and initiated a long line of Anglo-Norman barons who prospered in England and Scotland. These Baliol barons produced at least one claimant to the throne of Scotland and eventually the last American railroad tycoon to rival Hill or Harriman or Stanford—old John Marshall Baliol V.

Less than two years before the old man died Ralph appeared somewhat unexpectedly and, despite the lack of fatherly advice or example, grew up very much in the mold of John Marshall himself, a true descendent of that ancient Viking chief who had grabbed a nice chunk of Normandy when the French bought off Rolf and his

1

boys with real estate and a dukedom. But being the last of many children and therefore late to the grab bag, Ralph got little after prep school and Yale except a few million dollars and a marine corps commission.

The marines suited Ralph. He did two tours in Vietnam in the sixties, won a Distinguished Service Cross for heroism under fire, and traded in some Laotian opium for a nice profit. Ralph liked the war. He liked the sense of power every time he saw fear in the eyes of even friendly villagers, the thrill of triumph when he killed an enemy. He liked leading men into battle, he liked wheeling and dealing with few rules but his own—and the brass liked him. They showed a strong interest in his future, spoke in glowing terms of all he could accomplish for his country and the personal rewards of career military service. Ralph had more lucrative plans, saw far more opportunity to prosper in the civilian sector.

Heeding the horn call of his former Yale classmate, Fletcher Comrie, he hustled home after his second and final tour to join an old Wall Street brokerage firm where Comrie, who had seen no advantage in going off to war, had rapidly moved up. Ralph did well on Wall Street, quickly gained the necessary inside knowledge and marketplace experience, made the right contacts, and acquired the needed backing and credit to go out on his own. With a minimum of personal cash he bought a small management and investment company and set sail on the stormy seas of business.

Fletcher Comrie remained in the brokerage firm to become vice-president and partner. Together, he and Ralph wheeled and dealed through the dirty seventies and glorious eighties, acquiring and divesting, merging and spinning off, raiding and leveraging. They were a formidable team: Ralph Baliol found the prime companies to take over, and Fletcher Comrie supplied the river of cash through the brokerage's junk-bond empire. Out on the legal edge they cut a swath into the nineties, built empires, and left the financial landscape scorched behind them. The boy raiders of Wall Street, their older and more cautious colleagues called them. Financial Vikings forever sailing in search of solid assets and fat pension funds to conquer and rule.

But as the real old Vikings had learned, rivals return, victims rise from the ashes, and the enemy must be constantly reconquered. The nineties brought to the Wall Street wars the inevitable swing of the pendulum. In the white light of insider scandals, the collapse of the deregulation and risky investment binges of the eighties, Comrie's empire fell like the chimera it was. It turned out, of course, that wheeling and dealing on the legal edge hadn't been enough for Comrie. He'd sailed over that edge on more than one occasion, and ended under federal indictment.

Ralph Baliol's kingdom teetered. He was forced to sell off marginal holdings and shrink his company, but he slipped out from under serious trouble—until he was shot one sunny morning on the deck of his own Montecito mansion, his only son was arrested for the crime, and his former wife sent an urgent command to her third husband: *Come to Santa Barbara.*

PART I

Unfinished Business

1

The summons reached Langford Morgan in a village high in the green, cloud-covered mountains of Costa Rica's Cordillera Central. *Johnny arrested for attempted murder of his father. Utter nonsense. Need you immediately in Santa Barbara. Rachel.*

Despite the memories they brought of the highland jungles of Southeast Asia, or perhaps because of those memories, Morgan sometimes needed the solitude of the mountains and the cloud forest, often when he least expected it. Long weeks in the forest and clouds with people from a different universe. A need to drink with people who understood the need to drink. People who expected nothing from him but his companionship of the moment. He did not need the summons of an ex-wife he hadn't seen or heard from in five years.

At forty-six, Morgan still ran ten miles a day. Some days, if the mood was on him, he ran twenty miles. And when Rachel's message came his first impulse was to run. Ten, twenty miles along the narrow trails through the towering green solitude of the cloud jungle. He hated the outside world to intrude on his time in the mountains. So he ran, and when he finally returned to the village he tore up the message and scattered it to the clouds below, took a bottle of *guaro* from his backpack, and joined the villagers at their fires.

But later, around the fire with the bottles of *guaro* and the good companions who spoke no English, he began to see his ex-wife's summons in a different light. He realized he had no bad memories of Rachel. The end of their marriage had not been all her fault. He'd been too busy with his own problems in those years, away from her far too much. Now as the night wore on and the fire burned down to hot coals he found himself wondering if they had blown it back then, he and Rachel, never given it a chance. The prospect of a trip back to the States after five years seemed more attractive. Perhaps he owed it to Rachel. Maybe even to himself.

By the time dawn broke over the peaks and clouds Ford Morgan had decided that Rachel was unfinished business, and that something should be done about unfinished business.

Lareina said, "She whistle, this Rachel the ex-wife, and you run fast down the mountain, *sí, yanqui?*"

Lareina Clachar Alvaro was an actress, the only daughter of Don Emilio Clachar Alvaro, and Ford Morgan's lady of the last two years. Born on the family *finca* in the north of Costa Rica and educated at Bryn Mawr, she could speak English nearly as well as Morgan, but liked to play the unsophisticated *tica* with the charming broken English.

"Rachel," Morgan said, "is a Winrod. The Winrods are descended from the gods. Wodin, to be exact. They go back to eleventh-century England, and they don't let much stand in their way. Rachel would be down here after me in person next, believe me. It'll be easier to go up and see what she wants. After all, I suppose I did help to raise Johnny."

Lareina was not impressed. The Clachars and Alvaros had been in Costa Rica for over three hundred years, and had been rich and in power most of that time. She knew about baronial ancestors who got what they wanted, and her English had a way of improving dramatically when she was annoyed with Morgan.

"You have seen this Johnny Baliol four times in your entire life, Ford Morgan. Or that's what you told me. He was at college or in California with his father the two years you were married to this Rachel person. So now you must charge to the rescue when she whistles?"

They were in the living room of Morgan's hilltop house with its sweeping view of San José and the Meseta Central. After a lengthy and intense welcome home in the bedroom, when there had been no mention of Rachel Winrod or her whistle from far off, they were relaxing in the humid heat of a day that had not yet rained. They wore nothing except the cold rum coolers in their hands. (Rum coolers without rum—as part of her *tica* image, Lareina favored the native *guaro*, and had taught Morgan to do the same.)

"We will charge to the rescue," Morgan grinned. "Think of dry days and cool nights, good wine and secluded hideaways, shopping on Rodeo Drive. Beverly Hills, Hollywood, even New York if we stay past summer. We'll make it a vacation. I'll help Rachel with Johnny. After that we do La-La Land, then go on to New York for the theater."

Lareina stretched her long legs toward the wide picture window that formed the outer wall of the room and watched San José spread out below under dark clouds as the evening rain approached. The capital of the country Morgan had called home for five years, San José was a lively city but undistinguished, the plain sister, neither colonial nor modern, with nothing spectacular about it. Low, dull buildings with red corrugated-tin roofs all built in the last century, and new white-and-glass office towers.

"I have the many friends in Hollywood," Lareina considered, again putting on her accent. "In New York also. A vacation? Why not? Perhaps I get a very fine job in a big *yanqui* movie. And I am mad for the shops on Rodeo Drive. I live to shop, *sí?"*

She grinned at him over the *guaro* cooler that rested on her pale belly in the darkening room. It always surprised Morgan how much paler her skin was than his. She was Latin, he was Welsh—it was supposed to be reversed. Pale Welshmen and dark Latins. But there was a gypsy or two hidden in the branches of the Morgan family tree, and Lareina was Costa Rican. In this country of unconquerable Indians, native and Spanish had mixed far less than elsewhere in Latin America.

"Then start packing, *tica,* we'll leave tomorrow."

"Do not be so very eager, or I could think you are not telling me your real reasons to fly to the rescue of your Rachel. I will need a few days."

"Okay, take all the time you need. I don't expect Johnny Baliol will be going anywhere for a while."

Morgan had no need to risk her patience or jeopardize the easy relationship they had maintained for nearly two years. They were comfortable together and with their own lifestyles. He leaned his head against her naked shoulder and watched the darkening sky and oncoming rain outside the window. A few days would make no difference, since his interest in Santa Barbara had little or nothing to do with Johnny Baliol or his wounded father. Lareina could have all the time she wanted.

As for Morgan, once he had persuaded Lareina that the trip would be fun, there was little else he needed to do before they went. His import-export business ran itself. It was really only an excuse to live in Costa Rica with a plausible explanation of how he could afford his expensive lifestyle. That could be a touchy matter for a foreigner in Costa Rica, caught as it was between the intrigues and paranoias of larger nations north and south. And he had needed something to do when he wasn't up in the *cordillera* villages or hiking the cloud forest besides drinking and playing with Lareina and the women who preceded her.

As the rain clouds darkened over the central valley, he sipped his *guaro* cooler, played lightly with Lareina's bare thigh, and thought about Rachel Winrod and unfinished business. He had been the third of her four husbands: Rachel Winrod Baliol Senlac Morgan Wallman. She was his first attempt at any kind of a permanent relationship since a long forgotten wife of his early twenties and, as far as he knew, he was her only fling on the wild side with someone not from her background. Two years that had not been his best years. The years he'd finally parted from the CIA and everything else that had gone with it. Except, of course, the money.

Morgan closed his eyes and listened to the rain that finally began to hammer on the roof. For the first time in the five years he'd been in Costa Rica he felt a sense of excitement when he thought of returning to the States.

2

Rachel Winrod Wallman, tall, blonde, and elegant in a white summer dress, paced on the terrace of her borrowed beachfront house. Surrounded by the trees and seclusion of Fernald Point, in the exclusive Santa Barbara enclave of Montecito, the terrace was built of old brick and ringed with potted geraniums and thickly flowered climbing trumpet and bougainvillea vines. Surf broke on the beach less than a hundred feet away, and the view seemed to stretch all the way from Alaska to Japan.

"I don't do well with a husband who's somewhere else, Ford," Rachel said. "You were always running off to some goddamn country with jungles, for God's sake."

Rich and powerful people rarely pay if they can trade or borrow, and the house was Rachel's for as long as the owner was in Europe. The August day was sunny and warm, but compared to Costa Rica it felt as dry as a desert. The perfume of the flowering vines and exotic trees mixed with the salt and seaweed scent of the ocean. Stretched out, Morgan lounged on a redwood chaise and watched the surf. Pernod frappes and trays of hors d'oeuvres were supplied periodically by the silent Mexican woman who had come with the house.

Morgan was carefully dressed in proper gray slacks, an open-necked dress shirt, and navy blazer, the Akubra stockman's hat he'd taken to wearing in the sun of Costa Rica, and his cordovan high-heeled Western boots. He had come to talk about unfinished business between him and Rachel, and had dressed appropriately. Slacks, shirt, and blazer because they were what Rachel would expect a man interested in her to wear, the hat to show some dashing individuality, and the boots because she was a tall woman. But so

11

far Rachel hadn't sat down, or looked at Morgan long enough to notice his clothes, not even when he'd smiled and asked her directly why they had broken up five years ago.

"I suppose in the end I want too much attention, Ford."

She paced the worn bricks, and her voice was distracted, aloof with the arrogance and self-absorption of the Winrods. Her mind was not on any possible unfinished business between them. Morgan drank his Pernod and observed her as she stopped pacing and looked out toward the late afternoon sea. He could see the tiny marks on her neck and temples that showed the hands of the surgeon. In an era when appearance was more important than substance, the successful paid attention to how they looked more than to what they did. Celebrity meant image before accomplishment. But even without the surgical lifts and tucks, by all the old rules of age Rachel still looked a full decade younger than her forty-seven years. Except that the rules hadn't applied for a long time in upper and middle America and Europe. Those were rules made for a different time when life was harder and shorter for everyone.

"And all this time," Morgan said, "I've been thinking it was because I wasn't rich or important enough for you when the fling on the wild side lost interest."

She turned to look at him. "Why, Ford Morgan, have you been thinking about me? That's sweet. And I seem to recall you had plenty of money, although I did have the impression it tended to be high risk."

"But you never asked about the risk, or where the money came from."

"No, I expect I didn't." She finally sat down, crossed her legs, and smiled at Morgan with considerably less detachment. "It really wasn't important, Ford."

"What was important, Rach?"

She leaned back in the redwood patio chair, her blue eyes darker in the lowering afternoon sun. Her body relaxed under the white dress, and her mouth softened. "What was important was that you be there when I wanted you. You were away so much in those backwater countries God knows where down south. You even wanted me to move to some miserable village with mud huts or whatever they have down there in Costa Rica. Do you remember that? Can you see me actually *living* in such an outlandish place?"

Morgan laughed. "It's not that primitive, Rach. Costa Rica is a civilized country, probably with more of the old-fashioned aristocratic values you like than up here these days. Landowners who go back to the hidalgos of old Spain live on *fincas* with fifty thousand acres and two-hundred-year-old haciendas. Private jets, servants, peasants, all the privileges. Hardly any Indians at all. Indoor plumbing, the works.''

She lay back with her blonde hair spread out against the redwood, her long legs crossed at the ankles, and looked up at the high August sky. "Perhaps neither of us really tried all that hard to give it a chance. You seemed preoccupied so much. I often wondered what was on your mind, but you never said, and I suppose I wasn't used to your kind of life. It was too wide open, too precarious. I need to know that what I want and need will always be there.''

"Security and control, Rach?''

She smiled. "Probably. Up to a point.''

"What point?''

"Ah, now you have to figure that out, don't you? I'm not the man.''

Morgan felt the attraction her summons had brought back to him around the village fire high in the Costa Rican cloud forest. A palpable aura of heat from her smile that was warmer than the August sun. In the redwood chair, she still stared up at the sky as her eyes became speculative. "Two years. That wasn't very long, was it, Ford? We hadn't even acquired anything to fight over at the divorce. You were the perfect gentleman. Giving me the Central Park South penthouse, disappearing down to your Costa Rica.''

"It seemed like a good idea at the time.''

She continued to stare up at the high blue August sky while Morgan watched her in silence. Then, abruptly, she pulled back her legs and sat up in the chair as the silent Mexican maid who went with the borrowed house replenished their Pernod frappes and the hors d'oeuvres tray. When the maid left again, Rachel leaned forward, and her voice filled with the outrage and godlike anger of the ancient Winrods. "Johnny would not kill his father or anyone else! That kind of violence is simply beyond him. You understand that, Ford?''

"If you say so, Rach.''

"If someone tried to murder Ralph, it wasn't Johnny. He's immature and self-indulgent, yes. The result of a mother who was far too young, an imperious father, and the war between them ever since.

But he's basically a good boy, and he gets along well with Ralph. He would not shoot Ralph, and I want you to tell that to the Keystone Cops of this backwater town."

"I don't think the police are going to listen to me just like that."

"Then find proof. Evidence that Johnny couldn't have done it. I wouldn't put it past Ralph to have arranged the whole damn thing, for God's sake."

"Why not hire a detective?" Morgan said.

"When I have my very own? Don't be silly."

"I'm not a detective, Rach."

"Oh, CIA, intelligence, whatever. You know how to ask questions and make people answer. You can find out things people don't want you to find out. I want someone on Johnny's side who can end all this foolishness."

"Why do the police think Johnny shot his father?"

Rachel stood again, walked across the terrace in sunlight that was turning to a pale gold as the evening approached. She opened a black stone box, took out a cigarette. "They say his girlfriend Anne Neville and Ralph were screwing around. I don't put anything past Ralph, not even stealing his son's girlfriend, but Johnny isn't capable of caring that much about a girlfriend or anyone else, Ford, or of the anger and decision necessary to harm a fly."

Morgan knew little about Johnny Baliol, and cared less. He remembered him as an arrogant college boy who drank too much and was sullen when he came to New York to visit his mother in those days. But he felt vaguely sorry for any son whose mother had such a low opinion of his character.

"What makes the police think your ex-husband and this Anne Neville were playing house?"

Rachel smoked and watched the sun set to the west at the edge of the bluffs over the sea. "Anne was there in Ralph's bedroom the morning he was shot."

"She'd been there all night?"

"I suppose so."

Morgan tried not to look too amused. "Well, I'd say the police have a point about a possible motive then."

She glared at him, then glared out to sea without answering.

"What else do they have against Johnny?" Morgan said.

She continued to look out across the beach and the surf toward the oil rigs and the darkening horizon. "He was angry, he's admitted that, and he bought a pistol a few months ago. It was for Anne, for God's sake, but she doesn't know where it is and neither does Johnny. The police say it shoots the same size bullets they dug out of Ralph, whatever they call that."

"Caliber," Morgan said. "The police didn't find the gun that shot Ralph?"

"So they say."

"What does Johnny say, Rach? Where was he when all this was happening?"

"He says he was driving around alone all night over in the valley. In the morning he went to the mansion to confront Anne and Ralph." Rachel flicked her cigarette in a high arc into the garden beyond the terrace. Morgan recalled her doing that in their New York penthouse where the stub trailed sparks like a comet as it fell to the street and pedestrians below. "That's where the police found him."

"Found him? You mean at his father's mansion? When? That morning? When his father was—?"

"After Ralph was shot, yes." She took another cigarette from the obsidian box. "They found Johnny hiding on the grounds. But he had no gun, and they didn't find a gun anywhere on the estate." She lit the cigarette, turned to face Morgan. "And when they do, Ford, it won't be the gun Johnny bought and Anne claims to have misplaced."

Underneath some anger and contempt for this Anne Neville, Morgan heard simple certainty. Not the violent certainty of someone who isn't at all sure, but the total conviction that comes from absolute, real knowledge. Johnny had not shot his father. Rachel had no doubt at all. Which raised the question in Morgan's mind of why she had sent for him in the first place.

"So who *did* shoot Baliol?"

She waved the cigarette. "You don't have a notebook large enough to hold the names of every man, woman, child, or animal who might have wanted to kill Ralph. Since our very long-ago divorce he's never remarried, chases any woman in sight—single, engaged, or otherwise. Ralph is a shit, Ford. He respects no one but himself, uses anyone he can."

"Even Johnny?"

"Especially Johnny. To Ralph a son is a rival."

"Why the hell did you marry this guy in the first place, Rach?"

"My salad days, when I was green in judgment." She blew a harsh stream of smoke into the evening sunlight and the sound of the surf. "I was a child. He was strong, determined, handsome, rich, and getting richer. He was going far at whatever he wanted to do. My father said he was the one man among my suitors who was on the right path. What I didn't know was that Ralph has no room for anyone else with him on that path, except for momentary needs as the whim strikes him."

Morgan grinned. "Sounds like a sweetheart. If I'd known him, I might have considered shooting him myself. So you're sure Johnny didn't take a potshot at dear old Dad. In that case, the police'll straighten it all out sooner or later, Rach. You don't need me to—"

"Sooner or later's not good enough, Ford. They have Johnny sitting in a jail cell, for God's sake." She flicked her second cigarette out onto the sand of the beach in the orange twilight. "I've got this damned dreary dinner party to go to, Ford. Why don't you come with me? We could talk more later."

"I'll pass tonight." He had let her see what was on his mind, it was better to let her think about it for a day. And Lareina would not take kindly to eating dinner alone in a strange city. "Let's make it dinner tomorrow, just the two of us."

Rachel nodded. "Tomorrow it is." She sat once more on the red-wood chair, leaned toward Morgan. "The police know Johnny wasn't home all that night, and they know that was unusual. They don't believe his story of where he was, and neither do I. He was probably carousing, slept over somewhere, and doesn't remember where. But I want to know for sure. It could exonerate the stupid boy, for God's sake. I want you to find out where he was and what he was doing."

"I'll do what I can, Rach." He stood. "Why don't I come by tomorrow evening and tell you what I've found out over a drink or two. Then we can go and eat somewhere nice."

She smiled. "What a fine idea, Ford. I think I'd like that."

3

Morgan and Lareina had checked into the San Ysidro Ranch, the elite hotel of Santa Barbara. Class and taste instead of glitter and high-tech. At the ranch, you felt privileged and superior without having to fly to St. Moritz or some private compound in Jamaica. The lodging, food, and drink were of the highest quality, but the true elegance was in the secluded cottages. In a cottage you never had to talk to or even see another guest. You lodged in splendor and isolated luxury. Since the last century kings, princes, presidents, and other, more important people had stayed in the cottages hidden on the wooded grounds. Morgan had reserved the most isolated cottage, complete with living room, dining room, fireplace, kitchen, deck, and redwood hot tub. Lareina would expect no less.

After leaving Rachel he joined Lareina for rum coolers in the Plow and Angel bar below the dining room.

"She was as you remember her, *yanqui?*"

"Still a Winrod, Reina. I think my role is to light a fire under the police by my powerful presence and CIA connections."

"You think?"

"Knowing exactly what Rachel wants isn't simple. But what I do know is that she really believes Johnny's innocent."

"So? Then why does she then send for you, eh?"

"Probably to pressure the police into at least letting the boy out of jail."

Lareina sipped her rum cooler thoughtfully. "You will go again to your Rachel tomorrow, *yanqui?* Be the detective?"

"I suppose so."

"And you will be busy all day with the questions and the deductions?"

"Probably for the next few days."

"Then I will drive on the freeway to Beverly Hills to be with my friends. Shopping and parties, *sí*? You will be sorry." She held her drink up in front of her face like a crystal ball and looked deeply into it. "I think maybe you have more than the call of help with your ex Rachel, *yanqui.*"

"I'm wounded to the heart."

"It is all right. The Rachel Winrods are not when I worry."

"When do you worry, Reina?"

"I will let you know."

They had their dinner sent to the cottage. Morgan ordered a good Corton Renardes, and in the cottage dining room the red wine and white tablecloth reflected the candlelight. They ate and drank the wine and listened to the sounds of the night outside the cottage. Natural sounds, animal and mineral and plant. A trickle of water, the rustle of leaves and soft scurry of small feet. The only human intrusion was low laughter somewhere out in the cool August night, Morgan's hand that poured the wine, and their smiles as they watched each other over their glasses. They had an appreciation of each other, a pure pleasure that had few demands. There was never any hurry when they were together, nowhere they had to go or be other than where they were. When they each felt it was time, they left the table to go into the bedroom.

In the morning, as always, Morgan was up with the dawn. He ran five miles into the foothills along Mountain Drive and returned to find Lareina dressed, packed, and ready for breakfast. After a shower he put on jeans, a Guatemalan shirt, his most battered Australian hat, and his everyday boots. They had breakfast alone in the cottage, and Morgan carried her bags out to Lareina's rented BMW. He stood in front of the cottage until she had disappeared with a wave down the curving drive toward San Ysidro Road and the freeway.

He knew he wasn't fooling her for a second. She was giving him the space to do what he had come to Santa Barbara to do, to find out what he had come to find out. To give them both space and time to find out what they were going to do, here or in Costa Rica. And as Morgan went back into the cottage before going to play detective for Rachel, he suddenly felt not quite sure what it was he had come to Santa Barbara to find out.

He drove from Montecito into downtown Santa Barbara, enjoying the sweep of the city with its masses of trees. Flowers and red tile roofs and fifty varieties of eucalyptus rose up the steep slopes of the foothills. On a corridor between sea and mountains, Santa Barbara looked and smelled much like San José. Santa Barbara had the sea and the climate, but Morgan preferred the attitudes and priorities of San José, where love, eating, and drinking were the first three pastimes—and where everyone could afford to eat and get drunk as well as make love.

Over the next two hours in the periodical room of the public library, Morgan read every news report of the shooting of Ralph Baliol. The call to the sheriff's office had come in from a Gerald Kirsch at 8:59 A.M. on a Saturday two weeks ago. Deputies and paramedics arrived at 9:09 to find Ralph Baliol on an outdoor chaise, a private doctor working over him, Anne Neville distraught, and the chauffeur, Massimo Mancuso, crashing, gun in hand, through the dense trees and chaparral in search of whomever had shot Baliol.

Crash, curse, trample, swear.

"He usually swims alone in the morning," Gerald Kirsch tells the deputies. "Then he lies in the sun until he's dry. I was bringing the morning's faxes out to him when—"

Anne Neville knelt over the fallen man, "My God, he's been shot! Ralph? Say something! Ralph . . ."

"Sir, you shouldn't have moved him or—"

"So he could die in the proper place for your investigation, you idiots? I am Dr. Matthew Moran, I live next door. I am a friend of Mr. Baliol, and Gerald properly called me at once instead of waiting who knows how long for you people to arrive! Now, shall we stop being asses and get him to the hospital?"

Crash, curse, shout. "I've got the son of a bitch!"

The two bullets in Ralph Baliol had missed everything vital but were still nasty. Two more bullets were found in the wooden fencing of the deck. Dr. Matthew Moran had stabilized Baliol before the paramedics arrived, and insisted they take him to a private suite in Cottage Hospital. Dr. Moran took the bullets out with a coroner's doctor assisting. Baliol was unconscious or under sedation and on intravenous feeding for five days. He was still in the hospital.

The "son of a bitch" Mancuso had dragged out of the trees was Johnny Baliol. When they found a motive in the relationship between Anne Neville and Ralph, and he couldn't satisfactorily account for the missing gun or where he had been that night, they arrested Johnny for the attempted murder of his father.

A call to Cottage Hospital arranged a visit with Ralph Baliol. The wounded ex-husband of Rachel was as curious about Morgan as Morgan was about him. Morgan identified himself to the deputy guarding the door of the private suite. Ralph Baliol studied him as he came in, and Morgan realized Baliol knew all about him.

"How is our ex-wife?" Baliol said.

"Angry."

"I can believe that," Baliol laughed.

His laugh was strong, pleasant—and artificial. Behind the big, empty laugh he continued to study Morgan, comparing his own assessment with the reports he'd had from his sources. Morgan, who knew about artificial public faces, smiled and admired the array of business machines that filled the room.

"Business as usual even in the hospital?"

The room had been turned into an office. There was a laptop computer, fax, speakerphone, modem, plain paper copier, and closed-circuit TV to his main office in Silicon Valley. In bed in the center of all this, Ralph Baliol was pale and drawn under his California tan, and his dark graying hair was a shade long for most offices. For a man who probably had his hair cut once a week, the length was a mark of individuality and power. His handsome face was oval and full, with a large, thin mouth and a strong nose. His hands, folded on the lap of a black robe where he lay propped up, were small for his six-foot-two, two-hundred-pound frame. The same height as Morgan, a few pounds heavier and a few years older.

"You couldn't begin to imagine how much had to be put on hold the six days I was too weak to even sign a paper, or how damn much money was lost."

"I suppose I could if I tried really hard," Morgan said.

"Okay, right, you run a business too, don't you? In Costa Rica or somewhere. It must do very well. Rachel doesn't marry poor men."

"I'm not poor."

"All from import-export?"

"You could say that. Making money isn't all that hard with the right conditions. Mine sort of fell into my lap, came with the work and the territory."

Ralph Baliol wasn't pleased with that view. "I'd say making money wasn't easy at all in this day and age. You have to keep on top of your business and ahead of all the goddamn pissant dogs yapping at your heels from governments on down."

Morgan said, "Why do you believe your son shot you?"

Baliol folded his hands on his lap. "I don't believe my son shot me, the police do."

"But why do you believe it even could have been Johnny?"

"He was there."

"And shot you because of Anne Neville?"

"That part's hogwash. Johnny doesn't give a damn about Anne."

"Then why would he shoot you? Wouldn't a more obvious enemy be more logical? Someone with something more tangible to gain?"

"Probably. I'm sure I have many enemies. But the police don't appear to have found anyone else so far. Maybe it's like Henry the Second. His sons just wanted to take his place."

"It makes you feel proud to have a lot of enemies?"

Baliol shrugged, and grimaced with the pain the movement stabbed through his shoulder. He shifted his weight gingerly to get more comfortable. "In a way I suppose it does. If you play the game hard, you're going to make enemies. If you don't have enemies, it usually means you're not playing hard enough. Only the weak and the losers want to go through life without making enemies. Our ancestors wouldn't have survived if they were afraid of making enemies. And I'm sure there are people who wouldn't mind seeing me dead. The trouble is I can't think of anyone who'd actually do it. We don't have the iron for using murder as a tool of business anymore."

"I think our businessmen have more than enough iron if they really need someone removed."

"Then let's say I can't think of anyone who needs me removed that much, and Johnny was there for some reason."

"How about someone who hates you personally?"

"I've never bothered with that sort of thing. There isn't much to be gained by worrying about people who don't like you."

"You didn't get any look at the shooter?"

"Look, Morgan, I was standing up to turn over and this train knocked me down and out. I saw and heard nothing."

"No sound of an approach through all that thick brush? Is Johnny a hunter or hiker now, maybe a camper?"

Baliol laughed his artificial laugh. "I don't think Johnny ever hunted anything except girls and fun. The only places he camps is where the Maserati can be parked out front."

Ralph Baliol puzzled Morgan. He seemed to be taking the attempt on his life as nothing particularly important. Certainly nothing to worry about. Morgan had been shot at more than once over the years, he had taken none of those times lightly. The only people he'd seen who dealt easily with possible death were psychotics or people who were on the edge of being psychotic, and old warriors who knew what had to be done and accepted the risks. Baliol didn't seem to fit either description.

"You're not worried about all this?"

"I can handle it."

"How about your son? You're not worried about him?"

"When the police tell me Johnny did it for sure, I'll worry about him. Life doesn't wait for anyone to sit around being worried. It ruins today and won't stop tomorrow."

"Depends what you mean by life."

"*My* life," Baliol said. "I don't care about whatever *you* mean by life."

He never would care what Morgan or anyone else might mean by life. Or even what definitions other than his own there were.

"Can I take a look at where it happened?"

"I'll call my assistant and tell him you're coming."

The same odd sense of unconcern. Not worried about Morgan finding anything at his mansion, or, what was very different, unconcerned about anything Morgan *might* find.

Anne Neville's house was old Montecito. Under dusty oaks far back from a rural road near the sea, its white walls had the patina of years. The red-tiled roof had darkened and acquired a coating of moss from the morning fogs, and the wooden beams had split and blackened. All the windows had the iron bars the *hidalgo*s had favored as protection against hungry Indians, landless marauders, and their daughters' more ardent admirers.

Blonde and tanned, she stood in her doorway. "Morgan, right? Rachel's detective. Ralph said you'd show up."

"I'm not a detective, and the name is Ford."

"If you're not a detective, what are you?"

"Rachel's third husband. The closest thing to a detective she could get without paying for one."

Anne Neville laughed. "Come on in."

She walked ahead of Morgan along a low-ceilinged hallway into a large living room under a cathedral ceiling of dark brown beams. The walls were white, and the floor brown saltillo tiles. All the furniture was distressed pine, and the walls were hung with rows of native baskets from across the Americas.

"You like my Indian baskets? I collect things. The pine furniture too. When I find something I like, I want everything like it."

She pointed Morgan to a pine armchair with beige leather cushions as soft as cream, and sat on the matching couch. Her blonde hair was drawn back in an adolescent ponytail. It didn't suit her, made her long face show what Morgan decided were thirty or so years. No one had mentioned she was older than Johnny Baliol. A green silk shirt with a wide black belt and trim gray slacks fitted well on her sleek shape. African beads hung at her throat. She probably collected African crafts.

"You think Johnny shot his father because of you, Anne?"

"Not over me. He doesn't really care that much about me. We're used to each other, we live in the same world."

In what was a privileged and all-but-closed world, there was always another pretty face to display at parties, another set of broad shoulders and growing career to dance with, to hop into bed with. Love and passion were usually reserved for more important concerns like money, property, and status.

"Why else would he want to kill his father?" Morgan asked.

She shrugged. "Maybe they had a fight."

"Do you or Johnny know of any business trouble Ralph has?"

"I don't know anything about Ralph's business, and Johnny knows less."

Morgan remembered an old *padrone* in Guatemala who invited

him and the other CIA advisers to dinner at his *finca* any time they
felt the need to relax after a grueling week training the elite *kaibiles*
and paratroops in anti-guerilla operations and area-pacification
techniques. Sometimes the old Don's youngest son was home on a
visit from Vail, where he skied when he wasn't in Las Vegas gambling. While the Americans drank and ate, and his father related
the history of the enormous plantation and its operations, the son
watched television or left early to fly to Guatemala City for a night
of dancing and whoring with other local sons who had no more
interest in their fathers' businesses than he did.

Johnny had told her nothing about where he had been the night
before. She dismissed any idea of another woman. Johnny liked life
easy, no complications. His car, his clothes, his condo, his drinks
out on the town Friday night with whatever friends he ran into. He
would never look for another woman when he already had a per-
fectly serviceable one. She had no idea where the gun he had given
her was. She kept it in her bedroom, but carried it in her purse if
she expected to come home late. Since she wasn't coming home
that night, she hadn't taken the gun. It was missing when the police came to look, and she realized she hadn't looked at the gun in
weeks, had been too busy with Ralph and wondering how to tell
Johnny about her and his father.

"What did you tell him?"

"That I love his father, and his father loves me."

"Marriage?"

"Why not?"

Morgan was going to say because one bout with marriage seemed
to have been more than enough for Ralph Baliol, when the sudden
sound of metal striking wood echoed through the house.

Glass crashed and broke.

"It's my bedroom! At the end of the hall!"

The door at the end of the hall was closed. Morgan pushed it
open and saw a large bedroom in total disarray. Shards of a glass
vase lay on the tile floor. The french doors at the far side were still
swinging. Outside, he saw the man running away through the
trees. A short, thick man in a baseball cap, gray work shirt, dark
corduroy trousers, and heavy boots. A running man with a big
automatic in his right hand and a piece of paper in his left.

Morgan went after him. The stocky man turned and raised his
gun hand. The automatic pointed straight at Morgan. The eyes of

the stocky man looked straight at Morgan. *The man stood in the jungle shadows and looked straight at him over the barrel of the AK– 47 . . .*

Medic, shit, *medic.* The fucking safe LZ was fucking goddamn hot! All he could see were muzzle flashes. No faces, no black pajamas, no *bo doi* uniforms, no movement. Leaves showered down like rain. The goddamn *go-go* dragon ships blasted. Lieutenant: *The berm! The berm!* Sergeant: *Move out, move out!* And the man stood in the jungle shadow looking at Morgan, his eyes shining from some stray light through the vines and leaves. Morgan looked at the man. Nothing moved all around them where the platoon was running and the sergeant was shouting, *Move out! Move out!* and the lieutenant was screaming, *The berm! The berm!* and the chopper gun ships were flying low. Only the shadowed man and Morgan out in the sun. The AK–47 moved up and toward Morgan in long, soundless, slow motion, and his big M–60 moved up in slow, endless motion, and then the man in the shadows was gone and only the shadows were left.

Only the shadows and Morgan lay on the jungle floor, his elbows ripped on hidden rock or thorns or fucking metal left behind by some other fucking platoon some other fucking year at the same fucking LZ and Morgan fired at the shadows . . .

Morgan lay behind a big old oak. His breathing was shallow. He listened to the footsteps running away, felt the echo of the single shot like a blow against his ears, and the leaves of the old oak falling down on his back, and peered around the base of the tree trunk.

The heavy-set man had vanished into the dense growth of trees and thick underbrush between Anne Neville's house and the invisible neighboring house. Morgan stood up under the old oak, aware of a bruised left knee and two painful elbows and no weapon in his hands.

A second shot exploded ahead, and a third.

Morgan's knees bent . . . *Stay up, you motherfuckers! Stay up! They got fucking piss tubes! . . .*

And two short, sharp spits like the sound of a blowgun in some jungle.

Morgan eased ahead until finally he emerged from the trees and chaparral on the narrow blacktop driveway of the next house.

The short, heavy man lay face down, blood already pooling

around him. His automatic was still in his right hand, the piece of paper in front of his outflung left hand. . . . *Oh, shit, Sarge, oh shit, oh shit, oh shit* . . .

At the far end of the driveway, in the shadow of the house and beneath the shade of an enormous avocado tree, someone else stood motionless. A man in jeans and a light-blue shirt, solid and muscular but not tall. His face, shaded by the tree and a wide-brimmed Western hat, had sunglasses for eyes. There was nothing nervous or furtive about him. He simply stood there with what could have been a pistol with a very long barrel held down against his right leg, and watched Morgan like that single silent Vietnamese soldier so long ago. Then he too vanished, leaving nothing but the corner of the house and the empty shadows of the big avocado.

. . . *Morgan, take the fucking point. Move out* . . .

Alone on the driveway, Morgan felt naked. He had no weapon in his hands. He stood beside the fallen man in the pool of blood, and looked to where the silent figure had been. No one was there now.

He began to walk up the driveway to the rear corner of the house. Behind the house the trees and brush thickened into the usual dense old oaks and chaparral of Montecito. There was no sign of the second man, and no sounds.

Morgan moved into the trees. He felt his body pressing against a great weight that tried to stop him from moving forward. He knew the weight was in his mind, and that he had to force each foot down against the relentless memory of land mines and booby traps. Still he moved ahead, and a car started on the road behind the house and drove away with a squeal of rubber. When Morgan came out of the trees on the parallel rural road, there were no cars, and no one was in sight.

Morgan heard voices beginning to call to each other through the neighborhood, voices and people coming out of the houses hidden by the trees. Back at the fallen man lying in his own blood, he felt for a pulse and found none. He returned through the trees and chaparral to Anne Neville's yard. The big old oak he'd taken cover behind at the first shot from the intruder towered above the yard. Morgan stood and looked at the leaves the shot had knocked to the ground, and up at the high branches of the tree where the leaves had fallen from. Then he went on into Anne Neville's house and called the police.

4

Anne Neville had never seen the dead man before. The paper he had taken from her bedroom was where she had written the phone and room number of Ralph Baliol's suite at Cottage Hospital. The sheriff's deputies took her statement at the house, took the body to the morgue, and took Morgan to Detective Sergeant Koons at headquarters across from the county jail.

"This other man you saw, can you describe him any better, Mr. Morgan?"

"I'm guessing at what I told you already, sergeant. I barely saw his face, then he was gone."

"And you think he shot the dead man?"

"That's what I think, but I can't even say I saw a gun in his hand. What about the dead man? Who was he?"

"I was hoping you could tell me."

They had found no keys, no wallet, no papers, no driver's license. The John Doe's clothes were national brands without any local tags. The gun wasn't registered. He wasn't a missing person in the county or the state, and his prints weren't in NCIC. They had found no car. He had either walked to Anne Neville's house, or someone had dropped him off. Three shots had been fired from his gun. He'd been hit twice by 9–mm bullets from an apparently silenced automatic.

Morgan said, "He was there to locate Ralph Baliol. I think he shot Baliol and wanted to finish the job. He knew no hospital would give out that information, and that you people would be monitoring all calls. So—"

Koons put down his pen and sat back in his desk chair. "Are you a detective, Morgan?"

"I have some international investigating experience. Both crime and undercover."

"What experience would that be?"

"A lot of years with the Central Intelligence Agency, and some joint training with the FBI."

"You carrying a gun?"

"No," Morgan said. "Doesn't it stand to reason the dead man was the one who shot Baliol?"

"His gun's an old forty-five Colt," Koons said. "Baliol was shot with a thirty-eight. So if our John Doe was involved in shooting Baliol, he used two different guns or he wasn't alone. Maybe there were three of them, and they had a falling out. I expect we'll look into all of that without your help."

"Wouldn't business enemies, someone he hurt with his deals, be more logical than his son?"

"Sure, but we haven't found anyone like that. If anything, it was Baliol who got screwed in some deals."

"Screwed how?"

"For one, his buddy Fletcher Comrie manipulated stock in companies Baliol took over and made a bundle. Feds say it upped Baliol's costs in the takeovers by millions. Trouble is, that's a motive for Baliol, not Comrie, and Comrie has an alibi. Johnny Baliol doesn't."

"What's so important about where he was the night before?"

"Someone else was in the Maserati with him. Two different brands of fresh cigarette butts, and he doesn't even smoke. Beer bottles wet inside. Some pot roaches. He could have been with them in the morning. Now don't play any more detective, and close the door on your way out."

Morgan drove to the Brown Pelican at Hendry's beach for lunch. At least he knew why the police were so interested in knowing what Johnny Baliol had been doing the night before. If Johnny wasn't alone on the estate that morning, an accomplice could have escaped with the missing gun.

As he ate his lunch of shrimp and oysters he thought about the John Doe. The shot toward Morgan had hit nothing but leaves thirty feet over Morgan's head. As if the John Doe had missed him on purpose. That made him a strange kind of gunman.

And Morgan thought about Fletcher Comrie, Ralph Baliol's associate and unofficial partner. Sharks often nibbled on other sharks. That was the nature of sharks.

Ralph Baliol's mansion was an Italian *palazzo* built in the twenties by an Eastern banker to recreate the Tuscan hills in the cool summers and warm winters of Santa Barbara. Empty for years, the banker's acres of lawn, marble walks, statuary, and skinny poplars had crumbled and disappeared under a forest of oaks, sycamores, eucalyptus, and dense chaparral. The *palazzo* was invisible until Morgan drove through the gates in the high fence that surrounded the entire estate and up a long blacktop drive to the three-story terracotta-colored castle with miles of carved stone and a coat of arms above every door and window.

To be closer to the Pacific Rim, Ralph Baliol had moved Baliol Investments to Silicon Valley outside San Francisco in the eighties. The need for a showplace retreat brought him to Montecito and the Italian *palazzo* of the old banker. He rebuilt the interior in monumental modern to complement his collection of contemporary art, built tennis courts, an Olympic-size swimming pool, clubhouse, whirlpools, and a sauna. He kept the grounds the forest he'd found when he bought it, topped the fence with razor wire, and made the alarm system state of the art.

Baliol's personal assistant, Gerald Kirsch, waited to conduct Morgan inside. The walls of the huge living room were hung with giant paintings. Morgan recognized Rothko and Still, Johns and Rauschenberg. A staircase at the far end climbed to the bedroom wing. In the den, high windows overlooked the fence around the pool and the tangled trees and chaparral beyond. Rows of guns hung on racks with big game heads ferocious between. Framed photographs on the walls showed Baliol in Vietnam in camouflage fatigues, and in marine full dress at functions and ceremonies. A large Navaho rug and a mahogany-and-leather inlaid desk completed the den.

"How do you like your boss, Mr. Kirsch?"

"He is a remarkable man. You don't *like* remarkable men."

"What do you do?"

"You respect, admire, revere."

"Revere as in like a god?"

"Something more than most of us."

"What about his son?"

Kirsch gave the tiniest shrug. "There is potential. But he's immature and weak, never learned to respect his father."

"Would you have expected him to try to kill his father over Anne Neville?"

"Not really, no."

"Because he doesn't care that much about her?"

"I doubt if he cares much about anything other than his own well being."

"How about Fletcher Comrie?"

"Mr. Comrie? Why on earth would he shoot Mr. Baliol? They've been close associates and the best of personal friends for years." Kirsch looked up at the ship's clock on the den wall. "I really have work—"

"Go ahead. I'll look around on my own."

Morgan found nothing interesting on the first floor, only elegant rooms rarely used. On the second floor, Baliol's bedroom was as large as Louis XIV's in the palace of Versailles, but sleek and modern in rosewood and ebony, plastic and chrome. An audio-video center filled the high footboard, and walled the bed from the rest of the room like a separate world. The bathroom had two clear-glass stall showers, three marble sinks, a sunken tub with Jacuzzi, and a cedar sauna. Walk-in closets formed the entire interior wall. It reminded Morgan of the plantations of the French and their Vietnamese imitators back in Vietnam, the estates of the Third World rulers he'd had to work with, the Latin American military men and the Colombian drug lords.

The closets and drawers were crammed with more than a man could ever need. Except one closet where a blue bathrobe hung alone, and a pair of pale-blue woman's pajamas rested neatly on a shelf, new and unused, the sales tags still on them. A pair of woman's blue slippers in their original plastic packaging with a bill of sale dated less than a month ago. A hair dryer on a shelf, its electric cord still factory-packed for shipment, a sealed pack of emery boards, full bottles of dark brunette shampoo and conditioner, and an unopened box of maxi-pads.

Rachel had said Baliol made a habit of chasing every woman he met. It looked as if Anne Neville wasn't the only one with whom Ralph had planned, or hoped, to share his bedroom.

*   *   *

The two-story garage at the head of the driveway was made of the same terracotta stone, with a blacktop turnaround in front, openings for six cars and an apartment above. The chauffeur, Mancuso, wasn't in or over the garages in the apartment.

Morgan walked behind the *palazzo* where the pool, tennis courts, clubhouse, whirlpools, and sauna had been built in a U-shape with the open end facing the thick forest of trees and brush. Morgan found no traces of an ambush. What he did find were cut marks on a tall old sycamore that was in direct line with the pool deck. Deep cuts like puncture wounds in a single narrow row up each side of the thick trunk, stopping at a high branch hidden in foliage and in a direct line with the open pool deck.

Morgan looked at the marks for a long time. He had seen them before. Had made the same kind of marks himself. In the army, in and out of Vietnam. Climbing spikes. Someone had climbed the tree with a good clear range of fire to the pool deck.

It was nearly five o'clock, and he'd done more than enough to make his report to Rachel.

On the brick terrace of the Fernald Point house, Morgan and Rachel sat in the last heat of the August day. He had done laps for over an hour in the ranch pool; showered and shaved; called Lareina in Beverly Hills; changed into gray slacks, dress shirt, and blazer; and driven over. By then it was pushing eight o'clock, and Rachel had been ready. Cold beer this time—Thomas Kemper, a micro-brewery up in Paulsbo, Washington—to go with the hors d'oeuvres served by the borrowed Latina maid. Rachel wore silver tights and a loose black shirt that made her blonde hair a halo of pale gold.

"I made reservations at La Cananinna in town for nine. Tell me what you've found out about Johnny and Ralph and that night."

As he reported on the day, she shivered in the rising sea wind that was the glory of a Santa Barbara summer, the cool night wind you could count on to break the heat of the day in time for cocktails or a barbecue on the patio. Except on those rare occasions when the suffocating Santa Ana and sundowner winds blew down the mountain canyons and the heat remained far into the night. Morgan designed his report to indicate that Johnny was still in trouble, but with the entry of a new enemy there was a good chance of exonerating him, and that he Morgan was working hard.

Rachel heard the part she wanted to hear. "Then there you are! They have to let Johnny out of jail now."

"Not until they've got more than a dead man who wanted to know the room number at Cottage. And Johnny's done something he considers worse than being accused of shooting his father."

"What could be worse than trying to murder your own father, for God's sake?"

"I didn't say it was worse than *shooting* Baliol, I said it was worse than being *accused* of shooting him."

"What the hell's the difference?"

"The difference is that his refusal to talk about that night makes it more than likely he didn't shoot Baliol."

"How did you decide that?"

"He could probably clear himself of shooting Baliol by saying where he was, but whatever he did worries him so much he'd rather sit in jail until the police clear him another way."

"There, see? I knew you were a good detective."

Morgan drank the good beer, grinned at her. "On the other hand, Johnny could have done something else that night and still shot Baliol in the morning."

"I liked the first hand. Don't be too good a detective."

The silent Latina materialized from the night to remove the empty tray of hors d'oeuvres and leave a fresh round of Thomas Kemper pilsner. Morgan watched her as she glided away on soundless feet and went into the house.

"When did you come to Santa Barbara, Rach? Before or after Ralph was shot?"

"After, of course. I was in our Palm Springs house when Addison Berger called to tell me about Johnny. Max and I usually go to our favorite island in the Caribbean in August, but Max had business in Los Angeles so we had to come out. I didn't intend to sit around L.A. while he puttered with his dreary oil deals. I have friends at the Springs, and if you stay indoors with the air-conditioning up full it's not so bad."

The mountains of the Channel Islands were purple shadows out on the sea, and the lights of the oil platforms emerged with the night like so many fireflies. The good beer was strong, but Morgan felt unusually clear-headed and sober, the way he always had undercover no matter how much he drank. Only here on the terrace with Rachel it wasn't the adrenaline of tension, it was the adrenaline of anticipation. Rachel turned her face to the sea wind, put the cool of the glass against her pale cheek. Her golden hair took on the purple tinge of the air.

"Max and his stupid business." She took a long drink of the fresh beer. "I have the shittiest luck with men, you know that, Ford? I finally get my oil man and oil goes bust. Max Wallman is a nice man, but he's no Prince Charles, and now he's nowhere near as rich as he should have been. He has to work so damn much, for God's sake. First Ralph the shit, then Georgie Senlac the world-famous cardiologist who couldn't even take care of his own heart, now Max. You were the best of them, Ford, and there you were always brooding about some nonsense and trotting off to your mud huts."

"I'm not going anywhere now, Rach."

"What does that mean?"

"It means I didn't really come here to talk about Johnny, and I'm not all that hungry."

Her eyes smiled over her glass. "I always said that eating dinner at midnight was much more civilized."

"Or even later."

She put her drink down, stood with a small sway to suggest a shade too much alcohol, and stepped close to Morgan. He picked her up, surprised by her unexpected lightness—and at the same instant had the memory of always having had that moment of surprise when he picked her up to carry her to the bed. With the instant memory he was back in their New York penthouse and the bed she had put up on a platform so they could look out over the entire city and Central Park all the way to Harlem.

As tall and strong-willed as she was, she had always seemed so incredibly light when he carried her, her face hidden against his neck, her lips on his throat. When he lowered her to the high bed in the penthouse, or now as he carried her inside to the low bed in the borrowed bedroom with the sea wind cool through the windows. Light and smooth and pale where she lay and let his hands undress her, slide off her tights. Let his hands and his lips caress her breasts, her belly, the length of her hips and thighs, bury himself in the wedge of darker blonde hair. Let his hands spread her long legs and only then opened, slow and wide, her feet touching the wall behind her, her arms around his neck pulling him down and into her.

After the long moment of joining and isolation, they lay side by side in the quiet of the dark bedroom and another memory slowly entered Morgan's mind. A memory he didn't want to remember, not then, not ever. A memory of anger.

Her voice beside him was lazy on the night breeze through the windows. "You and Ralph were the best in bed. The two who lasted the shortest time. I wonder if that means anything? Says something about me, or about the men I like?"

Morgan could have said it probably told a great deal about her. About her concept of men and who and what they were. But he said nothing. He lay inside his unexpected and unwanted memory of anger as her voice drifted in his consciousness.

"Not just in bed, either. We get along. You're fun to be with." She lit a cigarette, the hand and the cigarette and the smoke floating as lazily in the dark as her voice. "But I can't wait for a man to get around to me."

It was an anger that had had little to do with her, but that had been pushed away and forgotten with her, and tonight it had come back with her and her blonde hair spread across the pillow. An anger and a memory he had left behind when he went to Costa Rica, and didn't want to remember now. Remember or even think about. He had not thought of the memory or the anger since he'd gone to live in Costa Rica, and he would not think about them now. He would think about what Rachel wanted him to think about.

"Who was Ralph's woman before Anne Neville?"

Her shadowy head turned in the dark room to look at Morgan. "The last one I heard about was a Mrs. Drysdale two or three years ago. She eventually went back to her husband, or left town, or something. Women don't have much future with Ralph."

"Two years ago is too long. There's a brunette somewhere in his life right now. Or there was." Morgan described what he had found in Ralph Baliol's bedroom. "New pajamas, a new hair dryer, the proper brunette shampoo, and menstrual pads are intended for more than a casual coupling."

"They certainly are." She rolled onto her side, her face propped on the hand that didn't hold the cigarette. "There *was* a woman I heard about. A story and a giggle at a party. Someone he was seen with at San Ysidro Ranch. Whoever told me the story implied that Ralph was hiding her. Why else would he stay at the ranch with his own house a mile away?" Her eyes took on the glow of her cigarette, and her whole body tensed like stretched silk with excitement because he had found still another suspect, or because she was thinking about the unknown brunette and Ralph Baliol alone in a hidden cottage.

Morgan touched the roundness of her belly. He took the cigarette from her fingers, dropped it into an ashtray on the side table and pulled her down on the bed. The excitement in her face changed to a slow smile. Morgan returned the smile as he went down to her once more in the sea night, and pushed the memory of anger out of his mind.

5

In the morning Morgan got up alone and ran barefoot along the beach. A few nude bathers splashed in the early surf, or sat up against the bluffs at Summerland. The rest of the narrow beach was deserted, and Morgan had to run through water up to his ankles more than once as the tide came in. The memory of anger had returned with the dawn, and he ran hard until he had run five miles from the Fernald Point house and had to run five miles back. Only the borrowed Mexican maid and a note were waiting at the house: *Find the woman. Tonight! Ciao. R.*

Back in his empty San Ysidro Ranch cottage, he had a dozen long-stemmed yellow roses sent to Rachel, called Lareina again in Beverly Hills, and had breakfast alone in the ranch dining room. *Cherchez la femme.* Find Ralph Baliol's unknown brunette. At least it sounded more interesting than looking for what Johnny Baliol had been doing. A hidden brunette in the life of a skirt chaser could have given someone the same motive as Johnny to want Ralph dead, or at least discouraged and dissuaded from his present course and action. Someone who perhaps didn't want to hurt anyone else and so shot into the air.

Or someone who used a silencer and shot to kill.

Morgan had a second pot of coffee. The party gossip Rachel had heard said that Ralph had brought a woman here to the ranch at least once. Lovers having a tryst at the ranch would arrange for a cottage, the more secluded the better. Each cottage had a book register for guests to sign, and the signatures of kings, presidents, prime ministers, and assorted lords of title and industry went back to the nineteenth century. Few could resist being in such important company.

36

Ralph Baliol had not resisted. It took some time and improvised stories about magazine articles for startled guests and uneasy maids to explain Morgan's snooping in the cottages, but he found what he was looking for in the guest book of another remote cottage with a private hot tub. A man who collected women would never overlook the possibilities of a hot tub.

It was only one page back: *Ralph Baliol and guest.* After all, who belonged among the great more than Ralph Baliol?

And guest. A boast. He had *had* her in this cottage, and that must be acknowledged somewhere in the universe, even if only by a few strangers who would see it and smile.

And guest. She was the one who was nervous.

Her name could be recognized at the San Ysidro Ranch. That eliminated almost everyone but the world famous or the locally prominent. Either way, she would in all probability move in the same public and social circles as Baliol. That would be how they had met, at a civic function or some charity party. They would go to the same parties, the same political events. Attend the same charity affairs, do the same civic duties. Photos would be taken, news stories would be written and the photos published in the local news media to edify the masses.

A call to Rachel got Morgan in to see her lawyer. The lawyer's office was on the second floor of a bank building at the corner of the city's main street, State, and Figueroa.

Addison Berger looked like a lawyer. Gray at the temples, he wore a blue pinstripe suit of conservative cut behind a desk so neat a single paper clip would have looked like chaos. A partner in the least-known and highest-priced firm in Santa Barbara, Berger handled the business and personal affairs of the oldest and richest families, and rarely came in contact with anything of a criminal nature. Berger wasn't at all happy to be in contact with a criminal case now. He had nothing to offer Morgan beyond what the newspapers and Rachel had told him.

"Then I've got a job you can help me with," Morgan told him. "I want you to send someone to the local newspapers and get all the public photos of Ralph Baliol over the last year and deliver them to my cottage at San Ysidro Ranch." It never hurt to impress a lawyer with your financial resources.

"Our staff is terribly busy, Mr. Morgan. I can't guarantee to get to it immediately."

"Do your best, counsellor," Morgan said. "For the Winrods."

"It may take some hours."

"Soon as you can, okay? Meanwhile, get me in to see Johnny Baliol. I suppose it's time I heard what he has to say."

Berger made the call that would notify the sheriff's office and Johnny Baliol that Morgan was coming out to talk to Johnny.

Built between Santa Barbara proper and Goleta, on the road to the county dump, the beige brick county jail had a new wing of bright cells with half-glass doors and video surveillance from a central room. There were no bars, and the hard clang of metal didn't dominate everything human. A decent jail, but a jail, and Johnny Baliol had never been inside a jail. An upper-middle-class American boy. Well fed, well groomed, well educated and well protected.

"I don't even know how to *aim* a gun, for God's sake, Ford. I only bought it because Anne wanted to learn to shoot. She's pretty isolated in that house."

Johnny had changed in the five years since his mother and Morgan had separated. A small young man not much taller than Rachel, his face was broader than his mother's and his hair had darkened. He was heavier than Morgan remembered, with the beginning of jowls.

"What were you doing there that morning, Johnny?"

"Showing them they weren't fooling me!"

"When did you find out about them?"

"Maybe a week before. Annie was acting funny, but I didn't think it was anything big until some guy told me he'd seen them."

"So what happened that morning?"

Johnny didn't want to talk about what had happened that morning. He tried to look determined and then tried a sullen sulk. Not even a fly buzzed in the tiny room. Morgan was experienced at waiting. Johnny Baliol wasn't. It was only a matter of time. He remained sullen, but he talked. He hadn't seen Anne Neville for three days so he called her house early that morning. He got no answer—at 7:30 A.M. on a Saturday. He was so angry he drove straight to her house. No one was there, so he drove on to Ralph's goddamn mansion and let himself in the door beside the gate.

He was inside the *palazzo* and headed upstairs to the bedroom to catch them in the act when he heard the shots. He knew Ralph took his macho swim in the morning, then lay around to tan the great bod. But Anne Neville ran out of the bedroom wearing one of Ralph's Sea Island shirts and not one damn thing else, and he ducked into a closet. He hid until she had run down the stairs, then came out and looked out the window. He saw Baliol on the deck and all the others around him, with Annie on her knees over the great man with her bare ass hanging out.

He saw nothing and no one else, was on his way out down the driveway when he heard a car. It was that doctor from next door. He didn't want anyone to find him, for God's sake, so he hid in the barranca. Then stupid Mancuso started patroling with his goddamn gun, and dragged him out of the barranca.

"Rachel says you got along with your father."

"Sure. He paid me my money, and I went over there whenever he wanted to show me off. The family man, you know? He didn't have to grab at Annie, make me look like a fool."

"Where were you all that night?"

"Nowhere! Driving around. I couldn't sleep so I went driving over in the valley."

"Then where did you call Anne Neville's house from, Johnny? You have a car phone?"

"I . . . I don't remember. A gas station. I was so damned mad I don't remember where I called from."

Morgan had seen fear and lying of every kind, and Johnny Baliol was both scared and lying. A boy who should have been a man but wasn't, and who was so worried about where he'd been and what he'd been doing the night before he'd rather have people think he had tried to kill his father.

In the San Ysidro Ranch cottage, Morgan spread all the photos from the local newspapers across the dining table and looked for Ralph Baliol with a dark-haired woman. She would be youngish, well dressed and good looking. She would be near him in many recent photos of public events, they would be seen together often.

After an hour Morgan sat back in his chair. There was only one possibility: Stanford graduate, former social worker, old-family Santa Barbara, active in the community. Thirty-eight, she had mar-

ried relatively late, had two children, aged eight and six. Her husband was CEO of an electronics firm with factories all across the
state, the nation, and in Europe. A proper churchgoer, he sat on
various boards and was chairman of the local Republican committee. A busy man. Sixty.

She had been photographed with Ralph Baliol twelve times in
the last year, five times in the last two months. In the later photos
their hands appeared nearly to touch. His smile was broad and self-
satisfied, hers was a little sad. Mrs. Barbara Allison Schoenhausen.

Morgan sat for a time and looked at the touch of sadness on her
face in each picture, a sadness in her whole manner as she stood
close to Baliol. A reserved manner, the proper clothes for the wife
of a prominent businessman at the particular occasion. A body and
manner held tightly. Morgan looked at each photo carefully one
more time before he put them back into the manila envelope. Mrs.
Barbara Schoenhausen had a problem, but was Ralph Baliol the
answer, the cause, or both?

Small in a reserved navy suit, she came into the afternoon cocktail
lounge near the shopping mall wearing a pearl-and-sapphire pin
that had cost ten thousand at least. She wore low-heeled navy
pumps, a pearl-and-sapphire ring on her right hand, and a plain
wedding band on her left. The smile she gave the men in the
lounge who stared at her was soft. Her voice was soft, with some of
the same sadness Morgan had seen in the photos.

"Mr. Morgan?"

"Mrs. Schoenhausen." Morgan stood up until she sat down in
the booth. "Drink?"

"That might be good. A beer?"

She spoke and moved with a diffident dignity that was controlled
without being stiff. Her blue eyes were so dark they were almost
black. Her full mouth was vulnerable, the lipstick eroded, and her
long hair was windblown. She hadn't stopped to fix her makeup or
comb her hair after Morgan's call. The fingers of her right hand
turned her wedding band around and around.

"I haven't told anyone else yet, Mrs. Schoenhausen."

"I'd like to tell everyone myself, Mr. Morgan."

The lounge was warm. She took off her suit jacket and laid it on
the banquette seat beside her as she faced Morgan with the soft

smile. Against the white blouse her long black hair and dark eyes shone like ebony. Her face was framed by the thick, slightly disheveled hair. She looked her thirty-eight years, and her narrow face with its prominent cheekbones had the same dignified control as her voice. A seamless texture to her face like a thin mask. A mature face. Vulnerable and not happy. An intelligent woman, with the edge of panic in her dark eyes of someone who stood on shifting sand.

"Why haven't you?" Morgan asked.

"I'm not sure."

The waitress came with glasses and two bottles of Beck's. Morgan filled their glasses.

"How did you meet him, Mrs. Schoenhausen? Ralph Baliol."

"Get involved with him, you mean?"

"All right, how did you get involved?"

"Do you have any idea what a large question that is, Mr. Morgan? How long? How complicated?"

"I've got an idea."

She turned her wedding ring around and around and looked down at the beer in front of her. She picked up the glass and drank it all. She refilled the glass and drank that. Morgan waved to the waitress. He felt her black eyes fix on his face. She wasn't accustomed to talking about herself, certainly not to strangers. Probably hadn't talked about herself in a long time. But as the new Beck's came, she began to talk. Morgan realized he was a release, a stranger who already knew the secret she hated and needed.

"We're an old family in Santa Barbara, Mr. Morgan. You know the kind. Daring ancestor comes West by foot, horse, or ship, arrives penniless, catches the eye of the daughter of the local *padrón*, proves himself strong and if necessary ruthless, and soon has land and money, becomes a power in the new state when the U.S. takes Alta California from Mexico."

"You don't sound impressed."

"I'm not impressed by power. If you start with advantages like intelligence, an education, the right appearance, and a rich *padrón* father-in-law, all you really need to get power is the burning need, some luck, and very little humanity."

"What are you impressed by?"

"Kindness, imagination, courage, individuality."

"Pioneers are supposed to have those things," Morgan said.

"Pioneer isn't exactly what I'd call Great-Great Grandfather Allison. Opportunist, perhaps." She drank her second beer as fast and hard as the first, but sat back in the booth and became more relaxed. Morgan couldn't tell whether it was the two quick beers or the release of telling her story. "Mother wanted to send me back East to her own school—private, all girls, much prestige. My father believed in learning about the world we lived in. They fought, but I wanted to go to the public high school, and I did. I think Father's regretted it since. I learned about the real world, the *barrio*, the poverty, people who were different. A bigger world than Santa Barbara or the Allisons. I let them send me to Stanford, Dad's alma mater, but I insisted they let me study social work."

Reliving her life, even momentarily, changed her more than simply easing the tension she had come in with. It took away the diffidence and some of the vulnerability, but not the sense of softness. "Then I worked in the San Francisco slums. It was hard work, mentally and physically, but mostly mentally. All those poor, hopeless people. You despair of seeing any real gains, of doing any real good. You come to feel helpless. What's the use? You get lonely. You get older. You meet a man. Alfred, my husband, is from a German family with an ancient castle. They lost all their power to the Nazis and their castle to East Germany. He's well off, secure, without any doubts. You feel good with him. Your parents see him as too old and a foreigner. You marry him anyway. You have babies, a big house, a full life. You should be happy, but you're not. You don't know why you're unhappy, so you blame yourself and go on, for the children if nothing else. Then . . ." The slim shoulders in the white blouse gave an all but imperceptible shrug. "The children alone aren't enough, you need something more. A man is the easiest choice."

"I wouldn't have thought that was true for you."

"You don't know me, do you, Mr. Morgan?"

The cocktail lounge had emptied. After lunch and before happy hour. Morgan was alone with her in the isolation of the afternoon bar with the day distant outside and a realization that he would like to know Barbara Allison Schoenhausen. He would like to know her very well.

"You fell out of love with Alfred?" Morgan said.

"I suppose that's what I did." She toyed with her empty glass and glanced around in the muted light of the cocktail lounge without really seeing anything. "Within his world he's kind and gentle. Being in America all these years has changed him, at least on the surface, made him more outgoing. Love does strange things. It's not exactly blind, but when you're in love other things don't matter as much. For men and women, but more for women in our society. We're raised that way. But something happened to me, and I seem to have fallen out of love."

"And fell in love with Ralph Baliol?"

"It would seem so."

"But there are the children."

"There are the children."

"And you're not all that sure about Baliol."

She looked away from Morgan. He was pushing her where she didn't want to go.

"Are you a detective, Ford?"

"Sort of a relative of Johnny Baliol's mother."

"Sort of a relative?"

"I was her third husband. It didn't last long, and it ended five years ago."

"But you're here helping her son? Ralph says you can never really be over Rachel, she won't let you."

"He's wrong. I was over Rachel the moment you walked into this lounge."

She held her smile on his face for a long time. Morgan felt himself smile back. An idiot smile. He felt her near him like a trembling inside. When he thought of Lareina he felt pleasure, and last night with Rachel there was excitement, but as he smiled at Barbara Schoenhausen and she smiled at him what he felt was close to pain. A great, wonderful pain. Perhaps great enough, big enough, to overwhelm any anger. Her hand reached out and brushed the back of his hand once with slow fingers. She returned her hand to her lap under the table, continued to smile for a time through her own sadness and apprehension.

"I think I needed that just now. You're a kind man, Ford, aren't you?"

He didn't feel kind. "Do you know about Anne Neville, Barbara?"

"His son's young lady? I've met her. Why?"

"She isn't his son's young lady anymore, she's Ralph's young lady."

The smile left her face. The smile and everything else except the seamless skin over the high cheekbones. And the control, a control so quick to rise to her aid that it could only have come from long practice. She said nothing. She opened her handbag, took out money to pay her bill, and stood up.

"She was in his bed the morning he was shot," Morgan said. "Bareass naked in one of Ralph's shirts, as Johnny so graphically put it. The police think it was Johnny's motive to shoot Ralph. But I doubt Anne Neville is serious, if that means anything to you."

"I wonder if Ralph's ever serious with a woman."

She had understood more about Ralph Baliol in the last minute than Anne Neville probably ever would or could. Or else she had already been wondering about Baliol's seriousness with any woman.

Morgan said, "Serious enough to prepare his bedroom with new pajamas and slippers in the right color for a brunette, the proper shampoo for a brunette, and maxi-pads for when he finally got you there."

A flush darkened her face. It wasn't embarrassment, it was outrage. "I'm sorry, Ford, I have to pick up my children."

"Could your husband possibly know about Ralph?"

"No."

"I'd like to talk to you again."

"Why?"

"Someone besides Johnny Baliol shot Ralph Baliol. I need to know all I can."

"Call me at home."

When she walked away from the booth in the dim lounge the bills she had intended for her share of the check were still in her hand, forgotten.

Morgan finished his second beer. He had been surprised by her permission to call her at home. Could Alfred Schoenhausen be that insensitive? Or that blind?

Morgan wasn't surprised that Ralph Baliol would play with a married woman as well as with his son's girlfriend. The risk involved with both would be part of the excitement to Baliol, perhaps most of the excitement. The thrill of small danger.

*   *   *

Morgan drove to the harbor and walked out on the breakwater in the sharp sea wind.

Santa Barbara wasn't a natural harbor, only a deep curve in the coastline where the Spanish galleons and Yankee hide ships had found precarious shelter, and had to stand out to sea if any onshore wind came up. The breakwater had formed the harbor with a marina behind it where sailboats, powerboats, and houseboats were massed along floating piers. A pier for sport fishing boats across the harbor reminded Morgan of his boyhood in Sag Harbor, New York, and his father's sportfishing boat where Morgan had cut bait and tended lines and chummed for bluefish every summer.

Flagpoles lined the wall of the breakwater, and the flags of many nations flew and snapped in the wind. Morgan leaned on the parapet and stared out to sea until his eyes watered in the wind. He thought of Barbara Schoenhausen. What she did and how she did it was important to her. Perhaps not to anyone else, but to her. What she did and what she was. She didn't think about what others thought of her so much as what she thought of herself. She was important to herself. She looked her age and took her actions seriously. An honest person. Real. Someone worth a possible future with no need for a memory of anger.

Morgan didn't go to see Rachel that night. He didn't phone Lareina in Beverly Hills. He ate dinner alone on the breakwater and drank his way back to the cottage at San Ysidro Ranch.

6

A high sun and the insistent ringing of the telephone roused Morgan from the depths of an alcoholic sleep the next morning. Lareina was too excited to notice that his voice was thick with sleep and hangover long past an hour when he was always up. It was necessary, even mandatory, that he come on the instant to Beverly Hills to meet a man who urgently had to talk to both of them about starring her in an important American film.

"I think he wants money, *yanqui*, but we will all talk. I will smile much and be the great actress. You will hear the small words, *sí?*"

"I don't know anything about movies, Reina."

"It does not matter. You will know what is between the big words this man is saying, and I will not. I will expect you by three o'clock, *sí?*"

He extended his arrival to four o'clock, and made himself run to the ocean and back. He ate a slow brunch in a corner of the dining room. He and Lareina had enjoyed each other far too long for Morgan to consider doing anything else but go to Beverly Hills. He called Rachel before he went because he would not have a one-night-and-run affair even with an ex-wife who brought unwanted memories to life. A message on her answering machine told him she had flown back to Palm Springs at five o'clock the night before, she would expect him to call her there to make his report. He smiled at his guilt, and left a message: he would be away for a few days, would call her when he returned.

On the pleasant and easy drive to Los Angeles, the mountain wall of the Conejo grade rose from the flat coastal plain beyond Camarillo like the escarpments of Africa where he had spent almost two years instructing the rebels in Angola and the army in Kenya.

From the top, the view back down to the plain had the same sweep and distance, but in Africa there had been no ocean or expensive housing tracts to break the flat brown land. Not then, but Morgan had no doubt the housing developments would come, complete with lawns and artificial lakes.

Lareina's movie mogul turned out to be an overbearing one-credit director of a cable movie with a baggy suit, big dreams, and a briefcase for an office. He had the dreams, Lareina had the talent, Morgan would put up the money. Expenses would start, of course, with salaries for everyone, especially the aspiring mogul. He was a shade better than the shabby hustlers who lived by selling shares in nonexistent projects, but not much, and Morgan had to tell Lareina that.

"His big movie is a fantasy, Reina. Or worse. It won't ever go into production no matter how much money he gets."

Lareina was depressed, and Morgan spent most of the next two days comforting her. Fortunately, she had enough old friends to take her to lunch or have her over for afternoon cocktails, and she soon cheered up. At night she and Morgan did the Beverly Hills–Hollywood party circuit through houses that looked more like art museums and furniture showrooms than places where someone could live. The guests were the most beautiful and most handsome, the slimmest and tallest and most muscular and best dressed. They were neither friendly nor unfriendly. They did not relate to anyone they didn't already know because they couldn't be sure if you were someone they could use, which was good and they must be friendly, or someone who would try to use them, which was bad and you must be avoided. They were people who talked only for themselves.

During the day, while Lareina lunched with her friends, Morgan swam and sat around the pool at her friends' house and drank rum coolers and thought much more about the shooting of Ralph Baliol and who might or might not have done it. He didn't think about it only for Johnny and Rachel, and on the second day he decided to contact some of his own old friends.

"Lang, *qué pasa?* Too long, *amigo.* Where the hell you been keeping yourself?"

"You trying to tell me Langley doesn't know exactly where I've been and what I've been doing?"

Hughes Bremner laughed. "So what is this, eh? You tired at last of sitting on your ass under the palm trees? Missing being in the swim? Maybe thinking of coming back to us? I mean, this is where it's at, right? Where the action is?"

"I couldn't stand the heat anymore, Hughes," Morgan said. "It's a young man's game."

"That sounds mighty like an insult."

"Some people never grow up."

Hughes Bremner laughed. A tip from Morgan had been the lead Bremner passed on to the Colombian military that eventually led to the ambush and death of Medellín druglord Rodríguez-Gacha, The Mexican. Bremner never knew how the tip had reached Morgan, but it had meant a big promotion for Bremner, and he had asked no questions. And in the CIA you never knew when a man might be useful again.

"At least come around sometime for old time's sake, Lang."

"Maybe I'll be in New York later this year. If I am I'll drop down for lunch."

"You got it. So what the hell's on your mind?"

"I need your best check on two men. Anything they might have done to get themselves shot, or make them shoot someone else."

"What men?"

"Ralph Baliol and Fletcher Comrie."

"Comrie's under federal indictment."

"And Baliol isn't. That much I know. But if that annoyed Comrie, putting Baliol on the hook with him would be more on the mark."

"Okay, Lang, I'll see if we have anything, and for you I'll even talk to the FBI under the table. I'll get back to you."

On Morgan's second call the man's name didn't matter, it wasn't real anyway. In Colombia his real name was well known. He was a member of a family that went back two hundred years, in and out of government but always in power. At the moment the aristocratic gentleman was out with Bogotá and in with Medellín and Calí. Power was power.

"I do not know those names, Señor Morgan."

"I would appreciate it if you would ask around, *padrón*. Any hint that either has any problems in your area, perhaps with guns, a little technical espionage. Any motive for someone to blow them away, or for them to do the blowing."

"I will call you."

By the third day in Beverly Hills Morgan wanted to go to the mountains for a year or run a thousand miles. No one had called back, and lying beside the pool of Lareina's friends he imagined the clouds and the villagers and the nights around the campfire with his *guaro*. Every nerve in him wanted to be somewhere else. Lareina had received a family invitation to fly to Cabo San Lucas for a few days. The invitation included Morgan, but Cabo San Lucas was not where Morgan wanted to be. Not Cabo, not beside a pool or at parties in Beverly Hills, not really in Costa Rica, the Cordillera, or the cloud forest. Barbara Schoenhausen had changed things.

"I ought to get back up to Santa Barbara, Reina. I did promise to help Johnny."

Lareina looked at him the way she looked at a dress she wanted but wasn't sure would be good on her.

"Something has happened, Ford?"

Her eyes searched his face for what had happened to him. She was an intelligent woman, Lareina. She knew when she knew, and she trusted her instincts. She would need an answer.

"I slept with Rachel. I'm sorry, Reina. I had it in mind when I came up. If you feel—" He heard himself apologizing, but was it Lareina he was apologizing to?

"Of course you slept with Rachel. She would have accepted nothing else. No, it is not Rachel."

"Perhaps it's Ralph Baliol. I don't like him much."

"The husband who was shot?" Her voice was not convinced, and her eyes searched his face for another moment before she smiled. "Maybe that is it, then."

She resumed eating her breakfast and talking about whatever they had been talking about. Something unimportant. They spent the day together in their guest room and around the pool at her friends' house. Morgan helped her to pack, and drove her to the airport to catch her seven o'clock plane to Cabo. At the airport she touched his face and kissed him before she went through the gate. Morgan watched until her jet took off. Alone, he got back into the rented BMW and drove north.

He ate dinner in a Mexican restaurant in Camarillo, reached the San Ysidro Ranch in time to have a few drinks in the bar and read his messages. There were four from Rachel asking where in God's name he was and what, for God's sake, was he doing, and one from Hughes Bremner. Morgan went to his cottage to call Bremner at home, only to hear him say that, with the exception of some questionable deals by Fletcher Comrie, neither Comrie nor Ralph Baliol had any visible motives to murder anyone or even to discourage them, and nothing special the CIA or FBI knew about to get them murdered.

In bed, Morgan tried to think about the shooting of Baliol, but soon gave up and lay with the image of Barbara Schoenhausen above him in the play of outside light on the ceiling before he finally fell asleep.

In the morning, when Morgan returned from his run along the endless curves of Mountain Drive, an older woman's voice at the other end of the telephone told him Mrs. Schoenhausen wasn't at home, and she did not know where Mrs. Schoenhausen could be reached.

Morgan ate breakfast in the cottage. He debated whether to call Rachel, which would mean he would have to go and see her because she would expect it, or to put the call off until later and go to the business school library at UCSB to research the operations of Baliol Investments, Inc. As he finished his coffee the library won, and he went out to the BMW.

And stopped three feet from the car. The passenger's door wasn't closed all the way. He was sure he had closed it after Lareina got out at LAX, and had had no reason to open it since. He stepped warily closer and circled the rented car studying it and the ground around it. Tiny pieces of colored wire lay on the blacktop beside the front wheel. He picked up two pieces, saw that the ends had been recently cut, and in the late morning sunlight thought about how long it had been since he last worried about booby traps.

He called Sergeant Koons from the living room of the cottage, and sat at the window looking out at the BMW until the deputies arrived in a caravan.

The bomb people and major crimes team came in separate cars. Sergeant Koons stood with Morgan as his men worked in and under the BMW. The bomb team lieutenant brought the small mechanism to them. "Pretty damn crude affair, but the wiring to the ignition was good. Whoever planted it knows electronics and cars better than bombs."

The bomb was small and with little power. It wouldn't have done

Morgan or the car any good, but it wouldn't have killed or crippled him. Cuts and bruises and a new engine. They could tell little about who had planted it. They would take it to the lab, but most of the parts were standard over-the-counter or even mail order. The explosive was old army C–4 plastic.

Morgan said, "It's the only present they left?"

"You'll be clean when we go."

Koons said, "Police work can be dangerous for civilians, Morgan. Someone doesn't like what you're doing."

"Johnny Baliol's still in jail."

"There were other people in his car with him that night, and they aren't in jail. Let's go in to headquarters and take your official statement."

"I'll tell Johnny's mother and her lawyer to meet us there."

Koons left with the others. Morgan stood and looked at the BMW with the same hollow in the pit of his stomach he had known so well in Vietnam, and in all the solitary undercover rooms of his life.

Morgan gave his statement to the sheriff's people in a room where a bright noon sun was hot through the windows. Rachel, her lawyer Addison Berger, and the district attorney listened in silence until he had finished.

"Obviously," Rachel said, "Johnny couldn't be responsible."

Addison Berger said, "You've got the wrong man, MacLeod. Isn't it time you accepted that and released him?"

Deputy District Attorney MacLeod was under double pressure. If he kept Johnny in jail and he turned out to be innocent, the power of the Baliols, Nevilles, and Winrods could put a squeeze on the mayor, the city council, and the district attorney. If he let Johnny out too soon and he was guilty, the prominence of the same Baliols, Nevilles, and Winrods could bring the public down on the mayor, council, and D.A. for giving the elite special favors, a different law for rich and poor.

MacLeod took the usual path. He tried to pass the buck. "What do you say, sergeant?"

Koons said, "We know someone else was in his car that night."

"You *know*?" Addison Berger said. "Can you produce these alleged accomplices? Can you prove anything?"

"We can prove he was at his father's house that morning. We can prove he was hiding from the police. We can prove he bought a pistol of the matching caliber. We can prove a motive."

"But you do not have the gun, you can show us no accomplice, and Mr. Morgan has been attacked while Johnny was in your hands under lock and key." Berger looked at MacLeod. "I doubt a judge is going to favor further denial of bail, Drew."

"If nothing turns up by tomorrow, we'll—"

"I want my son home tonight," Rachel said.

Berger looked at his watch. "You want me to bother a judge just as he's ready to go to lunch, Drew?"

MacLeod said, "Let him out, Koons."

Out in the parking lot, Rachel held Morgan's face in both hands, kissed him, and laughed happily. "Ford, you are a wonder. Come to the house right now."

"Maybe later, Rach."

"Are you spurning me, for God's sake?"

"We still don't know what happened at the mansion, or where Johnny was that night."

In a backless blue sundress with a full skirt that swirled around her long legs, she studied him as Lareina had studied him yesterday. "You didn't come up here just to help me exonerate Johnny or find out what he was doing that night. And you don't have to go on being the busy detective right now, for God's sake."

"Yes, I think I do."

He saw the surprise on her face, and felt a certain surprise himself. But he gave her a kiss, told her he would call later, and put her into her car. She didn't want to go, no one brushed off Rachel Winrod, but she went. Then Morgan drove up to the El Encanto Hotel, had lunch and several beers on the terrace, and called Barbara Schoenhausen again. A clipped male voice with a German accent asked who he should say had called.

"I'll call back."

"As you wish," the voice said, without much interest. "If it is urgent, you could reach her today at the office of social work in Cottage Hospital. She volunteers there twice a week."

She hadn't mentioned she worked at Cottage, so convenient to Ralph Baliol. *Volunteer* work, as the clipped and uninterested voice had made sure to tell him.

7

A fire-red Maserati sat in Johnny Baliol's private carport behind his beachfront condominium in Montecito. Crammed in behind the Maserati was a red Porsche with the license plate ANNE 1, and it was Anne Neville who opened the door to Morgan's ring.

"Am I interrupting something important?" Morgan said.

She grinned at him. "Not yet."

Johnny Baliol lounged on the balcony of the condo surrounded by a litter of beer bottles, food-caked paper plates, soft drink cans, and empty fast food packages. He wore the oversized white shorts that were the rage among the young this year, and his red canvas basketball shoes were propped on the railing. He sucked noisily on a bottle of Anchor Steam. Out of jail, his confidence and arrogance were all the way back.

"Who was in the car with you that night and morning?"

Somewhere between jail and the condo, Johnny's lank brown hair had been blown dry and carefully shaped. He winked at Anne Neville, and licked the neck of the beer bottle.

"What car?" he said. "What morning?"

Morgan leaned against the balcony railing and stared at the boy. "The police will find who it was sooner or later. They'll find out what you were doing that you don't want anyone to know you were doing."

"The police can't find what didn't happen."

"No one was with you all that night and morning?"

"Nope."

"You just couldn't sleep. So angry about Anne and your father, you went out driving the whole night."

"Bingo, Ford."

"The beer bottles and cigarette butts were left by friends the day before. Maybe you can tell me their names and the police can check that out."

"I forget who they were. You know how it is when you're having fun. I mean, hey, I have so many friends it's really hard to remember who I'm with on any special night, right?"

There was no fear now. Out of jail, protected by his mother, her lawyer, and even Morgan, Johnny was safe and smug on his hundred-thousand-dollar private balcony above the herd down on the beach. He could ignore everything but his view of beach, rocks, and blue ocean all the way to the Channel Islands.

Morgan moved away from the railing and sat on a white plastic chair, his face a foot away from Johnny's face. "I don't think you have enough real friends to half fill a Maserati. I don't think you had anyone in the car the day before, and neither do the police or your mother. Rachel says you were probably out carousing, got drunk, and don't remember where you were or what happened. I think you know exactly where you were, who was with you, and what happened but you're afraid to talk about that because it's worse than being accused of trying to kill your father. I think the people you were with don't want anyone to know what happened. I think one of them knows a lot about cars and electronics. I think one of them knows how to make a bomb. I think one or more of them made a bomb to scare me away from asking any more questions. I don't intend to go away, and the police never do."

In a heavy silence on the balcony, the voices of the volleyball players on the beach reached clearly from the distance. Anne Neville looked out to sea with studied neutrality. Johnny took a big gulp of beer, his face sullen again. "What the fuck do *you* know."

"I know that if whatever happened is as bad as you seem to believe, it won't stay hidden."

"I told you where the hell I was."

Anne decided to stop being neutral. "If we're going out, Johnny, you'd better get ready. I'll have to go home and change too."

Johnny eagerly took the escape, jumped up. "Shazam, you're right. Come on in and help me pick out just the right threads for the new shirt and tie Rachel got me."

He had an amazing capacity to ignore anything unpleasant the moment he didn't have to look at it head on. Morgan remembered that Rachel had had the same capacity. Ralph Baliol probably did too. All the Baliols and Winrods.

"You're going out together?" Morgan said.

"We talked it all over," Anne smiled. "We've known each other a long time, Ford."

"Have you talked it over with Ralph?"

Johnny grinned, "Ralph's in the hospital."

"Cute," Morgan said.

"There's no reason Johnny and I can't be friends, Ford," Anne said. "In fact, I'd say we have to be, wouldn't you?"

In sharp contrast to the litter of the balcony, the living room and kitchen were neat and clean as Morgan followed them through to the bedroom. The living room had been bought in a designer package and never used, and the kitchen was straight out of a Rodeo Drive catalog complete with a wrought-iron rack full of matching pans whose copper bottoms showed no marks of flame.

At his bedroom closet, Johnny studied the dark purple and forest-green Highland Brigade tie and blue Sea Island cotton shirt his mother had bought him. The bedroom was as littered with unwashed clothes, food wrappers, dirty paper plates, beer cans, and general debris as the balcony. Johnny Baliol lived in his bedroom, balcony, and car. There were more suits, sport jackets, and pants in the closet than furniture in the room. The life of a teenager. He and Anne Neville were two kids getting into mischief while their parents were away. Expensive clothes, pine furniture, Amerindian baskets, and sports cars. Life was a hobby.

"What do you think, Annie," Johnny said. "The fawn Italian suit, or the navy blazer and gray slacks?"

Morgan left them discussing Johnny's clothes, and went down to the parking lot. He walked around the building until he found a spot where he could watch the condo without being seen himself. Almost at once Johnny came out onto the balcony, the trousers of the fawn suit on one arm, a cordless telephone in the other hand. He spoke briefly, put on his pants, and went back inside.

In his BMW, Morgan looked at his watch. If he was right about Johnny and the fast phone call, someone should arrive within the next half hour, depending on how far away whoever Johnny had called lived. Probably more than one person, ready either to hold a conference with Johnny or to keep an eye on Morgan. If they came to meet with Johnny, Morgan would follow them until he found out who they were. If they came to watch him, with some luck he should be able to turn the tables.

After twenty minutes no one had appeared, and Johnny and Anne Neville emerged, Johnny fully dressed to go on the town. They drove away in Anne's Porsche. Morgan waited another ten minutes, then drove out of the condominium parking lot. He looked right and left as he passed through the gate to the street.

A single car was parked on the narrow road to the right—a small green Lotus. Morgan saw two heads in the two-seater, both facing straight ahead to where he emerged from the condo complex. He drove away from the Lotus, watched in his rearview mirror, and smiled to himself when it pulled out and fell in behind him. It remained behind him through Montecito Coast Village and onto the freeway.

Morgan got off at Sheffield Drive. The Lotus followed. Up Sheffield he drove past new houses, all size and no character, and through the golf courses on both sides until he reached East Valley Road. The Lotus stayed much too close. On East Valley he took a left, made the sharp right toward the mountains on Romero Canyon Road.

Whoever was in the Lotus finally decided they might be being obvious and dropped back. On the first sharp switchback in the mountains, Morgan pulled over. The Lotus had the sense to go on past, and the sense to turn off when they saw him get back on the road and come up behind them. But not the sense to do it soon enough, or to pick a place where they could easily return to the road. Morgan had the license number of the Lotus, had turned around, and was gone before they could recover and come after him.

In tan pants and a lightweight brown cashmere blazer over his thick bandages, Ralph Baliol sat in the bedroom of his hospital suite with his eyes closed, being soothed by a reclining massage chair.

He didn't open his eyes when Morgan came in. "You think because someone tried to bomb you and they let Johnny out on bail, you're entitled to ask me more questions, Morgan?"

"It's the American way. Pain and hard work rewarded. You have any thoughts on who decided I was in the way?"

"The police tell me Johnny could have had accomplices."

"Did they tell you about the gunman who wanted your room number? You have any thoughts about him?"

"None whatsoever." Baliol opened his eyes and looked at Morgan. "Why don't you concentrate on your fling with Rachel and leave me and my business alone? I mean, businessman to businessman. As a favor. Two Vietnam veterans. You don't really care who shot me, do you?"

He studied Morgan for a few more moments, then closed his eyes again and let the massage chair continue to stroke him.

Morgan said, "Have you considered it might have been someone who injured you? Perhaps cost you unnecessary millions? Afraid you'd find out, so shot first?"

For a time the rolling of the mechanical chair was the only sound in the room.

"Such as who?"

"Fletcher Comrie."

"Fletcher?" His eyes opened once more, squinted, and he raised a hand to block out the glare of sunlight in the room. "Close those damned drapes."

Morgan walked to the windows, pulled the drapes closed and returned to Baliol in the massage chair. The wounded man's eyes were amused.

"You're sure we're talking about the same Fletcher Comrie, Morgan? The Fletcher Comrie I've worked with for over twenty years? The one the government's crucifying because of some of our deals, not me? That Fletcher Comrie?"

"As far as I know, the very same," Morgan said.

"And in what way did Fletcher injure me?"

"It seems he made a financial killing for himself on some of your joint deals by manipulating the stock you had to buy for the takeovers. From what I've been told, that increased your costs and debt by millions."

"Told by whom?"

"Detective Sergeant Koons. The federal investigators working on Comrie's dealings told him."

Baliol shook his head in both wonder and disgust. "With the taxes we pay, you'd think the government could hire better auditors and investigators. All Fletcher's stock manipulations were part of our operation. Calculated in advance to pay him for his work, make him look good at his brokerage. You understand business,

Morgan. A profit arrangement we didn't make public, eh?'' Baliol
shook his head again at the ignorance of the world. ''If that's all
you have to tell me—''

''It isn't. I found some marks on one of your trees.''

''Marks? On a tree? What are you talking about?''

''Deep indentations in a sycamore directly in line with where you
were shot. A row going up each side of the trunk to a big branch
hidden in leaves. Close enough to the pool area for even a thirty-
eight pistol if the shooter were good. Marks I've seen before.''

''And what are they?''

''Climbing spikes. The kind of equipment used by telephone line-
men, rock climbers, lumberjacks, and tree trimmers. And soldiers,
special forces types like commandos and Green Berets. Maybe bota-
nists, environmentalists, ornithologists looking for birds. Surveyors.
Anyone who has to climb poles or trees uses them, and they leave
deep marks like those on your tree. I'd say that's also how the
shooter got over the fence unnoticed.''

Baliol thought about it. ''You're saying someone with climbing
equipment got over the fence by climbing a tree, sliding over on a
branch, and dropping down inside. He then climbed the sycamore
and shot me from where no one could see him.''

''That bring any particular enemy of yours to mind?''

''Not that I can think of.''

''You climb yourself? Rocks? Mountains?''

''No, and neither does Johnny. It seems you've done the job for
Rachel. If that tree does turn out to be where I was shot from,
you've exonerated Johnny. I owe you something myself.''

''I doubt it, Baliol,'' Morgan said. ''You knew the shooter wasn't
your son from the start. You never believed he had the guts or the
motive. You let the police chase an illusion and your son stew in
jail. You want to tell me why, or do you want me to guess?''

''It's your fantasy, not mine.''

''Speaking of fantasy, Anne Neville thinks you're going to marry
her. She doesn't know about Barbara Schoenhausen, does she?''

Morgan had seen contemptuous stares, but Baliol was a master.
''My private life isn't your business. Not any way at any time.''

''You better tell her before Mrs. Schoenhausen does.''

''Close the door behind you.''

Morgan went to the door. ''You know what I think? I think you knew who shot you from the start. You let Johnny stay in jail as a smokescreen to keep the police busy."

Morgan had dinner at an Italian restaurant in Montecito Village, Pan e Vino. The tables were small, and too many people came to gawk at the celebrities, to pretend they were celebrities or, if they were celebrities, to get their fix of being gawked at and pretending not to notice. But the food was good and different enough to be worthwhile. After dinner he sat over a third and fourth coffee. He didn't want to drink anymore, but he didn't want to go back to his cottage.

He wanted to talk to Barbara Schoenhausen. She had come to live in his mind. He wasn't sure if or why he really wanted her there or was ready for her to be there, but she was there. He wanted to see Barbara Schoenhausen or at least talk to her, but he knew it was too early to call a married woman with children at her home at night.

He went to a movie. Then he drank some more.

It was midnight when Morgan returned to San Ysidro Ranch and found two messages from Rachel waiting at the registration desk. There were none from Lareina, and that made him feel sad until he read the next message. Barbara Schoenhausen had called half an hour earlier. She wanted him to call her immediately. He hurried through the night to his cottage.

The moon was down, and the man came out of the deep shadow at the corner of the cottage. His face was a black blur with round white eyes. A face without features. A black face and white eyes behind the giant shadow that smashed into Morgan's face. A bolt of pain crumpled his side, and pain slammed into his shoulder, buckled his knees, and threw him backwards.

Morgan felt himself going over, but his body, hands, and feet did what his mind and the years out of action had forgotten. He caught the black cloth of an arm. He clawed, pulled, kicked, and levered, and heard the sharp grunt of the weight that flew over and behind him and slammed into the cottage wall. He rolled and came up—into another bolt of pain buried deep in his groin and the impact of crushing metal against the bone and flesh of his face.

He charged and hit the shock of his head against teeth and bone. A breathless grunt in the pitch dark:

"Fuck . . ."

Morgan's head was wet, and for an instant in a patch of ambient night light he saw the figure in black.

A lean, muscular man, not tall. Ski mask. White circles of eyes and a gasping red mouth, wet . . . dripping blood . . .

Then the moving shadow blocked out all light, and Morgan lay on his back without falling.

Why was he on his back?

The violent impact of the ridge of hard metal against his face and the dizzying pain came seconds behind his fall like a shock wave. A sword stabbed his ribs, his body tore like a rag, nausea in his mouth . . .

The black shape bent close over Morgan, and there were quick flashes of brief light in a hand. Large and long. The pain in his ears was like fire. Sticky, burning ears . . .

"Go home, Charlie."

Far to the left a silver edge of moon rested on the tops of the trees. Then there were squares of light. Voices somewhere. Faces looked down at him.

"The paramedics are on their way. Lie still, Mr. Morgan."

The pain radiated from his bones and muscles into his brain. The faces talked. Morgan didn't listen. He listened to himself, to his mind and his body. Listened to his mind and his body tell him that he had been hurt too easily, that only his reflexes had responded, not his mind and not his will. Physically, he was as close to being the soldier of twenty, the CIA agent of thirty, as a man of forty-six could be. It was his mind that was no longer ready to respond to violence. His mind and where he was, in the psychological present. It could never be the same for the civilian at forty as it had been for the soldier at twenty, for the secret soldier at thirty.

The paramedics went to work with their potions, tools, and instruments. People asked him questions, but he said nothing. The faces and the questions went away and he floated where there were no faces or voices. He rode in something that hurt whenever it bounced. He rolled into light and more voices, and hands that put needles in his ears, and then he rolled through lights to somewhere hard and cold where he lay quiet and soft with distant light in thin lines low and far away.

Morgan let his mind and body float until all sense of time slipped away into a suspended state without past or future, without yesterday or tomorrow. No care, and no thought. A cocoon out of time that had come to sustain him only once before. In the first days of the MASH hospital in Vietnam. A cone of silence away from a lifetime of thunder and screams. A void where there was only himself and solitude.

8

Rachel Winrod arrived in the room in St. Francis Hospital with a cold bottle of Dom Perignon and her own crystal flutes.

"They'd give us plastic glasses here, for God's sake."

She sent the nurse for an ice bucket, and sat on the foot of the bed in a red cocktail dress that was wrong for her coloring and style, made her look nearly as old as she was. But it was the proper dress for a banker's afternoon party. There were times for independence and disregard of convention, and times to acknowledge allegiance to the importance and power of convention. She reached to hold Morgan's hand and looked sympathetic.

"Does it hurt terribly?"

"It hurts," Morgan said. "Probably mostly my ego."

She leaned to kiss him, and then giggled. "You do look ridiculous with those two bandaged ears. My wounded bunny."

"That isn't going to heal my ego, Rach."

"I'm sorry, Ford, truly. The doctors say it's not serious, but you probably hurt, poor boy, and all for me and Johnny."

She kissed him again, opened the champagne and poured with a flourish. She handed him his flute, the champagne sparkling like a diamond with its cut crystal and masses of tiny bubbles. She raised her flute in a toast.

"To help you get better," she said.

Morgan said, "Someone paid a professional to discourage me asking questions about who shot your ex-husband, or perhaps about Johnny and where he was that night. That takes a reason and money. Johnny could have a reason—does he have the money?"

"You know how to spoil a party, don't you, Ford?" She drank the champagne. "Not unless he got it from Ralph or a friend. He certainly doesn't have that kind of money of his own."

"How about your money?"

"You think I'm protecting Johnny? For God's sake, Ford, why would I send for you to come up here and snoop around then? You're being ridiculous. Is that why you haven't come to see me again since that first night?"

"I didn't come to Santa Barbara alone, Rach."

"Oh, not your little *señorita,* for God's sake. She hasn't been at the ranch for days, and you went down to L.A. to meet her anyway."

"You have someone investigating the investigator?"

"It only took a few calls to the ranch. I do have contacts. And don't change the subject. Why are you avoiding me?"

"We're not in each other's future, Rach, you know that as well as I do. Why go on?"

"A week or so together on Fernald Point isn't the future."

The nurse returned with the ice, and Rachel wrinkled her nose at the white plastic ice bucket as she set the bottle into the ice. She wasn't someone who pleased nurses, but then, she didn't care about pleasing nurses.

"You're not going to tell me about it, are you, Ford? Whatever is stopping you from calling on a lonely lady in an empty house?"

"Lonely is one thing you'll never be, Rach. You're your own best company."

"Drink your champagne, I have to go." She stood and looked down at Morgan. "You know, I think you need to take life a bit more lightly, Ford. And don't give any champagne to the nurses, they won't appreciate it."

Alone in the sunlight of the overly warm room, Morgan looked out at the tops of trees and the high sky over the mountains. It was a far better view than the blank side panel of a MASH tent in Vietnam. For many, there or not there, Vietnam had happened, had scarred them, but had ended and they had gone on. These were the stronger or narrower or more whole. Or perhaps only the luckier. For too many more, Vietnam had never ended. Morgan's tour had not been the full horror, his wound had not been that bad. His scars weren't on the body or the mind, but they were the kind you carried with you. Scars on the soul, or whatever you called what made us different from all the other life on this planet. Scars he had buried until they broke out again in angry memories with an ex-wife, or at unexpected moments like last night's beating, or joined to an even more unexpected woman.

It was late afternoon when Lareina called. *"Querido!* You are all right?"

"I'm fine, Reina. Where are you?"

"In Cabo, where else would I be, *sí?* What is happen?"

Morgan told her what had happened in the dark outside the ranch cottage.

"I will come back at once."

"No need," Morgan said. "I'll be out tomorrow or the next day, and I'm still trying to get Johnny Baliol off the hook. Give me a few more days. I'll come down there. It's been years since I was in Cabo, or even Mexico. Perhaps only a few more days up here and I'll . . ."

Morgan was aware of his own voice talking, saying words that had little if any meaning, certainly not to him. When he finally stopped, aware of the emptiness of the words, Lareina was silent. Then her voice was quiet.

"You don't need a woman anymore, Ford?"

"You know that's not what I meant, Reina. Of course I'd like you—"

"Don't explain, Ford. When I return, or you come here, we will talk. I am glad you are not badly hurt, and hope you will take better care of yourself. *Ciao, querido."*

His hand rested on the receiver for some minutes after he had hung up. They had had good times, he and Lareina, but it wasn't Lareina he was thinking about.

As the long afternoon stretched silent and warm in the sunlight through the windows, Morgan thought about Barbara Schoenhausen and her call to the San Ysidro Ranch at nearly midnight last night. There were two explanations that came readily to mind: she had had a sudden late-night need to talk to him, or she had called to warn him, somehow knowing about the attack. He wasn't sure he was prepared for either. But he knew which he hoped was true, and he was thinking about talking to her alone in a dark room at night when Sergeant Koons of the sheriff's department closed the door and sat on the gray steel visitor's chair.

"A broken finger, a cracked rib, a concussion, and nicely sliced ears," Koons said. "I'm not even talking about bruises."

"I've got them."

"Let's talk about the ears. You're no lightweight to punch around, he was breathing hard and in a hurry. It was dark, he was bleeding where you got him a few good ones with your hand-to-hand and your head. His adrenaline was pumping. But the doctors tell me he sliced the outer edges of both ears as neat and clean as they could with a scalpel on an operating table, and without doing any important damage. He handles a knife like a surgeon, he used brass knuckles on your face and ribs, and he came dressed and prepared for the job. You need a telegram?"

Morgan said. "I think he was the same man who killed the John Doe outside Anne Neville's house. Have you identified the John Doe yet?"

"No. Go home, Morgan."

Morgan looked at a flash from high on the mountains where something moved and caught the sun. "Did you see those marks on that big sycamore near Baliol's pool?"

"Marks?"

Morgan described the deep cuts like puncture wounds on both sides of the tree on Ralph Baliol's estate. "My guess is they were made by climbing spikes. The sycamore's in good range of that pool deck."

Koons stood up. "Go home, Morgan."

Alone again, Morgan looked up at the pattern of sun and shadow on the white ceiling. Everyone wanted him to go home. Lying there in the hospital bed he realized he wasn't sure he knew where that was. Morgan closed his eyes, but sleep didn't come. After three or four minutes, he opened his eyes and looked out the windows once more and waited for the solitary flash to appear again high up where no one else was, but it never did. It could be hard to live that high and alone. It could be harder to live with others down on the valley floor.

Toward evening, the doctors came in and checked him over. With stern warnings to rest, stay off his feet, and give the mild concussion time to subside, they agreed to let him go home at noon the next day. The stitches would be removed from his ears in ten days, the splint on the finger of his left hand would stay on longer. The rib would heal by itself. He was advised to live a quiet life for a few weeks.

Morgan picked up the phone and dialed an outside line. This time Barbara Schoenhausen was at home.

"Last night," Morgan said, "you had to talk to me at once."

"I'm sorry, Ford. Call it late-night blues."

"You're not blue anymore?"

"Daylight does wonders."

"I've been trying to reach you."

"I've been out a lot, but I don't see what else I can tell you anyway."

"Have you seen Ralph Baliol since we talked?"

"Yes."

"Then we have something to talk about."

Her silence said she wasn't at all sure they had anything to talk about. "All right, Ford. When and where?"

"Sometime tomorrow. After lunch. Anywhere you want."

"It doesn't matter. I'll be dropping the children at a friend's in Montecito. Why don't I come up to the Plow and Angel at the ranch?"

"Three o'clock then."

She hung up. Something had changed. Five days ago at their first meeting she had insisted they meet in an out-of-the-way bar where she never went.

The night was long and Morgan's sleep short, and the next morning was even longer. He made one phone call while he waited for the doctors to make his release official. The important if nameless Colombian gentleman was sorry to have heard of his injuries, and wondered if the matter was anything he should be concerned about. Morgan assured him it wasn't. The Colombian accepted his word and got to the business in hand.

"The names you gave appear completely legitimate, *Señor* Morgan. Mr. Comrie has made small buys from a medium-level person as a favor for personal use. However, my sources inform me that this Mr. Comrie then used our product to intimidate those he himself had supplied by threatening to bring their superiors down upon them. He is not a nice man, this Mr. Comrie."

"I'll remember that," Morgan said. "Now I need another favor, *señor*. A gun and permit. Can you do that?"

"Of course. Give me the details for the permit."

Morgan gave him all the necessary data for a California pistol permit. "Can you have it delivered to the San Ysidro Ranch in Santa Barbara?"

"In a few hours."

"I appreciate the favor."

"*De nada.* You are perhaps returning to the employ of your government, *Señor* Morgan? And, of course, to us?"

"I don't think so."

"A pity. But, you are probably right. It is sometimes better to sit in the sun and drink *guaro* and make little gifts for one's children."

When the hospital finally released him, bandages, aches, pains, and all, Morgan took a cab to San Ysidro Ranch where the clerks stared at his bandaged ears and gave him a message from CIA man Hughes Bremner back at Langley. *The license belongs to a 1962 Lotus registered to Humphrey Bowan, 2727–A Ashley Road, Santa Barbara. 93108. Don't forget our lunch date.*

In his cottage, Morgan changed out of the bloody clothes he had worn into and out of the hospital, and washed as best he could standing in the bathtub. He shaved carefully, keeping far away from his bandaged ears. He put on his best gray dress slacks that were looser than jeans, and the biggest *jaspe* shirt he had to hide his bandaged ribs. It was purple, but it would have to do. At least it went with his boots and Akubra hat. There was nothing he could do to hide his ears.

He called room service for a rum cooler and sat on the deck of the cottage to wait for three o'clock.

9

In the Plow and Angel lounge Barbara Schoenhausen was already at a corner table, her head bent, her face framed by the hood of black hair. Morgan had been carrying her image inside his mind since she had walked out of that first bar a week ago. Her reality now was slightly shifted, like a double exposure. She wore large silver-rimmed aviator sunglasses, no jewelry except her rings, a dark blue blouse, black slacks and black sandals. Less precise and proper. The focus was harder, and the impact more blunt. The seamless maturity of her face was drawn tighter as she sat in the dim afternoon lounge seemingly unaware of him watching her, or of anyone else in the lounge.

He walked to the table. "Sorry I'm late."

Her eyes were invisible behind the dark glasses, but her face showed that she saw his bandaged ears and finger. "What happened?"

"Why did you call me last night?"

"I told you."

"Late-night blues, I know. But why me? You said I don't know you, and you don't know me. Not yet."

"You know about Ralph."

"It wasn't to warn me?"

She looked for the waiter, waved him to the table, and ordered two Anchor Steam beers. She turned back to Morgan. "I wanted to tell you Ralph was having you watched."

"By the man who attacked me?"

"I don't know who attacked you."

"Who else would want me out of the way?" He gave her the less graphic details of what had happened the night before. "I haven't

68

been around that sort of thing for a long time. I'm bigger than he was, in fair shape, and it was only a warning this time, so I came out of it without too much damage."

"I'm sorry, Ford. Finding me hasn't done much for you."

From behind the dark glasses she looked straight into Morgan's face. The full mouth was as soft as on that first afternoon, the dignity and the control were the same, but the diffidence was gone. That first afternoon she had come in with a husband and family all around her. Now, he realized, she acted more like a woman alone. Her face seemed thinner, deeper hollows below her high cheekbones. Her whole body was drawn tighter in a kind of fierce tension that radiated and vibrated. A tension she seemed to enjoy, or at least to accept as part of her.

"You're still seeing him? Ralph?"

The waiter arrived with their beers. When he had gone, she sat back in her chair. "He's the same man, isn't he? Ralph, I mean. He's another kind of Alfred all over again. Cruder, less polite, not at all kind, but the same man. All the men I've been with were the same man. I didn't know as much about myself as I thought I did."

"The same mistake a hundred times," Morgan said. "It's what we all do until, if we're lucky, we finally break out and get it right."

"Is that what you've done?"

"I thought I had."

She turned her head to look toward the entrance. "You came here and stirred a placid pond, Ford."

"The pond isn't all that placid. Something is boiling under the surface. Something that made you go to Ralph Baliol."

"Simmering, perhaps, not boiling. Boiling doesn't happen very often in our nice, complacent ponds. Boiling takes too high a toll."

"Simmering or boiling, something happened to you. That was what you said earlier. What did happen?"

"It wasn't all that dramatic, really. A small moment of revelation. About Alfred and about me. Nothing big or shocking, but it was important or I wouldn't have remembered it so vividly, would I? The trigger is so often a small thing. A laugh, a slap, an attitude finally understood." She drank her Anchor Steam. "A few years ago Alfred had to take a sudden trip back to Germany for a family crisis . . ."

*   *   *

That morning over breakfast, after the housekeeper had left their juice and returned to the kitchen for her yogurt and his eggs, Alfred said, "I must go back home again. It's Helmuth, my eldest brother. I'd like you to come with me. You have never met Helmuth."

They would make it a vacation. She had never gone to Baden-Baden, or seen the Schwarzwald. They could even go down to Italy for a few days. She had not felt comfortable with his family the few times they had been together, and didn't want to go. But she knew she would, so she smiled and told him what a wonderful time they would have.

On the jet he told her about Helmuth. She had met the other brother, Erich, the one his mother liked to call Graf even though the title had never been in their branch of the Schoenhausens. Helmuth was almost seventy. After the war, when they had lost everything, and Erich was a P.O.W. in England and Alfred only a boy, it was Helmuth who supported the family. It was Helmuth who pressured Bonn to award the family a small estate in compensation for what the Nazis had taken and the communists in East Germany had kept. But later Helmuth seemed to go crazy. He turned his business over to his sons and wandered off around the world. He went to live with a woman in East Berlin, became a communist and a painter. Alfred wasn't sure which of these three insults to the family his mother hated most.

Now Helmuth was dying in a hospital in the reunited Germany and the family would come together to bring him back into the fold. Barbara wouldn't have to go to the hospital or meet Helmuth at all. Alfred said this because he was a good husband, but Barbara knew his mother, Helga, would have a different view of what a wife must do. A woman with the face and manner of a statue in the town square, Helga wore long, dark dresses from the time of Bismarck, walked with a cane that was more weapon than support.

In the hospital, Barbara stood far back in the long room. Her German was good enough to understand what they said. There were eleven Schoenhausen adults. Helga in black with her silver-headed cane was the fulcrum. The others revolved around her. Alfred, silent and uncomfortable. Graf Erich, outraged beside his mother. The sisters—one a widow and two unmarried. The five grown children of Helmuth and Erich and the widowed sister. Facing them from bed like a prisoner in the dock was Helmuth, a bearded face Barbara saw intermittently as the family shifted and moved in front of her. The mood was anger.

Look at that beard! It is an insult, father. And your hair, Helmuth. Is that woman coming here? Mama could not come because of her. Will you be buried in that beard, Helmuth? This last from Helga, the matriarch.

Barbara didn't understand the trouble over the beard. She liked a beard on the right man. Helmuth's beard was full and black without a trace of gray. It gave the sick man a spiritual appearance without sacrificing what she sensed was a powerful dignity and conviction. He was alone among them all. A tremendous sense of isolation.

"You look like a starving Bolshevik! A white-faced rabbi."

"The walls have ears, old woman," Helmuth said. His voice was weak, an effort, but there was a fierceness in it too, like the black beard. "You want them to suspect an unreconstructed Nazi? They might take back the estate."

"The Nazis were low-class swine. This government knows who we are."

Helmuth's oldest son told his father to think of the family. He was urged to come home to the estate, return to his heritage. It was how a Schoenhausen should die.

"With or without the beard?"

When Alfred and Erich went to discuss Helmuth's situation with the hospital authorities, Barbara sat alone in the corridor. After a time she got up and returned to Helmuth's room. He smiled when he saw her. His English was only lightly accented. "You're the American. Freddie's wife."

"Barbara."

"So how do you like being a Schoenhausen, Barbara?"

"What's so wrong with a beard? Long hair?"

"Ah? You understand German?"

"Alfred helped me. Are you really dying?"

"I hope not, Barbara. So you like a beard?"

"On some men. I can't grow one."

Helmuth laughed, coughed, and held to the side of the bed. He breathed hard. His smile when it came again was half pain. "I saved the family. The hero of the Schoenhausens. An estate again, position, status, back in our anointed and deserved place. The Schoenhausens and Germany. All back to normal, everything as it should be. Smug, dreary, unchanged Germany, still Nazi in its soul. Smug, narrow, unchanged Schoenhausens, still medieval in body and mind and manner." His isolation was so strong it was tangible. "I had struggled to save us from what order and certainty had done to us, not to bring back the good old days of order and certainty."

"Long hair and a beard? East Germany?"

Helmuth closed his eyes. "A little chaos. The recognition of chaos. Of what we are. Of what is important. A radical, yes? A wanderer. A painter of what he sees. Bitter, horrific images. Disturbing visions. Disturbing to the Schoenhausens and the new Germany. All visions disturb those with no vision."

"What did East Germany see?"

"A new certainty." He opened his eyes, smiled that gentle yet mocking smile. "And some certainty that was not so new."

"They why there?"

"My Schoenhausens were in the West. My needle would stab more deeply from the East than from anywhere else. Now there will be only one Germany, one certainty. The old one and the Schoenhausens. Now I am dying and have a beard."

Barbara felt as isolated as she saw him to be. She sat down near the bed. "I don't think I understand."

Helmuth closed his eyes, breathed slowly. After a time, Barbara stood. He was a sick man, she had tired him. Alfred and Erich would be looking for her. She turned to leave.

He spoke without opening his eyes. "No one liked the Nazis among the elite of our village—the local party leader was the son of our butcher, *Gott in himmel.* But at least the Nazis gave order and patriotism to the nation, and showed respect for our position and traditions and estates. So we sat on our estates, observed our traditions, kept our heads down until such time as we had our power again as well as our traditions and estates.

"My father did not sit. He opposed the Nazis openly and loudly in speeches and pamphlets. He helped communists and Jews and democrats and labor leaders and anyone else they persecuted. Our land was confiscated, our privileges of centuries were canceled. The family was furious. My father had to make peace with the Nazis. Or at least keep silent. Wait for the wind to blow in another direction. He was a Schoenhausen, his job was to be a Schoenhausen, protect the Schoenhausens. People like us, Helga told him, do not tilt at windmills. People like us know what they have to do. My father did not make peace. He was arrested and killed. The family never forgave him."

A week later, on the train to Baden-Baden, Barbara asked Alfred what would happen if Helmuth kept the beard and the woman.

"He will certainly never be buried on Schoenhausen land."

Barbara thought of all she had been unhappy with in her marriage but could never say why. Alfred's assumption that their son would be Alfred Erich Helmuth, that their daughter would be Helga to honor his mother. It was what the Schoenhausens did. The clothes he bought for her, approved with a small smile and a nod when they shopped together. They were exactly the same kinds of clothes his family sent her for Christmas and her birthdays: good quality, reserved, proper for a Schoenhausen wife and mother. The same kind of clothes her parents sent her when she was first married. Mature, restrained. Not clothes she would have chosen for herself if she'd thought about it.

She said, "Alfred? What would you say if I went down to Nicaragua with our church group next year? They're planning to go and help in the coffee harvest."

"We don't want to give any support to those Sandinistas. Besides, picking coffee isn't something we do, is it?"

Alfred turned back to the window and the countryside of Germany. Barbara decided to think about going back to college, getting a graduate degree in social work.

The waiter brought their second beers.

"I did go back to college, got my master's, but it didn't really change anything. Alfred and I talked. We compromised on volunteer social work while the children were at school, and I made him buy me a two-seater 450SL, dark blue. A dissatisfied housewife's car." She drank, shook her head. Her black hair caught the muted light. "The turmoil is under the surface where we don't have to recognize it. That's the way most of us want it. Especially we middle-class women. We're unhappy, confused, alone, so we find an accommodation, a way to go on with the surface never showing a ripple. No one knows, the children are happy."

Morgan said, "You know, and the children know. They don't want to know, and they're not happy."

She removed the contoured silver-rimmed sunglasses and set

them down on the table between them. Her eyes were neither red nor swollen. Morgan saw some bitterness and a certain distance he hadn't felt in the other cocktail lounge that first time. Not a distance from him, a distance from what she had been. She pushed the dark glasses back and forth on the table with one finger. "Do you like them? They seemed to be something I'd like to wear, be comfortable with."

"What do Alfred and Ralph think about them?"

"Alfred hasn't noticed. Ralph has other things on his mind."

"Will you be there when Ralph gets home?"

She picked up the dark glasses, but didn't put them on. "Rachel Winrod is a woman who lives through men, isn't she? But not with men. She's alone with herself. Like Alfred." She held the dark glasses up to her face as a mirror. "When I told you it was all right to call me at home, you were surprised. You think most men wonder when a strange man calls their wife. You might find that less true than you think, but in Alfred's case there's a special circumstance. You see, Alfred came here, became a citizen, made money, married, fathered children, but none of that is really him. His wife is American, his children are American, but he is not American. He is *an* American, but he is not American. He lives with Bismarck and Goethe, Kleist and Barbarrosa. If he caught his wife in an adulterous affair, he would have to consider the problem. But I'm not in his mind enough that he would wonder if I *might* be involved with another man. It wouldn't cross his mind. Barbara Allison doesn't cross his mind, only Mrs. Alfred Schoenhausen, and then not often."

"Am I'm hearing a decision?" Morgan said.

She put her dark glasses back on and looked around the room that was beginning to fill as five o'clock and the cocktail hour came closer. The dark glasses in the low light of the lounge gave her the face of an ancient idol with its empty sockets blackened by the centuries.

Morgan said, "Can I tell you a story too? The story of my life?"

She still looked through the room at the laughing people arriving to fill the tables. Husbands and wives out on the town, getting drunk. Saturday night.

"Do you want to?"

"Mr. Langford Morgan? Telephone for Langford Morgan?"

Morgan had to take the call at the bar. It was the clerk at the front desk. "There's a package here for you, Mr. Morgan. It's hand delivered, the messenger insists you sign for it."

Morgan returned to the table, put his room key down in front of her. "I have to go to the hotel office. Why don't I meet you at my cottage? They'll send the beers. The story of my life can be long and dusty."

The messenger waited in the office—a dark man with blank eyes who looked hard at Morgan before he handed over the package and left. Outside his cottage, Morgan sat in the BMW and opened it. There was a compact Czech Vz70, two boxes of .32 ACP ammunition, a small belt holster, and the California pistol permit. It looked totally official. He left the gun in the car, locked the doors, and went inside.

Barbara Schoenhausen wasn't in the cottage. Morgan looked out on the deck, then all around the flowered grounds near the cottage, but she wasn't anywhere.

In the now crowded cocktail lounge a twenty-dollar bill lay on the table under her empty glass beside the bar bill and his room key, and the waiter said that the lady had left perhaps five minutes ago. Morgan went out to the small upper parking lot. She wasn't there, and he saw no dark blue Mercedes 450SL. The attendant told him a woman resembling her had gone down to the lower parking lot.

A small dark blue 450SL was pulling out into San Ysidro Lane as Morgan reached the lower lot. An old white Cadillac convertible with massive horns on the hood and a man in a cowboy hat sitting behind the wheel went out behind her. Morgan had seen the man in the cowboy hat before. Or he thought he had. At the corner of the house next to Anne Neville's house, standing in the shadows with what could have been a silenced pistol.

Back in his cottage, Morgan waited an hour and called Barbara Schoenhausen at home. The housekeeper informed him Mrs. Schoenhausen had not come home. At Cottage Hospital she had not been in all day. He knew nowhere else to call, and was too tense to sit in the cottage. If the cowboy in the Cadillac was who he thought he was, and was doing what he had a hunch he was doing —working for Ralph Baliol—Baliol wasn't going to tell him, but perhaps Fletcher Comrie would.

10

The narrow blacktop road off Romero Canyon climbed through the trees and dense chaparral of the first ridges of the Santa Ynez Mountains for a mile before Fletcher Comrie's house came into view around a sudden curve. White and abstract in right angles and flat horizontal surfaces, it perched high on a crag with a panorama of half the world. A modern aerie for a modern bird of prey, as inaccessible as any medieval fortress.

An electronic gate at the foot of a steep driveway announced itself. "Please state your business."

"Langford Morgan working for the ex–Mrs. Ralph Baliol. I'd appreciate a few minutes of Mr. Fletcher Comrie's time."

This far up into the mountain ridges the day was ten degrees hotter than down on the coast. The unshaded sunlight shimmered, and a pair of buteos sailed high on the thermal currents. The gate swung open.

"Drive up to the end."

The driveway curved up and around the house and ended on the roof. One level of the modern castle's main wing rose above the rooftop parking area. It had no windows on this side, only a single steel door. As Morgan approached the door he heard it click and watched as it swung open. He entered a bare room. A metal detector beeped.

"Leave all metal objects in the box to your left."

The lid of the steel box popped up; Morgan dropped his new Vz70 inside. The lid closed. Another steel door on the far side opened onto a spiral staircase in a circular shaft that led downward. He went down and emerged abruptly into space high above a living room that curved in a semicircle around the staircase. Its outer walls were all glass. Morgan felt he was hanging off the edge of the mountain.

"It's a hell of a shock the first time."

Below in the living room, a short man sat on a long couch. He wore a gray sweatshirt, baggy chinos, and black running shoes without socks. His head was too big for his thin neck and body, like a stick man drawn by a child. He had big ears and a dense growth of wild red hair, and one small hand rested on a series of electronic controls in the arm of the couch. On the single straight interior wall a massive video-audio-intercom-and-surveillance console took up a quarter of the wall. Morgan's parked BMW showed on one of the screens.

"Why not have visitors slide down a firepole?"

"Most of the ladies don't like the stairs as it is. Come on down, Morgan, and have a seat."

The living room was essentially one giant bay window. The only furniture was the couch, two armchairs, a glass coffee table on an oriental rug, and a small teak dining table with four teak chairs. The walls were bare, the surfaces empty. Morgan was acutely aware of the silence of the house as his footsteps echoed in the room the way they would in the lobby of a giant building at 3:00 A.M. Fletcher Comrie waved him to the other end of the big couch.

"So what did Rachel send you to talk to me about?" Comrie's voice was too loud, as if he spent most of his time alone and in silence.

"You live here alone, Mr. Comrie?"

"Is there any other way to live?"

"No attachments, no family? Not even servants?"

"Attachments come and go, no pun intended. The problem isn't making them, it's breaking them. Family is overrated. He travels fastest and so on. And all my houses run themselves. Hired hands maybe once a week. Technology and gadgets, that's my real weakness. Why does my lifestyle interest you?"

"It's unusual, iconoclastic and even antisocial, and I like to know who I'm talking to."

"So do I. You're pretty idiosyncratic yourself, and exactly what does Rachel want you to find out?"

"Who shot her former husband."

"I wouldn't have thought she gave a dog turd about Ralph."

"Sorry. I should have said she wants me to prove to the police that Johnny didn't shoot his father."

Comrie fiddled with the controls in the arm of the couch, and the whole couch revolved until it was facing the 300-degree view of mountains, coast, ocean, and distant islands. "It'd be a howl and a half if the kid did shoot Ralph. That's a hobby horse of Ralph's: the competition between fathers and sons. Maybe because his own father was so damned old he never seemed to know exactly who the hell Ralph was." Fletcher Comrie laughed aloud and let his eyes go distant and distracted at the same time. "You know, the first Comrie to come to this country back in the late eighteenth century was a slick conniver named Lucas. He got out of Scotland a skip and a jump ahead of an angry clan chief he'd sold out to the English. His father, Connal, not only disowned Lucas, he took his sword and other sons and rode with the clan to kill Lucas. The clan was understanding, didn't blame the father for Lucas's dastardly treachery. Connal disowned Lucas for looking out for Lucas, but was more than ready to help kill his own son to look out for Connal. My father doesn't speak to me, I'm not respectable enough. Old Lucas would laugh in his grave, wherever the hell it is."

"You know all about this ancestor of yours, but don't know where he's buried?"

"Unmarked grave. Comries don't go in for monuments. You can't use them, get rich on them, or buy anything with them." He looked up at his high ceiling. "He was quite a guy, old Lucas. Back then the path of glory, gold, and empire was West, right? But vision and glory wasn't what made Lucas tick, today's money and goods did. He intended to make his fortune digging in the pockets of the diggers and builders. Outsmart all the smug bastards from the noble clan chief to the last goddamn squire who thought he was God himself. He knew, Lucas did."

"What did Lucas know, Mr. Comrie?"

"It's not who ends up with the most toys, but who wins the most games. It's how much you kill, not how fat you get. Beat the other guy, the rest is shit. Nothing's permanent because you can't take it with you. When you're gone you won't know you were ever here. When the world's gone nothing will know it was here."

"You're not winning now."

"The game's a long way from over. We've got appeals, writs, motions, and depositions that'll make the feds dizzy. Even if I lose, what do they do to me? A whopper of a fine that won't even touch what I've really got. A couple of years in a federal country club not half as tough as the army. I catch up on my reading, get out, and it's business as usual. Hell, I'll probably write a book, make a billion, and get hired to teach business at a classy grad school."

To outwit the world, hoodwink the universe. The perfect predator, Comrie lived only to eat and so could never have enough. The *act* of triumph was what counted, not the result, so while he would never have enough, he would never be crushed by having nothing.

"The wolf on the fold," Morgan said. "Is that the way Ralph Baliol operates too?"

"Ralph can eat with us wolves when he wants to."

"Perhaps someone decided to get rid of a wolf? A business enemy. Can you think of any names?"

"Too many. People get angry when you beat them."

"Who's angry at Baliol who might use climbing spikes?"

"What the hell are climbing spikes?"

"Equipment used for climbing telephone poles and trees."

"Trees?" Comrie was thoughtful. "There's Stoke-Higham Timber up in the California redwood country around Gaul. Ralph did a leveraged buyout takeover back in 'eighty-eight."

"They didn't like being taken over?"

"Nobody likes a hostile takeover, but he left most of the management team in place. He sent in one of his own men to be CEO, but the old management still runs day-to-day operations. Profits have been up every year since Ralph took over, the mills're humming, employment's full tilt. They ought to want to kiss, not kill him."

"You were involved in that takeover?"

"Not directly. I never am. I peddled the bonds he used to raise the cash, and had some stock interest in the deal myself. That's all."

"Were those some of the stocks you manipulated to raise the price and cash in on? Incidentally raising the price Baliol had to pay for the takeover."

"Who the hell told you that?"

"The federal examiners told the sheriff's office. Sergeant Koons told me."

Comrie shrugged. "A nice piece of change in my pocket, and not even illegal." He grinned. "How did all that happen to come up between you and the police?"

"We were looking for other motives for someone to shoot Ralph

Baliol. Koons figured your manipulations were more a motive for Ralph to shoot you. But when I asked Baliol about it, he said it was all part of your working together. What do *you* say about it?"

Comrie sat up and looked at his watch. "I say I'm late for drinks and dinner. On business, whatever Ralph says, I say, okay? Anything more I can help you with, Morgan, come back or give me a call."

When Morgan looked back down before the staircase passed into the ceiling, Fletcher Comrie hadn't moved to go wherever he had to go, still sat on the couch looking out at his enormous view.

At sheriff department headquarters, Morgan sat across the desk from Sergeant Koons as the day shift hurried to close up shop and get ready to leave.

"Have you run across a company called Stoke-Higham Timber while you've been investigating the Baliol shooting? A redwood lumber company up north in Gaul?"

Koons worked. "I don't hear you, do I? You're in Costa Rica, or New York, or Shangri-la."

"Look, sergeant, I'm not a detective and I don't want to be one. I just wanted to make Johnny Baliol's mother grateful, but now I know Johnny didn't shoot anyone, and you know it, and I think Ralph Baliol knows it and always did. I think he's got someone of his own to help him 'handle' it. I think that's who attacked me and shot our John Doe. I'm afraid someone else could be caught in the middle. Someone I don't want to see hurt. Now I happen to find out Baliol did a hostile takeover and owns a timber company where they sure as hell use climbing spikes. Baliol never mentioned that, or Rachel, or you, or—"

"Who could be caught in the middle and hurt?" Koons didn't look up when he said it.

"A woman. Barbara Schoenhausen. You don't—"

"She's clear." Koons put his pen down, leaned back. "You think we're clowns, Morgan? All Baliol's private life is clear. The only people with any possible motive we know right now who aren't clear are Fletcher Comrie, Johnny Baliol, and our dead John Doe. There are a whole lot of people who could have motives we don't know about yet, and we're working on them. That's our job."

"Sorry, sergeant. I apologize."

The sergeant went back to his work. "You mixed up with the Schoenhausen woman?"

"No."

"But you'd like to be."

"I don't know exactly what I want with Barbara Schoenhausen except that I don't want her with Ralph Baliol."

"Maybe you shot him?"

"I didn't get here in time. What about Baliol hiring professional muscle?"

Koons gave up on his work, pushed it away, and sat back again. "What do you want us to do? Baliol's got security people all around his companies. You can't identify the guy who attacked you, or the one you think could have shot our John Doe, and we haven't a clue on either of those things yet. Literally."

"And Stoke-Higham Timber?"

"They're six hundred miles north of here. They've got a couple of hundred in the offices, a couple of thousand in the trees and mills. We've sent up the stuff on our John Doe, who else do we investigate? Their profit's way up since Baliol took over, they've doubled their shifts, are even hiring. We don't see a motive. Look, we missed those spike marks the first time around. You did good, and Stoke-Higham is a good lead, but it's not for Sherlock Holmes. If someone up there shot Baliol it's going to be a long job of knock on doors, dig, watch, and wait. Go home, relax, and think about the Schoenhausen woman."

It was, Morgan knew, good advice. He didn't give one real damn who had shot Ralph Baliol. Unless it involved Barbara Schoenhausen. Johnny was out of jail. All that was left he had to do was finish with Rachel.

"What about the bomb in my car?" Morgan said. "You have any clues yet on that?"

"No."

"I think maybe I do. If I'm right, I can lead you to who planted it, and to what Johnny Baliol was doing that night."

11

Ashley Road wasn't in Santa Barbara, it was in Montecito. Old Montecitans list their addresses as Santa Barbara, anything else would be ostentatious. Number 2727 was up near Mountain Drive on the slopes of the first mountains. A two-story Monterey with a second-floor gallery, it was set back from the road behind old oaks. A second mailbox was numbered 2727–A, and the blacktop drive branched before reaching the big house, with the narrower branch leading down into a barranca. Among the trees at the bottom of the barranca was the smaller second house rich Montecitans build for guests, retired parents, or grown children who never left.

Morgan, Koons, and the deputies in the second car parked up on Mountain Drive and walked back down. The garage was open and empty; no one answered their rings or knocks. At the back of the house a pool and patio were fenced from the trees. An automatic cleaning head moved like a turtle across the surface of the pool. The gate in the fence was open, so were the french doors into the house. Two mockingbirds and a jay watched Morgan and the police enter.

All the downstairs rooms were neat and clean, the work most probably of a cleaning person who came every day but who didn't do upstairs bedrooms. The first bedroom was neat under a layer of dust: a guest room. The second, at the front, had all the conventional mess of a male who has gotten up late and rushed to dress and run. In the third, on a table in a corner, there were rolls of wire, tools, plastic explosive, and a half-made bomb.

The Lotus and a sleek Jaguar came together down the drive to the house, pursuing each other like playful jungle cats, and produced two young men who lost their laughter when they walked into the living room and found Morgan and the police.

"You have names?" Koons said. "Mine is Koons, Detective Sergeant Koons, sheriff's department. Which one of you is Humphrey Bowan?"

The taller one swallowed hard. "I am."

"Francis Howard," the shorter one managed with more of a croak than a voice.

Two neat young men in business suits, ties, and white shirts. Well-mannered and well-dressed. In their late twenties or early thirties. Shock on their good-looking faces. Well-groomed hands with clean nails. One of them carried a full briefcase and the other a sack of groceries bought on the way home from the office, perhaps for tonight's dinner. A treat for themselves.

Morgan said, "Tell the sergeant why you and Johnny Baliol are so scared you plant bombs in cars."

Humphrey Bowan sat down and started to talk.

Their parents did business with each other, indirectly if not directly. They belonged to the same or similar golf, country, business, and social clubs. They went to the same parties, served on the same county boards, worked for the same charities. They belonged to the same political committees, alumni associations, fraternities.

Their boys grew up together, went to the same or similar schools, did the same drugs. Even those who went to private schools out of town or abroad came home to hang out in the summers. They did their Sunday school at the same or similar churches, joined the same Boy Scout troops. They were given the same or similar cars on their sixteenth birthdays, got into the same trouble, paid the same tickets.

Their colleges were mostly private and usually outside California. They felt no particular urgency to finish. They knew what their future was, what they would be expected to become. They knew who their wives would be, if not their final names. They knew where their houses would be, if not exactly in what town or city. So why should they rush through college and their youth? They would put on the suits and ties, wear the well-shined shoes soon enough, marry their destined wives, and carry the briefcases.

These were not the ambitious, the daring freebooters, the carvers of empires. These were the county officials, the city attorneys, the commission members and local politicians, the assistants to the king and his ministers. And sooner or later the time came when they had to fulfill their function, take their place, and begin the next generation.

That Friday night Humphrey Bowan had just returned from a two-week business trip. Two weeks as the most junior executive, at the beck and whim of all the others, had not been a lot of fun for Humphrey. Francis Howard hadn't had all that great a two weeks at his law firm where his uncle was the senior partner, or alone in the house on Humphrey's parents' estate. They had needed some laughs, a night on the town.

They had a few beers, smoked a few joints, and headed out to find bigger action at a Montecito nightspot where they knew they would find many friendly dealers in the happy flake. They were well known in the trendy bistro, had three or four more beers at the bar, and dickered with the dealers for the best price on the best cocaine.

Some people who were going to a party in a mansion down near the beach took them along. The party was crowded with glittering celebrities up from Los Angeles. Frank and Humphrey had more beer, did some lines, found themselves paired with two dazzling starlets from Hollywood and Beverly Hills. The starlets knew of another party being given by an important actor-producer up in the mountains above Toro Canyon. Frank and Humphrey agreed to drive the starlets.

The second party was smaller and duller. There wasn't enough beer, the blow ran out, and the starlets were far more interested in impressing the actor-producer and his friends than in two locals. Frank and Humphrey decided to go back to the nightspot and buy more cocaine. The crowd had thinned at the bistro, and they found Johnny Baliol alone at the bar brooding about Anne and his father. She had made a lame excuse for not seeing him that night for the tenth time in a month. They all had more drinks and agreed that women were royal pains in the ass. Especially all the goddamn cunts they grew up with who were too fucking in love with themselves and their goddamn pussies. They agreed on that one hundred and ten percent.

"Hey," the owner said, "I know a really great party. You guys ought to go over."

This was a different kind of party. It was in Montecito, but the people were not all from Montecito, or Beverly Hills, or Hollywood. The host was a rich eccentric with a vague past who invited all kinds of people to his parties. There was a lot of booze, and a lot of drugs right out in the open. Everyone was having a hell of a time. Humphrey, Frank, and Johnny joined right in and met Greta and Anita, two young women definitely not from Montecito or Beverly Hills.

They were pretty, Greta and Anita. They danced well and with wild abandon. They drank and snorted as much and as hard as any guy. They swore. They smoked. Greta wore orange stretch pants tighter than skin, a black tank top, no bra, and high-heeled silver ankle-strap sandals. Her breasts bounced every time she moved on the dance floor. Anita had breasts that didn't bounce in her red tank top, but pressed nicely against a man's chest when she danced close. She wore black short shorts spangled with rhinestones, and high-heeled red boots.

Around midnight Humphrey suggested Anita, Greta, and Johnny should come back to his and Frank's place and continue the party. The women hesitated. They didn't really know Frank, Humphrey, and Johnny. But when they learned the house was in Montecito, they decided the men were really "nice boys" and agreed to go. Humphrey took Greta in his Lotus, Johnny squeezed Frank and Anita into the Maserati. They opened bottles of beer, smoked, and blew a joint or two on the drive toward the mountains.

In the house, Frank took the women on a tour while Humphrey cleared space in the living room for dancing, and Johnny put CDs on the stereo. The women stumbled back giggling because Frank had flopped on the beds in both bedrooms and invited them to join him. The women said he was cute, but not that cute. All three of the young men were cute, the women could get to like them. Everyone danced, drank, smoked, and snorted until the women passed out. Frank was nearly out himself, Johnny was raving about Anne and his fucking son of a bitch of a father, and Humphrey wanted a woman.

Humphrey cursed the two starlets who had dumped them earlier and all the tight-ass cunts at the pool and country club. They had more vodka and beer and decided they all needed a woman. They shook Greta and Anita where they were slumped in chairs. It took a lot of doing, but they finally got the women on their feet and half carried, half walked them up to Frank and Humphrey's bedrooms. The women protested feebly, but they were too far gone with booze and drugs.

The men stripped them as far as necessary, took turns on each woman in each bedroom. Greta still had her silver sandals on. Humphrey took them both more than once. Frank made it with each and passed out. Johnny managed only with Anita; even semiconscious, Greta was too much for him. By 2:00 A.M. everyone had passed out: the two women on the beds; Frank on his bedroom floor; Humphrey out on the patio on a lounge chair; Johnny Baliol on the living room couch.

At dawn, Frank woke up cold and for a long minute had no idea where he was. Then he saw Greta's foot still in its silver sandal hanging off the bed above his head, and grinned. What a wild night! Downstairs, Johnny was up and stumbling around to reheat some black coffee made last night but never drunk. Humphrey awakened out on the patio soaked by the morning dew. Hungover, he came in to take off his wet clothes and put on a warm robe.

"They'll probably want some goddamn money. Better check our cash."

Humphrey went up to change and see what cash he had. When the coffee was hot, Frank took four cups up to his bedroom to check on his cash before they woke the women. Johnny drank coffee downstairs and brooded over Anne. In Frank's room, Greta moved on the bed, groaned, and mumbled. Humphrey came in. He was pale and still naked.

"She's dead! Frank, the other one's dead in my room!"

Frank ran into Humphrey's bedroom. On the bed Anita wasn't moving. No groans, no movement, no breathing. Frank shook her violently. Humphrey gripped his arm hard. Johnny had heard the commotion and ran up to join them.

"Christ, what do we do?"

Humphrey shook his head. "Shut up and let me think. It's not our fault. Too much drugs and booze together. That's what happened. We didn't have anything to do with it."

They agreed that what had happened couldn't have been their fault, and when they awakened Greta they were prepared. She was hungover, felt terrible, remembered little of what the men had done. But she remembered enough.

"You raped us. I feel like dirt."

"You loved it," Humphrey said. "We all did."

"We're sorry you feel bad," Frank said, "but everyone was having a good time last night, we didn't have to rape you."

Greta began to cry, shook her head back and forth repeatedly. "We were too stoned, you bastards raped us!"

"We didn't lay a hand on you, Greta," Humphrey insisted. "We didn't force you to do anything. Everyone was stoned."

Greta mopped at her tears. "Decent guys wouldn't never—"

"We didn't make you do a damn thing," Humphrey swore, "and we've all got more than that to worry about. Especially you. Your friend's dead."

The rest happened in a rush, a kaleidoscope of words and decisions and actions. A nightmare. A calculated, incredibly slow nightmare. A weird avant-garde movie. In black and white, but clear and precise. Frank emphasized he was a lawyer, and they convinced Greta she was as guilty as they were, part of the whole terrible accident. She had started Anita on the drugs and booze last night long before the three men appeared. She was in as much trouble as they were.

The four took Anita to the Isla Vista apartment she shared with Greta. They agreed on a story—Anita and Greta had gone out drinking and snorting cocaine, came home stoned, went to bed, and Greta found her dead in the morning. She would tell the police everything they had done, and everywhere they had been, except the party where they had met Humphrey, Frank, and Johnny. She would say she and Anita had come home from the last place before that party. The three men gave Greta a check for five thousand dollars, all they had in their combined bank accounts.

"Stick to the story, keep us out, and there'll be more."

They knew if the police even connected them to her she would tell everything. She wouldn't resist if the police had any doubt about her story. They warned her again that she would be in bad trouble if it came out, and left her with instructions to give them half an hour and then call the police. Frank and Humphrey drove back to their house to be sure nothing could incriminate them, and Johnny headed home to his condo.

Johnny never got home. On his way he remembered Anne and his father, flew into an even greater rage because it was their fault he'd been drunk and got mixed up with Humphrey and Frank and the two women, made his telephone call to her apartment, and drove to the mansion to catch his bastard of a father and the no-good bitch together.

Johnny was terrified when he was arrested, but Frank and Humphrey convinced him that since he hadn't shot his dad all he had to do was keep quiet and he'd be fine. But Johnny's stupid mother sent for her goddamn ex-husband who started to ask questions. Humphrey made a small bomb to scare him away. When Morgan didn't scare, Humphrey started to make a bigger bomb.

12

Since the morning of her friend Anita's death, and her relating of the constructed story to the police, Greta Goettinger had done little but sit in her Isla Vista apartment and wait for the police to return and arrest her. When Koons and his men did arrive, she still had the check the boys had given her to keep silent. She had known she'd never get to keep that much money, and told Koons the real story, with a few notable additions.

"Those bastards said their families were real important and no one was gonna believe me anyway. They said no one was gonna believe a nobody like me against them and their folks, and I could end up dead too."

An hour later Rachel, Morgan, Addison Berger, and a small, plump, cold-eyed lawyer from Los Angeles sat once more in the district attorney's office with Koons, Johnny Baliol, and the district attorney himself. The D.A. was pulling every string he had to convince the governor to appoint a special prosecutor for an investigation and trial of what was going to be a volcanic hot potato. The plump Los Angeles lawyer had been flown up by Ralph Baliol the moment he heard of the new charges against his son. Johnny had just told them all the third version of that night.

"At least," Rachel said, "it finally finishes the idiotic notion that Johnny shot his father."

"And I see no need for additional bail on this kind of minor matter," Addison Berger said.

The district attorney said, "The shooting of Mr. Baliol is Drew MacLeod's case, take it up with him. And I don't see this young woman's death and those young men's actions as being minor, Berger, and neither will the governor."

The Los Angeles lawyer had a voice as big and lean as he was small and plump. "I see no other possible conclusion than that which Mr. Berger has stated, Mr. District Attorney. You have a matter of nonviolent adult sexual activity without coercion, and a tragic accident that would have occurred without the alleged sexual activity. A regrettable incident, certainly, but one that broke no law and is not only minor but no charge at all."

"We have a bit more than that, counsellor."

"Nonsense," Rachel snapped. "Those boys were stupid, that's all. What they need is a good talking to."

"They're not boys," Koons said, "they're men, and they treated those women worse than objects. One woman died."

Addison Berger said, "The autopsy in no way suggests they contributed to the death of the woman. There is every indication the women were mentally and physically able to resist had they so chosen. Their personal sexual histories will—"

"Isn't all that for a court to decide, Berger?" the D.A. said.

"The newspapers, you mean," the L.A. lawyer said. "You wouldn't consider such a prosecution if they weren't from high-profile families. You're frightened of the political fallout. You're going to be prosecuting the families and their elite positions."

"Maybe they *should* be prosecuted," Koons said. "Those three guys thought they could get away with anything because of the families they come from."

"That's enough, sergeant," the D.A. said.

The L.A. lawyer smiled for the first time. "There you have it, Mr. District Attorney. The voice of prejudice. Those boys tried and convicted." He leaned forward in his chair and spoke directly to the D.A. "Look, what you have here is a revelation of the sexual and social mores of our younger generation, females no less than males. These activities are commonplace, believe me." He sat back. "And, you know, it doesn't worry me. People should be free to engage in any sexual activity they desire as long as it harms no one else. The death was entirely unconnected to the sexual actions."

Morgan said, "Her death didn't matter to them, only the problems it caused them. They didn't think of those women as human beings. I'm not sure most of you do."

"Who is this man?" The L.A. lawyer wanted to know.

"He's here with me," Rachel said. "Or I thought he was."

Johnny Baliol said, "We didn't hurt anyone. It was all just fun. Why'd that stupid girl have to go and overdose?"

On the brick terrace of Rachel's borrowed Fernald Point house a hot sundowner wind blew in gusts from the mountains. Rachel and Morgan drank Pernod frappes again. She had not changed into anything more comfortable even in the heat of the down-canyon winds. She stood with her drink in the same charcoal gray Paris suit intended to intimidate the police and the district attorney. She was not pleased with Morgan.

"Wonderful, Ford! Did you think I sent for you to find a crime Johnny *did* commit?"

The district attorney had refused to drop the rape, unlawful death, evidence tampering, failure to report a crime, and other charges. The three young men were out on bail, Greta Goettinger would be a prosecution witness. She had already found a lawyer to represent her against Humphrey Bowan, Frank Howard, Johnny Baliol, and their families.

"I'm not sure why you did send for me, Rach."

The silent Mexican maid padded up to them with her head down and face averted from Rachel's rage. She put down fresh Pernods and her ever-present tray of hors d'oeuvres, cleared the empty glasses. Rachel took a cigarette from the obsidian box, lit it angrily, and glared at the silent woman until she scuttled away like a crab.

"My son was in jail, Ford! That's why I sent for you. I didn't bring you here to help the police prove he did something else!"

Morgan drank the cold licorice drink and looked out through the hot wind to the lighted oil rigs that rode in space like distant aircraft carriers. "You knew Johnny didn't shoot his father, Rach. Baliol knew that all along, and so did you. You said that kind of violence isn't in him, and it isn't. He doesn't have the strength, and he never had a real motive. The only kind of violence he's capable of is the kind he and his friends committed."

She waved the cigarette like a fiery wand. "When you found those stupid boys you should have come straight to me, for God's sake."

"And that's why you really sent for me," Morgan said. "To get Johnny out of jail if I could, sure, but mostly to find out what he'd been doing that night he was scared to tell you or anyone else about. You don't like not knowing something that affects you, you don't like not being in control. You guessed whatever Johnny was afraid to tell had to be bad for him and for you, and you didn't want the police to find it first. So you called up your knight in armor. One of the family."

Rachel dismissed the accusation with an arrogant wave of her hand and the cigarette. Not denying it, only dismissing it's importance. "You *are* one of us, Ford, for God's sake. You were supposed to come straight to me, I thought you would know that. Then Ralph and I could have—"

"Ralph?"

"Johnny *is* his son."

Morgan nodded. "Close ranks and cover up? Send him abroad? A little pilgrimage as penance? Maybe join a crusade?"

"What are you talking about?"

"I'm talking about a nasty crime, Rach."

"Really, Ford. The future of those boys—"

"They aren't boys, Rach. Koons is right, what they did was despicable. They need to understand that."

"To women like that?"

"How are they different from other women?"

"We're talking about the futures of our children, Ford. *Our* futures, for God's sake. For two common party girls?" She paced the terrace in the click of her high heels, the last sunlight gone from the brick terrace leaving a red glow in the sky to the west. "You *have* been avoiding me since that first night. What is it, Ford? The pink glow of distance and separation taken away by reality?"

"In a way. Call it confusion. Then and now."

"You're saying we were a mistake?"

"The mistake was much earlier. The solution was wrong."

She lit a cigarette. The night was pitch black all around except for the distant oil platforms. "We *were* a mistake. I knew it the first year. You were tied up inside, I didn't know why. You were fascinating, exciting, but I came to realize quite quickly that you were wrong for me and I was wrong for you. It's amazing we lasted two years, but you really were the best in bed." She smiled. "You still are."

"Perhaps that's what we both wanted to be sure about the other night. That we were right, too."

"Oh, we were." The red point of her cigarette expanded and

contracted in the twilight, brighter than the house lights the maid had turned on, or the distant oil platforms.

"At least," Morgan said, "you were right about Johnny and his father. Maybe in more ways than one."

She tossed her glowing cigarette stub in a high arc toward the sea. It trailed sparks like a rocket to Mars. "Send me your expenses, I'll send a check to the ranch. Your *señorita* should be coming back any time. You haven't been very nice to her, now have you?"

"You don't want me to find out who did shoot Ralph?"

"Not really."

Morgan finished his drink, felt the hot wind try to push him from his chair toward the invisible sea. "I don't need your money, Rach. But Johnny and his friends need to know what they did, and if you and Baliol don't let them find out they'll never learn."

"I'll keep that in mind, Ford."

"And you'll have to meet Lareina before we leave Santa Barbara."

"Lareina? What a nice name."

Morgan gave her a peck on the cheek. She didn't respond. She lit another cigarette, and was still on the terrace pacing back and forth and looking out at the sea when he closed the gate and went to his car.

On the deck of the cottage at San Ysidro Ranch, Lareina sat in the hot tub, her long hair pinned up to keep it out of the foaming water. Her suitcases were dropped in the entrance hall, her traveling outfit flung on the bed. A new outfit with Rodeo Drive labels. Morgan undressed, slid into the steaming water facing her, and let the jets work on his cracked rib and bruises, on the tension knots in his back.

"How was Cabo?"

"It was Cabo, and my family was family. I would have liked both to be you."

"I'm sorry I couldn't get down. It got more complicated."

"So I see, *yanqui*."

She sat half in and half out of the tub, her breasts full and pink from the heat, her arms supporting her weight.

"I'm glad you're back, Reina."

"Do not change the subject. You have bandaged ears, a broken finger, and too many bruises. What have you done to justify such damage? Is this Johnny in or out of jail?''

"A little of both.''

Morgan told her all that had happened since she had called him in the hospital. Or almost all. Her breasts quivered with anger above the bubbling surface of the hot tub. The fierce rage in her eyes reflected the swirls of the water, and took on a surreal quality in the light of the single bulb over the deck.

"Those *cabrone*s! They will be punished?''

"Most juries seem to live in the same world they do. A combination of military school, the navy, Puritanism, Rogers and Hammerstein, boys will be boys, nice girls don't drink or go to bars alone, and women like that are asking for it. If a woman means no, she shouldn't look so sexy. Everyone knows women really want a man who doesn't take no for an answer.''

She slid under the water to her chin, floated across the tub toward him like a disembodied head with its hair up in pins and combs. He opened his arms to pull her body against him under the water, but she caught one hand, squeezed it, and floated to the side with her back against the tub wall beside him.

"It is the same or worse in Costa Rica. In all of Latin America. Our men, they all know what women really want.''

The night had begun to cool as the wind shifted to blow from the sea. They floated under the hot, swirling water for a time in silence. Comfortable with each other, if not totally comfortable with the subject. Aware of subtle differences between them, male and female, in understanding the mechanism of sexual relations.

"It is over then, *yanqui?* We will go to New York?''

"I don't think what Johnny and the other two did had any bearing on the shooting of Ralph Baliol,'' Morgan said. "Except perhaps to rub Johnny Baliol's nerves raw enough to make him actually care about having his girl stolen by his father and go over there to tell them off.''

"Then it is not over?''

"I'm not sure yet.''

She turned in the tub to look at him. Her hand came out of the water and touched the back of his neck. "You were where tonight, *yanqui?*''

"With Rachel. She fired me.''

Her hand massaged the back of his neck. "But then we cannot go to New York, or go home?"

Morgan took her hand from his neck, put his other arm around her and pulled her close. She let him pull her body to press against him, thigh to chest, under the hot water, but she held her face back and looked into his eyes. It was a question.

Morgan said, "Ralph Baliol never did think his son shot him, Reina, but he let everyone else go on thinking so. To buy time, I think. There's something about the shooting he doesn't want to come out."

"And you do want this whatever-it-is to come out? Because you don't like this man?"

"I just know it makes me angry."

"And that is why we stay here?"

"A little more time, Reina."

She let him draw her all the way to him, put her arms around his neck, raised her legs under the water, and opened her hips. He moved her legs around him. She closed her eyes as he entered her. The buoyancy of the water raised her high without effort, and they half-floated, locked together in the heat. Her lips were open, he kissed her throat and the place between her breasts and the breasts themselves. She breathed in slow sighs that matched the rhythm of their bodies. A rhythm that ended far too quickly under the hot water.

She opened her eyes. "My poor Ford."

13

Alfred Schoenhausen did not know where his wife was at eight-thirty in the morning, and he did not like that at all.

"You have called here before, Mr. Morgan. Perhaps if you told me what it is you require from my wife, I could help."

"You could if you know where I can contact her."

"I regret, but this morning I do not seem to. This is, ah, personal?"

Morgan improvised, "She's indicated she might be interested in doing social work for the county."

"So?" Schoenhausen's tone was both surprised and not surprised. "She has not mentioned that to me, but perhaps that is what she has been doing, then."

He had been unaware his wife was looking for work, which, of course, she wasn't, but he had been aware that it was something she might do. Schoenhausen's actual words added up to much more. Barbara might not be on his mind most of the time, but she was on his mind now. She had been acting in a manner far enough from her normal routine, and doing it long enough, for Schoenhausen to notice.

"If she comes in, perhaps you could have her call me." Morgan gave the cottage telephone number.

"I will tell her." Schoenhausen hung up.

Forbidden to run or work out for a week, Morgan had walked five miles, done isometrics in the misty morning sun on the cottage deck, and made his call to Barbara Schoenhausen's house while he waited for Lareina to get up. She said nothing about the morning phone call, and they went to the ranch's main dining room for breakfast. They talked about her stay in Cabo San Lucas, her Beverly Hills adventures, and the arrival of a friend from the Costa Rican consulate who was coming up to Santa Barbara for the day.

"You will have lunch with Rinaldo and me, Ford? Rinaldo's family owns the *finca* next to my father's. He is interested in Mayan culture and artifacts and such things. He could be useful to your business."

Morgan agreed it would be good for his business in Costa Rica to talk about Mayan artifacts with Rinaldo, and he would certainly be at lunch. But first he wanted to have another talk with Fletcher Comrie about his stock manipulations and Ralph Baliol's takeover of Stoke-Higham Timber.

A brown Nissan Maxima was skewed across the steep driveway of Fletcher Comrie's modern fortress. Sheriff's cars surrounded the Nissan, and teams of deputies worked around the house and on the rugged slopes of the mountain. Sergeant Koons stood beside the Nissan. Other deputies had removed two packed suitcases from the car and were examining the contents.

"Not much car for a millionaire financial wizard," Koons said as Morgan joined him.

"It's Fletcher Comrie's?" The small brown car didn't project the image of a captain of finance, and was therefore exactly what Comrie would drive. The game, not the name, was Comrie's obsession. "Are the suitcases his too?"

"Looks like it. I guess he was going on a trip. Come on up to the house."

Koons motioned for Morgan to follow him up the driveway to the rooftop area where more patrol cars were parked and the electronic door stood open. They went down the spiral iron stairs, emerged above the cavernous living room and the sprawled body of Fletcher Comrie in a gray chalk-stripe suit face down on the floor in front of one of his blank white walls. Blood had soaked in a wide patch around one enormous, ragged wound across his entire back.

"An army M–16 assault rifle," Koons said, "set on full automatic. It tore him in half. We dug fifteen bullets out of the plaster. Whoever it was ambushed him out there in the Nissan on his way to wherever he was going, forced him back inside the house, stood him against the wall, and mowed him down."

Perhaps, Morgan thought, offered him a last cigarette and a

blindfold, some final words before the execution. Because an execution was what had happened in Fletcher Comrie's spartan living room. Morgan saw that as clearly as he saw the anger and rage that had wanted the death of Comrie.

Koons said, "Did you talk to him too, Morgan? About Ralph Baliol's shooting and maybe stock manipulations?"

"Yes. He agreed with Baliol that it was routine business, but he also said Stoke-Higham Timber management wasn't happy to be taken over. That's why I came to you and asked about the company."

"That's all he said? Stoke-Higham Timber management wasn't happy? Nothing else about anyone from up there who could have shot Baliol?"

"Do I gather you're looking for a killer other than Johnny Baliol now?" Morgan said. "You think it was the same killer who shot Baliol, and you don't think it was Johnny anymore?"

Koons held out his hand and dropped a small object into Morgan's palm. For a moment it defied identification. A scrap of thin black cardboard, perhaps an inch and a half square, one end curled. There was printing on one side, silver ink on black. As Morgan studied the scrap of cardboard the printing came into focus: *Taffy's, Gaul, CA (707) 568–* It was the torn front cover of a matchbook from a tavern or restaurant in Gaul, California.

"Stoke-Higham Timber," Morgan said.

Koons held out a sheet of paper that had been torn from some writing pad. It had Fletcher Comrie's name and address written on it in a neat, precise handwriting. "Looks like someone who didn't know where Comrie lived and had to have it written down. We've already called the chief of police up in Gaul, and the company officials."

"Johnny's totally out of it? Because of this matchbook cover and a note?"

"He already was anyway. We found that gun he bought Anne Neville this morning."

"Where?"

"In the bushes at the Montecito tennis club the Neville woman goes to. She plays there at night. She must have dropped it over two weeks ago, but the gardener spotted it only this morning."

"You believe that?"

"Of course not. Someone had it hidden away and probably

planted it last night." Koons shrugged. "But it doesn't matter. It's not the gun that shot Baliol."

"Not the gun?" Morgan laughed. "Well, I guess that means I'm really retired as a detective. You won't miss me, will you, sergeant?"

"I've had worse around. Take a long vacation."

As he went up the spiral staircase, Morgan took a last look at the body of Fletcher Comrie sprawled in his bloody gray suit. There would be no monuments for this Comrie either. He'd had no family and only casual women. Few friends, many enemies, and not an especially grateful country. Those who were grateful to him, the corporations and financiers who had let him make billions for them while helping him make his millions, would not be anxious to be identified with him, and enemies rarely raised monuments. Who had killed him, the grateful or the ungrateful? Had he been leaving town on routine business or in sudden flight?

Morgan called down to Koons. "You know where Comrie was going, sergeant?"

"Not a clue. If he had tickets, they're gone. If he told anyone in his company, we'll find out."

Morgan went on up to his car on the roof of the modern fortress that had proven no more invulnerable than any ancient stronghold. He drove out to Romero Canyon Road. The mountains towered brown and dry over the red tile roofs and artificial green of Montecito. His eyes searched again for the flash of the solitary windshield high up, or the sweep of a buteo over the harsh and rocky slopes, but there was nothing. A land of dry mountains and chaparral, of desert and fire, where man was only another natural danger and Johnny Baliol had not shot his father and his mother knew everything he had been doing that night.

It was time to take Lareina to Palm Springs and New York. To do the theaters, the concerts, the galleries, and the finest restaurants. Catch Cabo on the way home. Return to his mountains, his successful business and his fine house on its hill. To his *guaro* in the Cordillera, and to his fine living room with its fine view and Lareina or whoever came out of his bedroom naked after Lareina had moved on to her own life, perhaps with Rinaldo of the Mayan artifacts and the neighboring *finca*. To lie back without worries or demands. Count his money. Relax.

Morgan looked at his watch. He still had half an hour before the time for lunch with Lareina and the Costa Rican.

The high chainlink fence around Ralph Baliol's Montecito estate had been built in front of the original stone wall. Razor wire topped the fence, and notices warning that the estate was protected by an alarm and a private police patrol were posted every ten feet. Seventy years ago when it had been built, the wall had been more than enough to protect against attack and depredation by the poor and violent outside. They had been under better control in those days.

A Toyota, a sleek red Ferarri, and a black limousine were inside the open garage doors. Rachel Winrod's red Mercedes convertible was parked in the turnaround. So was a battered white Cadillac convertible with a bleached steer skull flamboyant on the hood. The steer skull was the kind sold to tourists in every trading post on I–40 in Arizona and New Mexico, but the old Caddy had a California license plate. Morgan parked behind the Caddy, and Ralph Baliol's assistant, Gerald Kirsch, came out to lead him into the house and the den where a full-fledged meeting was in progress.

Ralph Baliol didn't ask him to sit down. "Discovered some new non-crime, Morgan? Now that it's clear that Johnny had no part in shooting me. No thanks to you, apparently."

Baliol sat behind his inlaid desk in full executive armor. A blue cashmere pin-stripe suit that didn't show a single wrinkle, even over his bandages. A Yale club tie and sapphire cuff links. Behind the desk of his own den, with the confidence of place and role, he contemplated Morgan with total indifference. Here, Morgan was less than unimportant, he was irrelevant. The others took their cue from Baliol, suffered Morgan's unwelcome presence in the impatient way people do any intrusion on an important meeting.

Anne Neville was seated across the office, blonde and ready for lunch in a backless yellow summer dress. Two middle-aged men with short hair and confidence sat in business suits and ties on the leather couch closest to Baliol. One was tall and one was stout. Rachel winked at Morgan from a big leather armchair. She was in her impressive but feminine mode. A plain black dress that showed her figure, with simple diamonds and opals at her throat.

"Fletcher Comrie's dead," Morgan said. "Or do you all know that already?"

As an entrance line it took their attention away from their meeting at least for the moment.

"Good God," Rachel said.

"When?" Ralph Baliol said. "How did it happen?"

"He was shot in his living room. Up against his wall, execution-style. I don't know when. The police are there."

Rachel was outraged. "What is going on, for God's sake, Ralph? What did you two *do* to someone?"

"What do you think?" Morgan asked Baliol. "The same person or persons who shot you? The same motive? And how long did you have the gun Johnny bought for Anne there? She left it here after some pleasant tête-à-tête, right? Then forgot she'd even brought it with her."

Ralph Baliol flicked an invisible speck from his cashmere trousers, smoothed the beautiful cloth. "Johnny needed a lesson, a message. I think he got the message. He did, didn't he, Annie?"

"Oh, he got it." Anne Neville smiled innocently at Morgan. "Now we're all friends."

Rachel said, "You always were a shit, Ralph. Your own son! Not to mention me. Did you enjoy it? Make you feel like King Henry the Second again?"

"Johnny needed a good hard scare. Hassling Annie, sneaking around here looking into bedrooms. I've been a lot closer to him than you have, I know more about what he needs. There was no harm done, we've cleared the air, and it's all over."

"And me?" Rachel snapped.

Baliol's laugh was almost genuine. "You got to visit Santa Barbara, show Johnny how much you care about him, and have your one-more-time fling with Morgan. No harm and maybe some good, eh? Johnny had an adventure, you and Morgan had fun, Annie and I got Johnny off our backs."

"And you got space and time," Morgan said. "With the police looking at the wrong man, you could follow your own agenda on the shooting, handle it your own way. Why? Afraid of the motive being exposed? That would be one reason to keep the police going in the wrong direction. And that, by the way, is a crime too."

Baliol shook his head in disbelief. "You really are good at finding trivial crimes. Too bad you're not better at the big ones. Rachel really could have saved her money and her time."

"You should have told her that. You were the one who knew where the gun was and who didn't shoot you."

The room moved restlessly. Morgan was delaying what they had come to do. Anne Neville wished Morgan would stop prolonging the meeting and keeping her from being alone with Baliol. Rachel had better things to do than sit listening to two ex-husbands face each other down. Johnny was no longer involved in Ralph's shooting; she had no more interest in who was involved. The two strangers wanted to get on with whatever Morgan had interrupted. Kirsch found it all in poor taste, and Baliol was irritated.

"If you have anything you want to accuse me of, Morgan, do it to the sheriff. Only don't bother him with more non-crimes you can't prove anyway. Gerald, would you escort—"

"You think withholding evidence from the police and what Johnny and those other two did are trivial non-crimes?" Morgan said.

"I think they're no crimes at all. Dreamed up by overpaid bureaucrats with nothing better to do to justify their bloated paychecks. Those boys and I hurt no one."

"A woman, an unknown man, and Fletcher Comrie got hurt. They're dead. The woman who was raped got hurt."

The taller stranger suddenly came to life. "What rape? What did those women think the boys wanted to take them home for at that hour? To meet their mothers?"

His blue shirt was monogrammed on the cuffs: *GB.* Bowan, George or Gerald or Guy, father of Humphrey of the Lotus who knew how to make bombs.

"Thirty-year-old boys, Mr. Bowan? Perhaps that's the trouble. No adult ever told them that no matter what a woman wears or how she acts, where she goes or what her history is, yes is yes and no is no. Anything else is violence, and that's rape."

"Not to decent people who can see what those women were," Bowan said. "Not to normal people, Mr. . . . Morgan, is it? Not, we hope, to an honest and respectable jury."

"Close ranks, raise the drawbridge. Right, Rach? Ralph's a shit, but the tower is under siege."

Rachel said, "Don't search for the holy grail, Ford, it never did exist. We have plans to make here that don't concern you." She smiled. "You came when I called, for that I'm grateful. I'm happy we got to meet again, but now it's time for us to get on with more important business of our own. I'm sure your Lareina will welcome you back warmly."

"I suppose I appreciate your coming to help Johnny, too," Ralph Baliol said. "Even if you did a hell of a lot of damage by not coming to Rachel with what you'd found. We'll see what we have to do to minimize the damage, and why don't you stop out at the Valley Club and play a round before you leave town? We'll talk."

Morgan said, "I think I want to talk now. In private. No sense boring everyone else. They can plan their war strategy for getting the 'boys' off without you."

"I can't think of anything more we have to talk about." Baliol waved Kirsch forward. "Gerald—"

"I can think of a lot more," Morgan said.

Morgan smiled at Gerald Kirsch. Kirsch stopped, stood nervous and hesitant and not moving at all. Physical action wasn't Gerald Kirsch's strength.

Rachel said, "For God's sake, Ralph, talk to him and get it over with."

Baliol wasn't pleased. "Say whatever you want to say here, Morgan."

"All right. Are you going to marry Anne there, or just string her along?"

Baliol's voice was like thin wire. "Why not ask the lady?"

"He can save his breath," Anne Neville said. "It's none of his goddamn business."

Morgan said, "Does she know about Barbara Schoenhausen?"

"She knows," Baliol said. "Does it bother you, Annie?"

"Not anymore. I even feel sorry for her. She lost."

Baliol tented his hands. "Anne didn't have me shot, Morgan, if that's what you're after. Neither did Barbara Schoenhausen. Barbara and I are still good friends, but she made it too hard, you understand? I liked her, we had a lot that was good until she got too demanding. There were too many complications. She understands that now. No one was hurt."

"Just like your 'boys,'" Morgan said. "You hurt no one."

Baliol knocked his chair back into the wall behind his desk as he stood up. He went chalk white and hung onto the desk bent forward—he had forgotten his wounds. He breathed hard, but managed to deliver his message: "Get out, Morgan. Now."

"Fletcher Comrie might be alive if he'd known someone at Stoke-Higham Timber wanted him dead."

The cold, hard shine of Baliol's pale eyes caught the sunlight in the den where he held to the desk. "The police still know nothing for sure about Stoke-Higham or anyone else. And I certainly don't."

Morgan shook his head. "You knew where the shooter or shooters came from, and you know why. You always did. For some reason I don't know, you plan to handle it all yourself."

Baliol sat back down slowly and gingerly. "Do I have to call the sheriff?"

"I'm going," Morgan said. "But while you're not hurting anyone, be sure you don't hurt Barbara Schoenhausen any more than you already have. That clear enough?"

"There, I knew it!" Rachel said, pleased with herself. "Barbara Allison, for God's sake."

"Be careful, Morgan," Ralph Baliol said. "I'd think hard about becoming too involved with our Barbara. She says she wants a different life, but she doesn't. She's exactly the same as the rest of us. She wants what she has, and more. She just doesn't know it yet."

14

The man in the cowboy hat circled the old white Cadillac in front of the estate's garages like an airline pilot on a walkaround before takeoff. The weathered gray hat was pulled down low over his eyes. A hat older than the Cadillac, but a broad hatband heavy with silver and turquoise indicated that both hat and Caddy were probably old by choice, not necessity. The empty-eyed stare of the bleached steer skull on the hood seemed to follow the man as he kicked each tire.

"What do you think, Charlie? Do I need to get new ones, or what?"

His chinos had faded to a thin white, but his blue denim shirt flew an embroidered eagle across the shoulders, and his Western boots were lizard skin. Not tall, he was solid from shoulders to hips, muscular in the thighs and without any fat. A thirty-year-old body under a forty-five-year-old face that had no visible cheekbones. The nose had been broken, the mouth and cheeks scarred, and his eyes were pale tunnels into a great depth with nothing at the end. A thick brown mustache didn't hide the recently stitched wounds on his mouth and nose.

"I guess I can thank you for these." Morgan touched the bandages on his ears. "How come you let me walk away at Anne Neville's house?"

The man smiled but said nothing and went on circling the Cadillac. He took out a red bandanna to flick leaves off the hood and the bleached steer skull, and stood back to admire the old car.

Morgan said, "Sergeant Koons liked your handling of the knife. Especially under the conditions. Where do you carry it? The boot?"

The man stopped his circling and leaned against the dented grille of the Caddy. He touched his stitched lips and nose. "You got a real hard head, Morgan. All ways."

"Ford," Morgan said. "What do I call you?"

"Roy Shepherd. You was a Sneaky Pete, right? Green Beret, spit and polish, the works. Over in country, I mean. One of the sci-fi boys up at Nha Trang."

"More of an A-team grunt in the bush and out country in Laos and Cambodia."

"The career type," Roy Shepherd nodded. "You liked it, Charlie? The lifer game?"

"Not as much as Ralph Baliol. Joining up was what I thought I had to do at the time."

"The good grunt." Shepherd waved the red bandanna like a flag. "Go get 'em, men. Gung-ho. All the shit."

"The whole latrine," Morgan said. "Not you, right?"

Shepherd smiled. "So how'd you get out? The million-dollar hit?"

"Maybe half a million. I was lucky on the hit, and my spin came up. By then I was ready to take it."

Shepherd leaned against the front of the old Caddy, the steer horns on each side of him. His was the unhurried and unworried manner of someone who has no need to explain himself, not even to himself. But who didn't mind talking about himself either, if that was what he wanted to do. He rubbed each steer horn like a talisman. "I got into it for the money and the angles. Never could see riding on a tractor in a cloud of dust for the bank or anyone else. Sweatin' some damn assembly line, powering on nuts and bolts. Around my town, you didn't have a business yourself, everything else was picking, packing, McDonald's, and washing bedpans. Uncle Sam looked pretty good right then." Shepherd smiled once more, perhaps remembering with an amused wonder how good the army had looked. "It was all shit and colonels, but I worked it okay. I angled myself into the MPs and some schooling before we got sent over in country. Right off the airlift they stuck us in CMZ-Saigon working with the white mice cops, and that was fine. I was a great Saigon warrior, found a really sweet kid I could teach English so she could do more than fuck and wash my socks. We had a couple of clean rooms in her family hootch."

Shepherd still smiled but looked into a distance beyond Morgan, and the tunnels of his pale eyes were darker. "Some marines hassled her, hassled me. I had to rough 'em up, and they threw me into the LBJ Ranch. When I got out I told the colonel I was going to marry her, stay in 'Nam after my tour. He sent me up to play tunnel rat with the section we got detached to the Cu Chi national guard. I said fuck the army, went back down to Saigon and figured to move in with her and hide out."

He flicked the bandanna against his knee. "Some bastard who'd lost it down the delta and bugged out to Saigon had shot her dead. I went looking for him, but the colonel shipped him out so I broke up our HQ and they stuck me back in LBJ. The colonel talked to me like a father. I told him flat out what I'd do when they let me out, so they shipped me back to the world and give me a bad conduct for the good of the service."

The dark in his pale eyes was almost solid, but he still leaned lightly against the Cadillac and the steer skull, still smiled that small smile under the mustache. Morgan had begun to realize the smile was permanent, unchanging no matter what Shepherd thought, did, or said. An amused smile, faintly mocking. The world, himself, or both.

"I'm sorry," Morgan said.

"Hell, it got me liberated. Best thing ever happened to me in service. I never could make a go of it with the brass's hired hands."

"I meant the woman."

Shepherd arched an eyebrow. "That's okay then. I was sorry as hell back then too. She was real, you know? No way they could ever've let it happen." He thought about it, then pushed away from the old Caddy and walked around it again, studying the worn but lovingly cared-for leather under the early afternoon sun. "CIA too, right? Saigon HQ? A regular Cass commando?"

"Mostly in Laos. Phoenix program stuff."

"That dirty?" The grim work of the CIA's Phoenix subversion and assassination program in Vietnam impressed Shepherd. "You must of liked it, right? Signed up to spook on the world."

"It still seemed like a good idea. I learn slowly."

"A gung-ho hardhead, the worst kind. Only now you live down over the border somewhere. I mean, you got out of the whole country?"

"Costa Rica," Morgan said. "I got tired."

"You got tired? That's the whole story, Charlie?"

"It's all you're going to get," Morgan said. "You've worked hard to learn a whole lot about me."

"Part of the job."

"Know the enemy?"

"Do what the big chops tells you to do. You think you're the enemy?"

"I think Baliol thinks I am."

"Is he right?"

"That might depend on what he plans to do, and to whom."

Shepherd thought about that. "I guess he figures if you talk like that you already are, you know? I mean, what he does, and who he does it to, got to be none of your business."

"Is that what you think?"

"I don't think on a job, I just do it."

"Is spying on Baliol's ladyfriends part of the job? Sort of pimping for the boss? Keeping the harem?"

"Whatever."

"Anything the paymaster tells you?" Morgan looked for a reaction, but there was none. "Anything the brass wants?"

"Anything I want."

"If you don't want to do something?"

Shepherd shook his head. "Look, Charlie, be smart. The kid's clear, the ex-wife's happy. You got a nice woman. What's the problem?"

"Perhaps I just don't like how Baliol treats people, how he thinks about other people. Like father like son."

"Okay, the kid's a turd. Not a clue how to treat a woman. You helped fix the crud's wagon, and that's okay. But the rest of the honcho's business ain't your problem."

"You'll handle it? You and Baliol?"

"It's no big deal, okay? You don't need this."

"Maybe not," Morgan said as he walked past Shepherd and the old Caddy to his rented BMW. He looked back as he opened the door. "I'm still sorry about the Vietnamese woman."

"I hear you."

"And Baliol says he and Barbara Schoenhausen have called it quits. You won't have to follow her anymore, right?"

Shepherd draped the bandanna over one steer horn. "That important to you?"

"I guess it is."

"She's a cool lady," Shepherd said.

Morgan got into his BMW. He drove away without looking behind him. Roy Shepherd would be the kind of hardhead who always let you know what he had to do to you before he did it, give you a chance to run.

The afternoon sun still high over the trees, and a beer in his hand, Morgan sat alone in the warmth of the San Ysidro Ranch cottage with the television turned on to some Western he had seen when he was a teenager. He recognized the actors but couldn't remember their names or the plot of the picture or exactly where he'd been when he saw it. It was either at home in Sag Harbor on some rainy summer afternoon when his father's boat didn't go out, or in basic training on a rainy day between the end of training and the time to ship out to special forces. He remembered the rain, and seemed to remember he had liked the film.

September first, no longer August. In Santa Barbara there was no discernable difference outside the window of the warm room. He had called Barbara Schoenhausen twice and gotten a busy signal both times. Lareina had not returned from lunch with her Rinaldo from the next *finca* who was interested in Mayan arts and crafts, and who was probably interested in Lareina, or at least in the proximity of their family *fincas*. For five years there had been no questions, problems, illusions, strings, or promises. Five years and forever . . . more than the past had been over and forgotten when he met her; the future had been over too. For five years there had been only a present where he lived comfortably and did what he wanted to do and had no need of a past or a future. He sat alone in the warmth of the room, thinking of Lareina, the past and the future, and didn't know how long the telephone had been ringing before he heard it.

The voice on the other end was calm and cold. "Mr. Morgan? Alfred Schoenhausen here."

"Yes, Mr. Schoenhausen?"

"Is my wife with you, Mr. Morgan?"

"Why would you think your wife was with me, Mr. Schoenhausen?"

Beneath Schoenhausen's calm voice was an anger under tight control. "The telephone number you left and I am now calling is the San Ysidro Ranch. The San Ysidro Ranch is not an office of social work."

"She isn't with me, Mr. Schoenhausen."

When Schoenhausen's voice came again, it was rigid. "Who and what are you, Mr. Morgan? And what is your exact relation to my wife? You are, I think, not a social worker."

"No."

"That is all? No? My wife has not come home since eight o'clock this morning. She has not called. She has missed things she should have done. She has not been to the school to bring our children home. Where is she, Mr. Morgan, and what do you know of her?"

Morgan breathed long and slowly. "I'm a friend of hers. I've been looking into a situation that involved my former wife and turned out to involve your wife too. I don't know where your wife is, but I do know some facts that might help you with the answers you need."

Alfred Schoenhausen was having trouble maintaining the control that was so important to his image of himself. "Perhaps you should tell me these . . . facts."

"Can I come over?"

"You know where my house is?"

"Yes."

"Then I will wait for you."

Alfred Schoenhausen was having difficulty with more than his rigid control. He was having a great deal of trouble sorting out what had to be a cascade of new and unexpected information. A type of information he was unaccustomed to dealing with. Unknown information about the wife he had been sure he knew very well indeed. In a different time and place, he would have known precisely how to act.

Time and place had changed for Alfred Schoenhausen.

15

The Schoenhausen house wasn't the regal Italian *palazzo* of the Eastern banker and Ralph Baliol, but it was lordly enough behind wrought-iron gates. An imitation Tudor manor with half-timbers and a gabled slate roof visible over rows of non-native white oaks and a broad lawn. There was no razor wire or alarm system, and the gate stood open without the need of a barrier intercom. Neither high-tech nor paranoid, only exclusive.

Alfred Schoenhausen stood waiting for Morgan at the top of the semicircular drive. A tall man in steel-rimmed glasses that flashed in the sunlight as he moved his head, he had the pronounced forward lean of certain tall people in the habit of peering closely at everything. Hands folded behind the back of his soft gray flannel lounge suit, a deep crease between his close-set blue eyes as he peered at Morgan's BMW. Expectation in the eyes and tension in the rigid face. His face was narrow and his nose was large, but a heavy brow balanced the nose. His dark blonde hair was brushed straight back.

"Mr. Morgan?" Schoenhausen did not click his heels, but Morgan felt as if he had.

"Mr. Schoenhausen."

They went into a pleasant entry hall full of pale wood and sunlight from a fan-shaped transom. A cantilevered and open staircase of polished maple seemed to hang in space as it curved up to the second floor. Schoenhausen opened a door on the left and ushered Morgan into a sunny family room of old and well-used furniture, a big-screen color TV, children's scattered toys, and a large leather armchair and footstool with a pipe stand and chess table beside it. Schoenhausen inclined his head toward the armchair. Morgan sat.

Schoenhausen didn't. He stood and stared at Morgan's ears and finger. "You have been hurt?"

"Nothing serious."

Schoenhausen understood reticence, didn't pursue his obvious alarm that Morgan's injuries had some relation to the absence of his wife. Instead, he returned to the point. "You say you are a friend of my wife?"

"Have you heard from her yet?"

"No. Our housekeeper had to take the children to school this morning and pick them up this afternoon. That is not something that has ever happened, not without arrangement, and the children are understandably upset. You say you know things that might tell me where my wife is, and what she is doing."

"I said I know what might help find an answer." Morgan heard his words and knew he was stalling. How did you tell a man his wife had been having a torrid affair with someone he probably knew? "You've tried everywhere you know that Barbara could be?"

"My wife is Barbara to you?"

"I hope we're friends."

"Yes, I see." He didn't see at all, but continued to peer at Morgan. "You think I should know somewhere my wife would be, Mr. Morgan?"

"For your sake, I hope so."

"For my sake? Not for her sake?"

"That too. This isn't easy, Mr. Schoenhausen."

"So? Perhaps you would like a beer? Something to eat? I am not the best at this either, Mr. Morgan. It is what my wife should be here to do."

"A beer would be good."

Morgan sat in the comfortable room in what would be Alfred Schoenhausen's chair. The room was full of the children and the father, but not of the wife. Their toys and his chair. A television for all. Couches and chairs for everyone. Nothing for her alone. This would not be a situation, condition, anyone had planned, least of all Schoenhausen, but it had happened and Morgan was thinking about how often it happened unplanned and unthought about when Schoenhausen returned with two Becks and a plate of crackers and Muenster. He poured the beers into large pilsner glasses, set the cheese on the chess table. He raised his beer in a brief salute, but still did not sit down. He had no interest in the cheese or crackers.

"Perhaps I can help you, Mr. Morgan. You are telling me that my wife has some reason to go away. Some reason I don't know. But a reason you know."

"A reason, or a cause."

"Cause? You imply by that she could be in trouble? What trouble? Where? With whom?"

"I don't know, not for sure. I . . . . Where is your brother, Mr. Schoenhausen?"

"My brother?"

"Your older brother. Helmuth, is it?"

Schoenhausen sat down on the couch. Collapsed would have been a better word for anyone except Alfred Schoenhausen. He put his half-full glass of beer and the bottle carefully on the coffee table. The anger and the stiff control were back in his voice. "My wife has spoken to you about my family?"

"It came up when she talked about your marriage."

"Our marriage?" His eyes were large and unbelieving behind the steel-rimmed glasses. "My wife talked about our marriage? To you, or to someone else?"

"Probably both. I guess it's been on her mind. Your marriage and your family. And you, I suppose." Morgan tried to think of any way to try to prepare Schoenhausen for what he had to tell him. "Tell me about your brother Helmuth. Where is he now?"

Schoenhausen stared at him in silence. "Helmuth is dead. This will lead somewhere, Mr. Morgan?"

"Is he buried with all the Schoenhausens? On the estate?"

"No."

"Why not?"

Schoenhausen was silent again. "Yes, I see. My wife liked Helmuth. She did not understand about the beard. She does not like my mother or my second brother. She is American, she does not understand these matters."

"What doesn't she understand?"

"She does not understand what a family means. A noble family. Its rank, its history, its continuity. Of place and obligation. Most Americans are without continuity. Now that the Marxist stupidity has left Germany our lands and castle will be returned. We will go back to where Schoenhausens have lived for over a thousand years.

We always knew the communist rabble would disappear the same as all the other rabbles before it. These people come and go. They try to take our place, but they always fail and we go on."

"Even in America?"

"For those who are like us here."

"Not for you?"

"It is not my land."

"But you're a citizen. You have a wife and family."

"That is me. I live and work here. So of course I am a citizen. But that is not the continuity of the family."

"And Barbara isn't German."

"No."

Schoenhausen waited for Morgan to continue saying whatever he was going to say that would somehow lead to something about his wife. Morgan finished the Beck's. There was no more he could do or say but tell it.

"As I said on the phone, I came here to help my former wife look into a situation and found your wife was part of the situation. I don't know where she is, but I have an idea where she could be." He stood up. Somehow it wasn't something you told a person while comfortable in his own chair. "She's been having an affair with a man named Ralph Baliol. I don't know how long it's been going on, but in all probability some months at least. Baliol acts as if the affair were over. I have no way of knowing if that's true or not. Ralph Baliol says and does whatever is to his advantage. But . . ."

"But?"

"But I don't think she's coming back to you even if the affair with Baliol is over."

Morgan watched the rigid control of the tall man as he held himself together. "That is not possible. Perhaps she will not wish to continue the marriage; I am not sure I would wish to. But she would not go away without the children. If she does not come home, it is because she cannot. You have said yourself my wife could be in trouble. It is the only possibility."

Morgan knew it was far from the only possibility, but it was a possibility. The cowboy ex-soldier with the bad conduct discharge hadn't reassured Morgan about the future or safety of Barbara Schoenhausen. And then somewhere out there was whoever had shot Ralph Baliol and killed Fletcher Comrie.

"Two weeks or so ago, Mr. Schoenhausen, someone tried to kill

Ralph Baliol. Someone did kill one of his business associates. Another man, who may have been one of those who wanted Baliol
dead, was also killed. I think this last man was shot by a man
working for Ralph Baliol. It's possible—"

"My God, Morgan, what is my wife involved in?" Schoenhausen
was on his feet. "Murders, killings, sordid affairs! Is she in danger?
Is she—" He stared down at Morgan. "This Baliol was shot? Do
they think my wife—"

"The police say she isn't under suspicion, and neither are you.
But there may be another reason."

"Me?" Schoenhausen blinked at him from behind the steel-
rimmed glasses. "Ah, the injured husband, yes, I see. And of course
I have met Mr. Baliol once or twice. Casually, yes, but it could be
said I know him. But no one has talked to me, asked me any questions."

"Sometimes the police can be discreet. They were probably able
to rule you out without talking to you. Where were you on August
tenth? A few days either side?"

"The tenth? Of August? In Tokyo. For two weeks. That would be
simple to find out." A bitter second thought entered his voice. "Two
pleasant weeks for my wife and this man."

The self-flagellation had begun. The imagining his wife in every
possible intimate place and position with the *other* man. Laughing
with the other man. Laughing at *him* with the other man, while he
slept, oblivious, in Tokyo. A necessary ritual to accept the end.
Make it so painful now, build such an anger, that the pain of the
final end must become less in the long run.

"It's possible your wife knows something about the crimes and
Ralph Baliol, or about the crimes and someone else, and they want
her out of the way. They could be holding her, and not necessarily
in Santa Barbara. Have you seen anyone unusual or suspicious
around the house? Strange cars parked too long near your gates?
Yesterday or this morning? Did she talk about seeing any strangers?"

"There are always strange cars, but I recall none that seemed
important. I will speak to the housekeeper and the maid."
Schoenhausen picked up the telephone on the coffee table beside
the couch, dialed an intercom connection. He spoke low and for
some time. Morgan heard voices upstairs, children and adults.

Schoenhausen hung up. "They can recall various automobiles, but none that made a great impression."

"You'd better call the police. Sergeant Koons in the sheriff's department."

Schoenhausen blinked once more behind the steel glasses. "If she does not return or call by this evening, I will call the police, yes." He had something to do, something to keep him busy. "Ralph Baliol, he would abduct her?"

"It wouldn't shock me," Morgan said.

Ralph Baliol wouldn't hesitate a second if he had a reason, and the unknown killers would probably take even less time to think about it if they needed her silenced.

"My wife, she is still important to what you are doing for your former wife?"

"In a way, yes."

"You will continue to look for her?"

"The police are better equipped to do that."

"Yes," Schoenhausen nodded, "of course."

Morgan stood up. "You have to remember it's possible she's simply gone off with Baliol, Mr. Schoenhausen. In fact, the police will probably tell you that's a lot more probable."

"I understand."

Perhaps he understood, but it wasn't what he wanted to hear or think about. Morgan wasn't sure what he wanted to think about, but as Schoenhausen walked him to the door the housekeeper, a thin middle-aged woman with a retainer's careful eyes and her hair tied back in a tight bun, hurried down the stairs toward them.

"Mr. Schoenhausen? You asked about anything strange around the house recently? Well, young Freddie saw something. His mother had brought them home from school yesterday and he ran down to the fence because he thought he saw a squirrel, you know how he is about animals?"

"Do you have a point, Elly?" Schoenhausen was more tense and tired than impatient.

"He saw this bizarre automobile, and mentioned it to me, but I forgot it. It was an old white convertible with some horned animal's skull on the hood! Can you imagine? I'm sure it was nothing. It was just passing by along the road, but—"

"Yes, thank you, Elly."

The housekeeper went back upstairs.

"Ralph Baliol's hired man," Morgan said. "He's been following and watching everyone connected to Baliol. It could mean something or nothing."

The sun was low over the trees to the west, and Morgan was back in the cottage with his third Red Tail ale. He sat on the deck this time. Trees and a view of the sea were preferable to old movies he couldn't remember. Lareina still hadn't returned to the cottage, and Morgan felt alone. Except for the years undercover in alien cities, he had never felt alone, had never really been alone. Few people were alone, or allowed themselves to be. There was a hollow at the center of being alone that was easiest to fill with other people. For Lareina as well as for him.

This time the telephone rang when he was looking at his watch for the tenth time, wondering if perhaps something had happened to Lareina too.

"Lang? Hughes Bremner. Listen, how close are you tied to this Ralph Baliol? What's the story there?"

Morgan told the CIA man about Johnny Baliol and his father. "Unless something's happened to a woman I met here, the police take it from now on."

"Then you'd better tell the local police to watch their backs, because if your Ralph Baliol is the big-money California businessman the FBI investigated for the S.E.C. a year or so ago, I just got word from them that he's hired a character named Roy Shepherd, supposedly to do some bodyguarding. Which is what Shepherd says he does for a living."

"Says he does?"

"It seems Shepherd's got a record that looks like both Bonnie and Clyde. Juvenile assault, armed robbery, some possible killings no one's pinned on him. A general bad boy. Lived in the stockade in the army, got a bad conduct discharge, went back to his real trade. He shot a guard and was shot himself in a Barstow holdup. For some reason he got off with five to ten and was out in four years. That's his last conviction for anything, but the FBI says they don't think it's because he got religion but because he got smart. He hires out his skill and firepower to well-heeled clients who need one or both for one reason or another, usually on the wrong side of the blanket. But the FBI says he doesn't work all that much because he's a first-class nut case who doesn't take orders well, is unpredictable as hell, hard to control, and still keeps his hand in some banditry to beat the monotony of working for other people."

"A bad conduct from Vietnam isn't automatically a sign of bad character, Hughes," Morgan said, "no matter what Langley thinks. You have an address on Shepherd?"

"He's got an office in Los Angeles, the door is always locked, and on the phone you never get anything but a recording. He calls you. Otherwise, he's a ghost."

"Give me the address and phone number."

"I thought you were out of it?"

"On what I came here to do, I am. But something else has come up. Don't get coy on me, Hughes."

The CIA man gave him the information. "Be very careful with this guy, Lang. Shepherd listens to a little green man in his head no one else can hear. A real loose cannon."

When Lareina finally returned Morgan still sat alone on the deck of the cottage in the last light of the setting sun. He heard her cross the living room, her high heels tapping on the wood, and stop in the doorway behind him. She went back inside and the cottage became silent.

Morgan looked over the trees to the violet evening haze above the sea and the distant islands. It was one of those times when the aspect of the earth itself made Morgan feel all human needs and concerns, desperate imperatives and rock-solid certainties, weren't worth the hope or attention of a second. Or perhaps that was only his reluctance to talk about what had to be talked about. When she came back out she had her shoes off, a rum cooler from room service in one hand and his sixth Red Tail ale in the other. She sat beside him and faced out toward the violet sky.

"Sorry about lunch, Reina."

"Rinaldo—he is the idiot. He think it would be *mucho* wonderful for us to marry, and he would then own two *fincas*. *El cabrón!*"

Her *tica* dialogue could become excessive when she was upset without being really angry.

"That makes me even more sorry, *tica*. I abandoned you to an idiot and a pig."

She smiled without looking at him, and they both watched the sunset sky of spreading reds and purples.

"You know, *yanqui*, they look at the same sun over the same ocean from the same side of the world in Costa Rica."

"That means it's not so far away, doesn't it?"

"And very far. You did today what you had to do?"

"Some of it. Too much."

She turned her head to look at him. The beauty of the *tica* with the exotic Latin eyes, full lips, and thick light brown hair piled in ringlets had never been so unnerving.

"There's a woman," he said. "She could be in trouble." He told her the story of Barbara Schoenhausen and Ralph Baliol. "She's been gone all day without a word to her husband, without picking up her children. Baliol says they broke up, or he broke it off, and that she would go back to her husband because that was where she really wanted to be. That doesn't sound like the woman I talked to, and her husband has no idea where she is. She appears to have said nothing to anyone about going anywhere, and her husband is certain she wouldn't stay away from her house and her children unless someone made her stay away. One day isn't much, but for this woman in these circumstances I think it could be."

"Without a word even to you, *yanqui*?"

"There's no reason she would have told me, Reina."

"Would you not have hoped she would tell you before she went off without a word?"

Morgan knew the moment she said it that, yes, that was what he would have hoped.

"I don't believe Ralph Baliol, Reina. It looks to me like he was shot and another man killed by people from a town named Gaul up in Northern California. People probably connected to a company named Stoke-Higham Timber. Baliol isn't acting like a man who is going to let the police do their job. My guess is he's hired a professional thug named Roy Shepherd to help him handle those people personally."

"And you think this Shepherd has abducted your Barbara Schoenhausen for the arrogant Mr. Baliol?"

"She's not my Barbara, Reina."

"But you are worried, *sí*? For this Barbara?"

Behind the line of trees to the far right the sun was intermittent glimpses of blood-red orange. "I feel somehow responsible. Perhaps they've taken her hostage. She could be more involved in the shootings than I know. She doesn't strike me as a woman who would let Baliol shoo her away easily."

"Unless she has another man, *sí?* Or knows there is another man who would want her very much."

"Her husband wants her very much."

"For him it is too late."

"I don't know," Morgan said. "I don't trust Baliol, he's doing a hell of a lot more than he pretends, and Barbara could be part of it. I do know where I think Baliol and Roy Shepherd are or will be soon. Up in Gaul snooping around the town and Stoke-Higham Timber."

"Perhaps this Barbara wished to warn the people up in this north of California. Your Mr. Baliol would not want that, would have this Shepherd take her with him to watch her, *sí?*"

"That's about what I've been thinking."

"Then this Gaul is where you must go also."

The whole sky to the far horizon was layered with long low clouds in shades of violent pink and lavender.

"No New York?"

"New York is a place, Ford. So is Costa Rica. They will be there for a long time. Go and find your Barbara."

This time Morgan did not correct her, and they sat in the darkening dusk until the only light was the distant halo over the small night city at the edge of the sea. Then they walked to the restaurant for dinner. They would sit long over coffee, sleep a chaste night, and in the morning Morgan would drive north.

PART II

The Redwoods

16

There are two ways to drive north from Santa Barbara. Each is beautiful in its own way, and both take the same time, give or take a few minutes and depending on the traffic.

The longer freeway, which follows the coastline and the sea before turning inland at Gaviota, is faster and safer. The mountain pass and back-country two-lane road is shorter, slower, and has more varied scenery. Morgan took the pass. It seemed to suit his uncertainty better. He had eaten breakfast alone at the ranch, and Lareina had still been asleep when he'd come back to pick up his single bag. He hadn't awakened her. He wasn't sure how he felt about her sleeping or about his leaving.

The pass road rejoined the freeway beyond Los Olivos, and from there north the drive alternated between the dusty brown inland valleys and the foggy green coast, with mountains always somewhere to the right or left or both. A pleasant land, Southern California, with gentle days and easy rhythms, where the only extremes were earthquakes, floods, fires, and *homo sapiens.*

North of the Cuesta grade near Paso Robles he stopped for gas, and by King City he was ready for lunch. In the dusty interior, King City was one of those small inland cities of California that seemed to have no particular reason to exist except to provide fast-food stops and gasoline stations for the stream of travelers on the freeways. Morgan drove on with the sensation of existing nowhere, a human King City. A feeling that in leaving Rachel behind once again he was leaving the past, and in driving away from Lareina he had left the present.

By dark he was north of San Francisco. He stopped at a motel somewhere in Sonoma, had dinner in the motel restaurant, and went to bed early. He lay awake in the bed with the presence of his comfortable Lareina and the memory of himself as the eager boy working on his father's charter boat out of Sag Harbor thirty years ago. He watched mindless TV sitcoms and dramas with the image of Barbara Schoenhausen beside him. With Ralph Baliol and Roy Shepherd and a young Green Beret in Vietnam. With the captains and the generals and the CIA directors. With the gulf between the boy on the charter boat cutting bait and dreaming of the future, and the man of forty-six with his self-exile and his money and his memory of anger and his self-imposed no future at all.

The redwoods came to meet him north of Leggett.

Before dawn at the Sonoma motel, Morgan ran for the first time since his injuries, despite the aching pain in his cracked rib. He did the full ten miles on rural roads, showered long and hot to ease the pain, ate a quick breakfast, and drove on north through the vineyards of Sonoma and Mendocino counties with their purple-black bunches of small wine grapes waiting to be picked. Through the rich farm country and up into the Coast Range valleys of pines and hardwoods and, both gradually and suddenly, into the redwoods.

Tall, straight trees in a forest so thick it was difficult to pick out individual trunks even close to the highway. Driving under them was to drive in a tunnel with the gloom of ferns and vines vanishing up the massive trunks. Occasionally the forest receded from the highway and the mountains appeared topped by ragged crests where the masses of trees met the sky. Redwoods are not tidy trees with neatly upraised branches and symmetrical pointed crowns. Their branches spread flat or droop downward like an osprey's wings, and they claim their own space at the top where the crowns are often stripped bare by lightning. They paint a wild and unruly profile against the horizon. But their glory was in the thick trunks rising from the dim hush of the forest floor to tower straight and bare so high above they vanished into their own darkness even at noon.

This was what Stoke-Higham Timber was all about: broad forests of tall, straight trees up to two thousand years old. The only one of the three survivors from the prehistoric redwood forests of the northern hemisphere to have any extensive area of growth left. Native to the fog belt of the Coast Ranges from Monterey County north into Oregon, the coast redwood, *sequoia sempervirens,* close cousin to *sequoia gigantea,* the big tree of the Sierras, was among the world's tallest and largest trees. It often exceeded 300 feet in height, achieved trunk diameters of 25 feet and more. With age, the lower limbs dropped away and left a columnar trunk to the height of 100 feet or more before the first branch. The heartwood was reddish brown, fine-grained, strong and durable. Heavy cutting began in the 1860s and drastically reduced the original 1,454,000 acres. To-day, yields ran about 150,000 board feet per acre in normal stands, but cuts as high as 1,500,000 board feet per acre were on record. The tree that had survived since the age of the reptiles, with an immunity to fire, disease, and animals, was threatened by the only enemy that could destroy it. Its other cousin, *metasequoia glyptostro-boides,* the dawn redwood, had been known only through fossils and considered extinct until an expedition discovered a single grove in a remote area of China in 1945. There were many who feared *sequoia sempervirens* too would be known in a hundred years only from photographs or a rare stand fenced and exhibited like a museum.

The first great piles of logs began appearing along the highway, then changed to stacks of finished lumber in Caernarvon five miles south of Gaul where Morgan saw the first light-blue-with-red-trim buildings of Stoke-Higham Timber. The highway became a semi-private road of slow-moving logging trucks all the way into Gaul and the big river that ran through it. The long, high-roofed mill buildings of Stoke-Higham stretched like a wall between the town and the river, all painted light blue with dark red trim. The trucks, gates, and lampposts, the bridge over the river and the houses, were all painted light blue with red trim. Orderly rows of identical company houses and clean streets, with the mountains close around, and the redwood forest coming down to the edge of town. The single main street paralleled the river and crossed the bridge into a different Gaul.

Here it was a mixture of styles, colors, and past eras, with a busy main street of Victorian gingerbread houses turned into tea rooms, shops, and offices that stretched away from the river to the wooded western mountains. A few brick buildings painted white or yellow, and windowless cement block taverns with neon Coors signs. Fast food chain outlets, discount drugstores, mini shopping malls, and motels.

Morgan had reserved at the Mill Inn in the company part of Gaul. The inn was the company hotel. First-class, it had been built in the 1800s as a private mansion for Samkin Stoke. Like its more famous rival, the Carson house thirty miles away in Eureka, it was a mixture of Italianate, Eastlake, Stick, and Queen Anne building styles. Four stories high, it had two sixty-foot towers with steep witch's hat roofs, seven gables covered with intricate moldings, spindle work, stained glass palladian and eyebrow windows, and endless other gingerbread decorations.

The elegant lobby spoke only one word: *wood.* Carved wood, shaped wood, and paneled wood. Wooden floors, wooden ceilings wooden walls, wide wooden stairs, all glistening and shining. A broad marble fireplace encased in golden polished wood. There was no doubt what and who ruled in all parts of Gaul. But somewhere in the town, east or west of the river, someone did not like the new rulers of Gaul, and Morgan wanted the town, the company, and that unknown someone to know he was there.

He had asked for the best suite. This was the Royal Suite, named for a nineteenth-century crown prince of Sweden who came to Gaul to study the latest lumbering methods for his forested country. In the suite, the bellman looked curiously at Morgan's Costa Rican tan and Southern California clothes, announced the bar and restaurant hours, the free tours available at the Stoke-Higham mill, and started to leave.

Morgan said, "What time does the mill open?"

"Day shift goes on at eight."

"Any trouble at the mill lately?"

"Trouble?"

"Someone unhappy with management?"

"I wouldn't know."

"Isn't this hotel owned by Stoke-Higham?"

"Yessir, it is."

The bellman didn't want to be questioned, and Morgan didn't push it. "Where's a good place to eat dinner? Outside the hotel. Perhaps across the river."

"Stoke House Tavern's pretty good."

Morgan unpacked his bags and hung his extra clothes in the bedroom armoire. The suite had two bedrooms, a sitting room, and a large bathroom. He chose the bedroom with the four-poster of polished redwood. He showered, dressed in baggy designer jeans, his purple Guatemalan shirt, a white summer silk jacket, and purple running shoes. The quintessential Hollywood look. He went down to drive across the river to the Stoke House Tavern.

Morgan walked along the main street among the evening people the way he had walked so many undercover years along other strange streets among alien people. Aware, always, of who and what he was, of what he was doing and what could happen the next instant. A gun snug and reassuring against his spine, as the little Czech Vz70 in its belt holster was now. He had carried a gun more than half his life with easy familiarity and the glow of power.

They noticed him, the people of Gaul. The stranger in Hollywood clothes. Tree huggers and tourists came from Southern California. Tree huggers, alfalfa eaters, dolphin kissers. No one good came from Southern California. Even the tourists with their dollars were an evil not everyone thought was necessary. So they eyed him, looked over their shoulders as he passed, stared over beards and from under Western hats. He looked in the shops, bought the proper postcards, and found the Stoke House.

On a corner one block from the river, the tavern served drinks at a long bar with booths, and dinner in another room of tables and booths. Or you could do both in either room. Two long narrow rooms of dark wood paneling and photographs of redwoods as they used to be. Faded photos of the Stoke-Higham logging railroad, the lumber schooners and full-rigged ships of the last century on Humboldt Bay, the fishing boats and the dairy farms and cattle ranches on the flat delta land at the south end of the bay. A lively tavern crowded with young and old, loggers and non-loggers, men and women.

The only empty stools were at the far end of the long bar. Morgan sat down beside a skinny older man in work clothes and a John Deere hat. The man drank Budweiser out of the bottle.

"They have any imported beers in here?" he asked.

The older man shrugged. "Never asked."

A woman in jeans, denim shirt, scuffed cowboy boots, and short red hair took the next empty seat. "Beck's. That's all the excitement we can stand here."

When the bartender came the woman ordered a margarita, and Morgan ordered Beck's and a glass. He spoke to the skinny man.

"Pretty small town you have here."

The man looked at Morgan's clothes. "Big as we want it."

"And everyone works for Stoke-Higham, right?"

"Not everyone."

"How about you?"

"Thirty years."

"That's a long time."

"Tell me about it."

"You like the new management?"

The man turned to face Morgan. "How do you know we got new management? You from around here?"

"Costa Rica."

"Where the hell's that? Down around L.A. somewhere?"

"Central America."

In the context of Stoke-Higham and the tavern, Central America meant nothing to the older man. "How come you askin' questions about the company?"

"Some people want me to invest in Stoke-Higham, so I came up to check it out."

Investment was territory as exotic to the man who had worked thirty years for Stoke-Higham as Central America. He had no way to relate to it except with suspicion. "What people?"

"Ralph Baliol and Fletcher Comrie."

Morgan saw heads turn along the bar, and the skinny man looked him up and down again. "Well, ain't you some shit? Baliol, huh? Friend of yours, right?"

"Just someone I know in business."

"Yeah? Well you tell *Mister* Baliol he maybe better stay a helluva long way outa Gaul he knows what's good for him."

The man turned away to brood over his beer, the conversation over. Along the bar and from some of the booths people still looked at Morgan and the skinny man. A few continued to stare even after Morgan had seen them. The red-headed woman with the margarita on Morgan's other side spoke again behind him.

"What's it like in Costa Rica?"

"Hot and wet, but pretty nice."

"You must be rich."

"Just a businessman. Export-import."

"Bananas?"

Morgan laughed. "Artifacts. You know, arts and crafts. They

probably even sell Central American crafts in Gaul. It's a small world."

"Very small," she said. "You know Ralph Baliol owns Stoke-Higham? Or at least his company does."

"I know."

"Do you personally check out every business someone wants you to invest in?"

"Not always."

She waved for another margarita. "What's your name?"

"Langford Morgan."

"I'm Jenny Stoke."

"Stoke?"

"The town's full of Stokes from both sides of the sheets, don't let it impress you. There hasn't been a Stoke high in the company for a hundred years."

"How about Highams?"

"They're still there."

"Even after Baliol bought the company?"

"Some of the old management stayed on."

"Happily?"

Her margarita came, and Morgan ordered a second Beck's. The bartender forgot his glass, had to get one. While Jenny Stoke drank and he waited, Morgan looked over the room again. For the first time he noticed men in suits and ties in the booths, a few even at the bar, and watched better dressed men and women enter and go into the dining room section on the other side of the ornate divider wall. Executive and mill-hand hours in Gaul were different. His glass arrived.

"What's your impression of Stoke-Higham so far, Mr. Morgan?"

"I haven't looked at it closely yet. I'll probably do that tomorrow. You know, take a tour and look around unannounced. The company seems to know its business, but I'm not so sure about the morale among the workers and in town."

"It's a company town. Our fathers, grandfathers, and great-grandfathers worked for the company. We've had changes, and I guess we all think we know how the company should be run."

"That implies some people don't like the changes or the way the company's being run now."

"You could say that."

"Does that include the old management?"

"Some were unhappy. They left. The ones who stayed take their checks and shut up."

"What made the unhappy ones unhappy?"

"You don't seem to know all that much about the company."

"Only what Baliol and Comrie and a skim of the prospectus told me. Is Fletcher Comrie unwelcome here too?"

"I never heard of Fletcher Comrie. There's no one named Comrie around Stoke-Higham. Have you had dinner?"

"I planned to have it here. Why don't you join me?"

"Having just about invited myself, why not?"

She had a big, open laugh that was exactly right with the jeans, denim shirt, and short red hair. Relaxed, indifferent to appearance or propriety, someone who would invite herself to dinner if that was what she wanted to do.

"Good," Morgan said. "From the look of the clientele, the food should be fine."

"Best in town, which isn't saying much. Except for the Mill Inn, of course."

"We could go there if you prefer."

"Wrong side of the river. You'll do a lot better here for food almost as good."

Morgan ordered more drinks, and they took them to a booth that had come open. The prices were high but not unreasonable. He ordered the poached salmon with hollandaise sauce, fresh asparagus, and new potatoes. She had the vegetarian plate. In a logging town, that told him a lot more about her.

"An alfalfa eater?" Morgan said.

"And a tree hugger," Jenny Stoke said. "I'm not always popular around here."

"I shouldn't have had the salmon."

"I try not to push it, Mr. Morgan."

"Ford. What don't I know about the changes at Stoke-Higham that make people here unhappy?"

She had a good appetite. "Nothing that isn't fairly common knowledge. You could have gotten it out of the prospectus with a little help."

"Why don't you give me that little help?"

"You'll need another Beck's. It's a long story."

17

Sometime in 1850, four young men left their impoverished villages in the English Midlands to sail to Australia. In a stroke of fate, they wound up instead in California in the middle of the gold rush. They were bold lads and bright. None had known the others until they met on the ship, but on the long and difficult voyage they became friends. In California they staked claims together and hated the work together. They were farm and village boys, not diggers in holes in the ground, and their skills were with plants, animals, and people.

They managed to squeeze a little gold dust out of the poor claim, earned more by tending livestock, and heard of a new strike three hundred miles north. They recognized the knock of opportunity and reached the Trinity County field in a month. They staked a better claim, made a good strike, but still had no love for mining and did not get rich. They noticed that those who did get rich tended not to be the miners but the ones who sold the miners what they had to have. They also noticed the vast forests of giant trees more majestic than anything in nature they had ever seen. Inexhaustible forests in a country where waves of people arrived every day, towns sprang up overnight, and no one made bricks or built with stone.

They went down to Humboldt Bay and put all their gold into the equipment for a sawmill. For power they bought a steamship and ran it ashore. They used the ship's cabins as their first bunkhouses for millworkers. The demand for lumber exploded, and by 1855 there were nine mills on Humboldt Bay, and 140 schooners carrying the lumber down the coast as far as San Francisco. In 1860 the four partners bought their first 10,000-acre tract of prime redwood forest and built a second mill and a town for their loggers and millworkers up-river from the bay.

By this time one of the four, Roger Higham, had married an educated lady who taught school in the growing metropolis of Eureka. She had taught him to read largely through the study of Julius Caesar's *Gallic Wars*. The new town was duly named Gaul, the partners moved their headquarters there, and for the next 130 years Stoke-Higham Timber sold redwood lumber to a growing America and the world. Eventually it owned more than 250,000 acres of redwood forest in Humboldt County.

All four became rich and then took divergent paths. Samkin Stoke built his giant mansion, traveled, gambled, lived high and extremely wide. He married more than once, strayed innumerable times with ladies of the mill and town, and died in a fall from his horse while riding to hounds in the baronial sport he had introduced to a land totally unsuited for it. Jedediah Lines built his mansion in more elegant Eureka where he plunged into shipping and fishing and cattle, went bankrupt within five years, and was killed in a duel with a rival. John Hordle sold out to Roger Higham, took his wealth to San Francisco and New York, gambled in many ventures, and died penniless. Roger Higham had only his one schoolteacher wife, built a modest mansion, stayed at home, and eventually owned the company alone.

Roger always remembered his homeland where the original vast forests had vanished centuries ago. A village man, he held the love of the land in his genes. He knew what happened when the land died. So for the whole 130-plus years he and his successors, Highams all, cared for their workers and their forests as they did their children and their farm animals. These rulers were benevolent and patriarchal, and in those days Stoke-Higham Timber amounted to a large family in a private town. There were family squabbles, but there was never a war. Stoke-Higham was their world, they needed no other empire.

Through the succession of Highams the company finally went public, but its practices and policies never changed. By the 1980s their logging and milling operations were so conservative they were one of the few timber companies in the county never to have had trouble with the environmentalists. They cared for their trees better than the tree huggers could, never clear cut an acre of redwoods, and meticulously reforested every year. There would always be trees on Stoke-Higham land, and they would be redwood trees. The company owned more old growth redwoods than any other timber company, had almost no debt, and carried a rich pension fund on its books.

Enter Ralph Baliol and Baliol Investments Corporation. Stoke-Higham, rich and conservative, with an abundance of cash and little debt, was perfect fodder for the takeover binge of the eighties, a virgin jewel ripe for the corporate Vikings to plunder. Ralph Baliol swung into action, launched his buying raid on Stoke-Higham Timber. The conservative management tried to fight back, but it was no contest. The junk-bond fountain was turned on and gushed its river of cash to pay for the company, and Baliol Investment bought it for a billion dollars, give or take a million or two. Ralph Baliol knew nothing about the timber business, but that made no difference. Takeover operations were about money and numbers, had nothing to do with producing or making anything.

Unfortunately, the timber business was more than money and numbers. It was trees and mountains, land and people, watershed and erosion, the environment and the future. In the last year under its 130–year-plus management, Stoke-Higham produced a substantial profit of some $60 million. After his takeover, Ralph Baliol had put so much junk-bond debt on the books he needed twice that profit every year just to pay the interest, and even more profit to pay a return to his own company and himself. The result was inevitable.

Baliol told the former management they could stay on to run the daily operations he and his people couldn't, but he'd send his own CEO up to instruct and watch them. The instructions were simple—double, even triple profits. There was only one way to do that. Production would be doubled, then tripled. And there was only one way to do that: clearcut the ancient forests that had survived perhaps millions of years before the Europeans came, and 150 years after that in the hands of Stoke-Higham. Trees dating back to the time of the original divider of Gaul, Julius Caesar himself, would come down to feed the takeover.

The future was clear. As the chainsaws roared through the forests, the trees would dwindle faster and faster on Stoke-Higham lands. Birds and animals would die, watershed would erode. The air would lose its oxygen, and the people would lose their jobs. In the end, there would be no trees and no work and perhaps no air.

*   *   *

Morgan sat in the booth with Jenny Stoke and drank coffee. She had said nothing since she finished the story of why the people of Gaul were unhappy with Ralph Baliol. A story that was common knowledge. At least in Humboldt County, and probably in the offices of the S.E.C. But nowhere else, and to dig it out of the prospectus you would have to have known the history of Stoke-Higham Timber.

"It's strange," she said at last. "I doubt anyone here ever heard of a corporate takeover or junk bonds or stock equity or any of that financial wheeling and dealing. I doubt anyone knew anything about Wall Street except the name. But what no one knew could destroy the company and everyone who works for it."

"That's the name of the game, Jenny."

"Everyone and everything loses except the top dogs."

"What do you and the town plan to do about it? The loggers and the tree huggers?"

"Nothing, probably. Face a future without the trees. I do know it's got the loggers and millhands together with the tree huggers for the first time I can remember."

"Nothing like being in the same boat."

"I guess not."

She stirred her coffee more thoughtfully than unhappily, but Morgan had little doubt which side she was on.

"I also came up here to talk to some people. A man and a woman." Morgan described Barbara Schoenhausen and Roy Shepherd and the old white Cadillac. "Have you seen a car like that around town?"

"No. You couldn't really miss it, could you?"

"If you happen to see it, would you call me? Tell any of your friends. I'm at the Mill Inn."

She drank her coffee. "What do the woman and the funky Cadillac have to do with your interest in the company?"

"They're associates of Baliol's. He told me they'd be here, would contact me at the hotel. There hasn't been any message."

"If they're from down south they'll probably be staying in Eureka where there's more to do. No one stays in Gaul if they don't have to."

"I'll have to wait for them to call, I suppose. You ever go to somewhere called Taffy's, Jenny?"

"I've been there. It's a roadhouse out west of town. It has dancing, mostly younger people go there." She looked at her watch, smiled at him. "I have to go. Thanks for dinner. I'll keep my eyes open for a strange brunette and a white Caddy with horns."

"Maybe we can do this again. I could use a tour of the town. Do you work for Stoke-Higham?"

"In a way. I do public relations for the county. I'll call you at the inn."

Morgan watched her leave. Standing, she was taller than he had thought. Long legs in the jeans, broad shoulders in the denim shirt. She took long strides in the scuffed cowboy boots. Her short red hair had been tinted, and she wasn't all that young. Forties. She hadn't sounded all that young, and Morgan didn't think for a second she'd believed his whole story of why he was in Gaul. She was an environmentalist. How much were the loggers and environmentalists together in Gaul, and how much were they against Ralph Baliol?

Outside, night had brought a wide sky of stars, colder and clearer than in Costa Rica. Morgan stopped in all the shops along the main street where Barbara Schoenhausen might go. He had made copies of a clipping of her and Baliol, showed it to the clerks with her face circled. No one remembered her, no one asked questions. He left the copies and the number of his hotel room. He returned to his BMW and drove west along the main street. It gradually lost its street lights and became a county highway through the dark mountains and the redwoods until he saw a neon sign with a bubbling red-and-blue cocktail glass: Taffy's.

The crowd inside wasn't large on a Monday night, despite a wall of signs announcing cheap specials, but it was young. Young people who paid little attention to a visitor in gaudy clothes and concentrated on their dance rituals that had a great deal of violent and tortured originality but little contact. All the dancers appeared to dance alone no matter how much they twisted in front of each other. Like the dancers of oriental nations, they danced for each other, not with each other, if they danced for anyone but themselves. At the end of the twentieth century, the ritual was little different in Los Angeles or even Costa Rica, thanks to the miracles of motion pictures, television, and a shrinking world of dying cultures.

A few older men at the long bar could have been loggers or millhands, attracted by the cheap specials or the pleasures of watching young women dance in wild abandon with their eyes closed. There were no older women. Morgan ordered a Coors and described the John Doe in Santa Barbara to the bartender in a voice loud enough for the older men to hear. The bartender showed neither recognition nor interest, but one of the older men showed both.

"Sounds sort of like Dan Derbyfield. Comes in here regular, Dan does. Ain't that right, Luke?"

"Guess he used to come in," the bartender said, "Ain't seen Derbyfield in a while."

Morgan got little else. Dan Derbyfield was a retired millhand, had no family except a sister who'd moved to someplace up in Oregon, no special friends any of the older men knew about. He liked to drink, and liked to listen to dance music. One old man thought Dan might have been some kind of musician. Another said Dan was a nut who liked to hang around with nuts and tree huggers. When Morgan added a description of Roy Shepherd and the white Cadillac with the horns, the older men and the bartender began to look at him with suspicion, and he got nothing more.

His final stops were in West Gaul's cinderblock saloons where country-and-western music played on ancient jukeboxes, no one danced, and the activities were confined to loud drinking and silent drinking and low, serious conversation. In the first two, the loggers and millhands at the bar fell silent when Morgan walked in. They looked at his clothes and up into his face, and went back to their beers and laconic conversation. They didn't particularly resent him, and they didn't include him. He was there, and he wasn't there. A stranger. In some of the bars they stared at him longer and with more hostility, and in all the bars he asked the bartender about the white Cadillac with the steer skull on the hood and left his phone number at the hotel.

There was no reaction beyond suspicion and silence until a shabby saloon on a dark side street. A shaggy blonde man in work clothes and boots, with a thick voice and drunker than most, took strong offense at Morgan and everything about him.

"Fuckin' hotel, huh? Goddamn company hotel."

"A place to stay, friend. I don't own it."

"How come you got clothes like some fuckin' clown?"

Morgan drank his Coors, looked at the bartender. The bartender did nothing.

"You a goddamn cop?"

"Just looking for a friend."

"Shit. White Caddy with goddamn horns. Guy like that we run outa town. Hotshot son of a bitch. You're a hotshot son of a bitch. We don't like no hotshots aroun' here."

The man swung a big fist faster and with more accuracy than Morgan had thought he could. Morgan caught the wrist and elbow as he slipped the punch, leaned into the drunk and put him on the floor, still holding the wrist and elbow. No one else moved. They seemed to be judging Morgan's skills. The drunk cursed and tried to get up. Morgan put some pressure on the elbow and the man howled in pain and sat down on the floor. Morgan released him, thanked the bartender, went back to his BMW, and drove back to the Mill Inn. He would be remembered in the bars.

He left an 8:00 A.M. call at the desk, went up to his room to get a good night's sleep, and found the room had been searched.

It was a good job. Almost everything had been returned to where it should have been. But he had changed from his Western boots into the purple running shoes before he left, and dropped the boots on the floor. Now they were neatly together beside the bed.

Someone had already noticed he was in town.

18

Long before the telephone rang with his wake-up call at eight, Morgan had been watching the dawn grow lighter over the valley as he composed a message in his mind to convince Stoke-Higham's president to meet him. The final message: *My name is Langford Morgan, a detective working for the family of Fletcher Comrie. It looks very much as if someone from Gaul, perhaps an employee of Stoke-Higham, is involved in the recent murder of Mr. Comrie, and I would really like to talk to Mr. Higham before I go to the local police.* Polite, with a suggestion of self-interest, a shade of menace, and a hint of threat.

Baxter Higham's secretary took his room number and assured him in an edgy voice that, yes, she would deliver the message in person. He dressed in his best three-button tropical silk suit and his proper cordovan oxfords, with striped blue and white shirt and regimental tie, and his appointment came through before he had finished breakfast downstairs in the airy dining room.

Morgan drove the few blocks to the mill. The old Stoke-Higham had not indulged itself with the trappings of wealth and power or the elaborate security of modern corporations. Behind a plain cyclone fence at the end of the main street, the giant mill had no armed guards or badges, and an elderly millhand on a chair directed him across the gravel yard to parking spaces in front of the three-story frame headquarters. Inside double front doors a receptionist at a desk in a cool wood-paneled foyer greeted him with a smile.

"Mr. Baxter Higham, please. Langford Morgan, I have an appointment."

The receptionist made a call. "Mr. Higham's secretary will take you upstairs, sir."

The secretary who came down had the cool, brusque manner of

someone who had been with Mr. Baxter Higham a long time. She did not shake hands, walked in front of Morgan to lead the way. The president's office was on the third floor, and there was no elevator. Only wide wooden stairs with the space and elbow room of many old Western office buildings from the turn of the century when both wood and space had been cheap. She didn't apologize, took the stairs at a brisk pace without a hard breath, was both surprised and a little annoyed to see Morgan easily keep pace with her. She was accustomed to more effete visitors to the asceticism of Stoke-Higham. Construction at the far end of each floor had all the signs of an external elevator shaft, suggesting someone high in the company wasn't accustomed to frontier rigors and had no intention of becoming accustomed.

"In here, Mr. Morgan." The secretary offered no *sir*, and Morgan heard a tight anger in her voice as she led him into an office with as much wood, air, and space as everything else in Gaul. Old California lived on among the redwoods.

"Mr. Morgan, I'm Baxter Higham. Please sit down. The armchair there should be comfortable."

Baxter Higham stood graciously behind a redwood desk. He was a middle-aged man with gray hair and a soft pink face. The office was as spartan as the stairs, had high windows and a wooden ceiling fan. Comfortable Victorian furniture was set far apart. A relaxed office. Baxter Higham wasn't relaxed, and he wasn't alone. The two other men in the office had to be the cause of his tension, and probably of his secretary's tight anger. Morgan nodded to them, got no response, and sat in the wooden armchair with its old-fashioned cushions.

Baxter Higham sat behind his desk. "Exactly what is it you want to discuss, Mr. Morgan?"

"Who shot Fletcher Comrie and Ralph Baliol down in Santa Barbara?"

Baxter Higham glanced at the two other men. One stood in front of a cabinet decorated in intricate scroll and spindle work. All shoulders and chest and thick hips, he had a ramrod stance and a waist that had once been narrow but had expanded. Morgan had seen at least one of him at every police interrogation or intelligence briefing and debriefing. Every inch a former officer, law or military. But he wasn't in command here.

The third man was the one who gave the orders. "You forgot to mention Ralph Baliol in your message, Mr. Morgan."

Overweight and short, stout in the middle where his black Italian silk suit barely covered, the third man sat in a leather armchair. He had not stood up as Morgan came in, and he would be the one who was having the new elevator built. Younger than Baxter Higham by at least ten years, he had thick black hair and had tried to give his round face more age and authority with a rectangular black mustache.

"I'm not working for Baliol."

"You're aware that Baliol Investments owns this company?"

"Why else would I be here?"

There was a silence. Baxter Higham broke it. He was one of those people who lived by proper form and good manners. "Mr. Boyle is our new chairman, Mr. Morgan. He asked to sit in on our meeting. Mr. Chandos is chief of security for the company."

"I'll explain myself, Baxter," the seated man said.

Baxter Higham nodded stiffly. "Of course, Daly."

Daly Boyle, who didn't value manners or form, would be the CEO sent up by Ralph Baliol to take charge in Gaul. He would set the schedules and give the orders day-to-day management had to carry out and explain to the county, the EPA, and the workers. Daly Boyle didn't have to explain anything. Not here. Baxter Higham was used to that by now, had settled for what he had. He assumed as neutral an expression as Mr. Chandos, the ex-officer security chief. It was Daly Boyle's show. He had decided that by being there.

Boyle said, "Exactly what do you want, Mr. Morgan?"

"Whatever I can get," Morgan said. "You know Fletcher Comrie was murdered?"

"Comrie had no connection to this company."

"That's not exactly true, is it? He had a big connection to Baliol Investments."

"He had a financial connection to many companies."

"But Ralph Baliol was shot too, wasn't he? Probably by the same people."

"If you have some specific questions, Morgan, ask them."

"The police have reason to believe the attackers were from Gaul. Who in Gaul would want Baliol and Comrie dead?"

"I suppose there could be many," Daly Boyle said. "You're not suggesting some executive of the company? One of us?"

The sound from Chandos was ominous. Boyle didn't look toward the security chief; he was too intent on intimidating Morgan with a stare that challenged him to suggest the murderer could be one of the company executives, old or new. The same suggestion put Baxter Higham in a trance behind his desk, his glazed eyes seeing what no one else could see in the spacious office. A fantasy, perhaps, of himself riding gun in hand to right the terrible wrong done to Stoke-Higham. Shoot Ralph Baliol and Fletcher Comrie. Something he might very much have liked to do but could never have done. The Baxter Highams of this world rarely act for good or evil. A reasonable man, as he would have said himself.

"Has there been any serious trouble at the top in the company?" Morgan asked. "Differences with Ralph Baliol?"

"There were some differences as to the future direction of the company. It was made clear there would be no discussion, and those who disagreed left. Right, Baxter?"

"Some of the old management didn't like the new policies," Baxter Higham agreed. "They resigned rather than do what, in good conscience, they couldn't do."

"Perhaps some of them would like to return," Morgan said. "Have the company back the way it was."

"Most of them have other jobs now, Mr. Morgan, and almost all have left the county," Baxter Higham said. "And they aren't the kind of men who shoot people."

Daly Boyle demurred. "I don't know, Baxter, some of those old country boys had more good solid hate in them than you, eh?" He liked this idea, nodded in pleased agreement with himself. "Revenge. Now, that's a good, honest motive for murder."

"Saving forests and jobs can be a powerful motive too," Morgan said.

"Forests," Boyle said, "take care of themselves, and no jobs are in danger at Stoke-Higham. In fact, we're hiring people and boosting production over a hundred percent."

"Close to two hundred percent, from what I've heard," Morgan said. "Clearcutting to pay off the junk-bond debt. Maybe even selling off forests. That won't do a lot for jobs in the future, or for the redwoods."

"Don't believe everything you hear in a saloon, Morgan."

"How do you know I heard it in a saloon?"

"Because I told him," Chandos said.

"Spies?"

"The Stoke House is a popular place," Daly Boyle said. "A lot of people drink and eat there."

"Company spies in the town. That's interesting."

Chandos allowed himself a faint smile. "It's our town."

"Not everyone out there would agree," Morgan said. "Didn't your spies tell you that?"

"What the town thinks is irrelevant," Daly Boyle said. "They're our workers, we bought them along with the company. We set the plan, they carry it out. For years this company generated one-third of the profit it should have. They underused all resources, were grossly inefficient, robbed the stockholders, and denied the country the lumber needed to build homes. This country needs all the building materials it can get, and under our management it's going to get them."

"Clearcutting your forests isn't efficient, Boyle."

"Of course it is. We reseed. Redwoods grow from the stumps of cut trees, it all comes back sooner or later. And does anyone really need a meat-eating owl and a five-inch sea bird no one ever heard of?"

Baxter Higham said, "That's not correct, Daly. I've told you. The trees depend on the birds and animals, the whole forest depends on everything in it. It has for millions of years. No one can change that. If you break the cycles of the forest, nothing will be the same."

"And I've told you to decide which side you're on once and for all."

"I know what side I'm on, Daly. I'm on my side. I decided that when I stayed, didn't I?"

"That's the side everyone's on. Remember that."

When the telephone rang, Baxter Higham made no move to answer it. If Daly Boyle wanted to take over his office, he could damn well answer the telephone too. We all fight back in our own ways, small as they might be. Chandos had to quickly cross to Baxter Higham's desk to pick up the receiver. He listened, then held it out to Boyle who had to stand to take it. Boyle listened, spoke low, listened again, and hung up. He sat on the edge of Baxter Higham's desk, his back to the company president, and stared at Morgan.

"So what do we really have here? Maybe I should call the police, eh?" He was pleased with that thought, too. "Let's talk about what you're after, Morgan. Some blackmail? A muckraking magazine piece: Civil War in the Redwoods? Some spying and infiltration for the tree huggers?" He nearly rubbed his hands with satisfaction. "Bob, you'd better escort our friend out. He isn't any kind of detective, and the late Fletcher Comrie didn't even have a family. Goodbye, Morgan. Don't come back."

Morgan got up. "It was worth a try."

"Bob," Daly Boyle said.

Chandos took a step. Morgan unbuttoned his suit jacket and let the security chief see the little Czech pistol in its holster. Chandos stopped. Morgan walked out and down the three flights of stairs without hurrying. No one came after him, and no one was in the gravel yard as he went out into the morning sun except a tour group on their way to the mill. The only person who could have called Daly Boyle and told him about Morgan was Ralph Baliol. He should have realized Boyle would call Baliol to report this man who wanted to ask about the murder of Fletcher Comrie. The call that had just come into the office would have been the return call. Where had Ralph Baliol called from? Morgan got into his BMW, but he didn't start the motor. He wanted to see who came through the gate in the next few minutes.

What came through the gate was a light-blue-and-red police car. The two uniformed policemen who jumped out had their guns drawn and aimed at Morgan.

"Out of the car! Now! Hands up and against the car! Spread the legs! Do it!"

The one stood with his gun nervous in both hands, the other found the Czech Vz70 in Morgan's belt holster. He took it even more nervously. They handcuffed Morgan and put him in the back of the patrol car behind a metal mesh and with the usual lack of door handles on the inside.

19

Headquarters of the Gaul Police Department is an ornate two-story building on Main Street with columns to hold up the overhanging second story. The columns are made of whole redwood trunks.

The patrol car took Morgan to the parking lot behind the building, the two officers pulled him out and walked him into a room with desks all the way to the front where there was a small fenced-off waiting area. A male and female officer sat at two of the six desks. The male was in plain clothes.

"Take the cuffs off, Davis."

The man who told the two patrolmen to remove the handcuffs from Morgan's wrists was in his fifties, short and neat in a seersucker summer suit and bowtie under graying hair. He looked like a small-town lawyer.

"Follow me, Mr. Morgan."

They went into a private cubicle tucked into a corner of the single room. Inside the office, windows looked out on the room as well as on the mill and river outside. The man told Morgan to take a chair, then sat in the chair behind the only desk in the cubicle and leaned back with a creaking of springs.

"Jim Walker. I'm the chief. You have a first name, Mr. Morgan?"

"Langford."

"That's quite a mouthful. What do people usually call you?"

"Ford, Lang, Morgan, take your choice, chief."

"You have some trouble with the Stoke-Higham brass, Ford?"

"I was talking to them about this problem I've sort of gotten involved in. They didn't think I should be talking to them."

"Do you always go armed to talk about problems with businessmen?"

"That would depend on what the problem was and who the businessmen were. I've got a license for the gun."

"I don't doubt you, and we'll look at it. But we don't get a lot of strangers with concealed weapons up here. When we get a call reporting an armed trespasser it makes my men nervous, they tend to overreact."

"That's understandable, chief."

"It looks like you made some other people nervous recently. Those are pretty nice bruises there, not to mention the ears and the finger. Was it the same problem?"

"More or less."

Chief Walker pondered as he glanced out his rear window at the parking lot and the river beyond. "Generally, we're about the last place Daly Boyle or Bob Chandos would call for help. You really must have worried the hell out of them."

"If I hadn't worried them I'd never have gotten in to see them."

"I can relate to that. Would it be the same problem you were asking about all over town last night?"

"You've got spies too?"

"I'm supposed to. They didn't get a lot of details, though. Why don't you give me some?"

The Santa Barbara sheriff's department would have contacted him about the shootings and maybe about Barbara Schoenhausen. Morgan told the chief all he knew about those problems, and about Roy Shepherd and what had brought him to Gaul.

Chief Walker nodded. "That's about Santa Barbara's story. We've had no crime committed up here, and they're still working down there. They want to send someone up, and that's fine with me. But they don't seem to have much evidence to go on. We did identify that John Doe as Dan Derbyfield, right enough. He was a retired mill foreman, and he did hang out at Taffy's. He was pretty much of a loner, a woodsman, and kind of eccentric. Santa Barbara insists there has to be another killer from Gaul, but so far I haven't found anyone."

"Would this Dan Derbyfield have had reason to kill Ralph Baliol?"

"I wouldn't know. Derbyfield kept to himself. But it sure looks like it, doesn't it? Now here you're up here too. Would you know something the Santa Barbara sheriff doesn't? Especially about that Fletcher Comrie. Who was he, anyway? Did he have some connection to Gaul or Stoke-Higham? Why would someone from here want to kill him?"

"You don't know Fletcher Comrie?"

"Never heard of the man."

"Then I don't know why someone from here would want to kill him."

"That's too bad."

"Did Santa Barbara contact you about Barbara Schoenhausen?"

"They mentioned her, nothing official yet. It's only a few days she's been gone. What do you know about her?"

"I know she wouldn't leave on her own without her children, not without telling her children and her husband."

"Know, think, or hope?"

"All three."

The chief found that information interesting. "She feel the same about you?"

"That's why I'm here. I want to ask her."

"Knight on a white horse to the rescue? They tell me it even works with women sometimes. What makes you think she could be up here?"

"What Ralph Baliol told me about their breakup doesn't sound like the Barbara Schoenhausen I talked to."

"Maybe they didn't break up."

"He made up the breakup story for my benefit? I've thought about that, but that's not what Ralph Baliol does. With women or anything else. He uses them, they don't use him. I expect he'll use you when he gets up here."

"He's already called today."

"From where?"

"I didn't ask. It was a short call."

It was the second time the chief had implied that he didn't have a particularly good relationship with the new Stoke-Higham management. Morgan wondered what relationship he might have with the enemies of the new Stoke-Higham.

"A woman I talked to last night, Jenny Stoke, said loggers and tree huggers were getting together up here."

"You talked to Jenny, did you? What'd she tell you?"

"That some people are opposed to the new policies of Stoke-Higham. Perhaps a lot of people."

"She ought to know. She's one of the leaders of an employee and

town group called the Save Trees, Save Jobs Committee. They protest, picket, and try to raise capital to buy the company back from
Baliol Investments. My assistant chief is a member."

"Not you?"

"It wouldn't be appropriate."

"How are they doing?"

"As far as I've heard, Ralph Baliol has refused even to meet with
them."

"What have you heard about people who might want to do more
against Stoke-Higham than talk?"

"Not much." Chief Walker creaked in his chair. "So you came
up here because you think the people who did the shooting in
Santa Barbara are up here and could be holding this Barbara
Schoenhausen?"

"I think it's possible. It looks to me like two, maybe three from
up here went down to Santa Barbara with more on their minds
than a protest. I could use some names."

"I don't know any names."

"Not even one?"

"Not even one."

It was a difficult time for the chief and the whole police department. Stoke-Higham owned this building, and the buildings and
streets outside. The funds for the police came from taxes on those
streets and those buildings, and Stoke-Higham probably funded the
department more directly as well. A civic-minded company would
want the very best equipment and uniforms for the police who
maintained law and order in their town. But the chief had grown
up with the town and the old management. He would keep the
law, do his job, but he wouldn't jump for Ralph Baliol and his
seneschal, Daly Boyle. To Baliol this would make the chief of police
his enemy.

The old white Cadillac with the bleached steer skull was parked in
front of a bookstore across the side street from the parking lot as
Morgan left police headquarters. Its top down, the car was empty.

Before Morgan could start toward it, Roy Shepherd emerged
from the bookstore, vaulted into the driver's seat, and drove off
with a squeal of rubber, one hand on the wheel and one arm
draped lazily across the back of the front seat. Morgan ran to his

BMW and followed. Stopped at the corner of the main street, Shepherd didn't act like a man in a hurry. The vault into the saddle and the squeal of rubber was probably the way he always drove.

A half mile beyond the mill gates where the town came to an abrupt end, the road narrowed to a tight two lanes without a center line and dropped down toward the river. The Caddy slowed for the narrow curves, the sharp rises and descents, as the road followed the winding course of the river and the contours of the ridges. There wasn't a house or a shack along the road as it wound through the tall trees and river brush. Morgan held position where he could glimpse the Caddy's white tail from time to time. Far above, the guardrails of the freeway were visible like something not only in another world but another century. Eventually the road angled right and crossed the low September river on a narrow iron bridge with a redwood board roadway that rattled under Morgan's BMW.

On the other side the road climbed for half a mile before turning to parallel the river once more. They were now among the redwoods, the Caddy only brief flashes of white through the giant trunks and low ferns. Morgan felt small yet somehow safe in the shadowed peace under the trees that smelled of the damp soil, humus, and needles of an evergreen forest. Scattered cabins began to appear in the forest gloom. Weekend cabins for people from somewhere else. The blacktop grew narrower and the white Caddy vanished ahead.

Morgan pushed the accelerator and the narrowing blacktop forked. The right fork climbed steeply uphill through the shaded sepulchre of the trees where the Caddy flickered white and on upward. Morgan followed. The road became steep enough to shift the BMW's automatic, and the Caddy seemed to have slowed. It stayed in sight through the giant trees as the ridge line of sky appeared above, and Morgan began to think he wasn't following, he was being led. Not the hunter but the hunted.

He reached behind him under his silk suit jacket, took out the compact Vz70, and laid it on the seat beside him. The road turned sharply left again to follow the ridge with the sky close on either side through the trees until the BMW passed an open clearing where the white Caddy was parked in front of a large A-frame lodge with a high deck that faced the wide sweep of the next valley. The Caddy was empty again.

Morgan parked where he could see the Cadillac. He refocused his side mirror until it looked at the edge of the trees to the left. His rearview mirror covered the road behind him. The bulk of the clearing was to the right. He held the small Czech pistol on his lap, and studied the A-frame. Tire tracks in the forest duff led to a garage on its right, and then circled away again to rejoin the road. The dirt brought up from under the duff was still soft and wet in the tracks. Redwood needles littered the front deck, there was no smoke from the metal chimney, and all the windows were dirty with forest dust. Through the dirt on the window to the left of the door, Morgan saw Roy Shepherd in his cowboy hat looking out at him.

A clock inside Morgan's head ticked off the minutes. He'd had that clock since the Green Berets in Vietnam, and it had been his most useful tool through the endless hours of waiting undercover, the violent minutes of action, the brief seconds of decision. Now it was one of those seconds of decision. He put the Vz70 inside his pants under his belt on his left side, buttoned the suit jacket, and got out.

Morgan walked to the house and up the two steps to the deck, opened the unlocked door, looked to the right away from where Shepherd still stood at the window, unarmed and watching Morgan with obvious interest. The single large living room was empty, the furniture all covered for the winter. Morgan walked in, sat on the arm of a covered chair, took out the Czech pistol, and rested it on his raised leg.

"Armed ourselves, did we?" Shepherd's amused smile was still there. It was as much a part of him as the pale tunnel eyes and the cowboy hat and the high-heeled boots, dark brown this time.

"It seemed like a good idea."

"I'll buy that. So what is it, Charlie? Shoot-out or talk?"

"You led me here, so I'd guess you have some call in mind."

"If you figured that, you could of broken contact and gone back to base, so you got to have something on your mind, too."

"I came to talk," Morgan said.

"Then we talk."

Shepherd pulled the cover off a leather couch and sat down, his legs crossed and one boot swinging. He was comfortable, a man without worry, peaceful and relaxed and ready to talk openly man to man about whatever Morgan had on his mind. Morgan wasn't ready to talk.

"Why don't we get everyone together first?" he said.

Shepherd laughed. "Come on in, Krajic."

The young man who stepped through the front door wasn't smiling and he wasn't amused. Dark-haired, pockmarked, thick everywhere, he was twenty years old, as sullen as Johnny Baliol and carrying a big .45 automatic that looked like a cannon in his pale hand.

"I done everythin' you said, Roy! I swear he don't hear me. No way. I mean—"

"It's okay, Krajic. Put the piece away and go sit down."

"Don't go too far, Krajic," Morgan said.

Krajic sat down and glared at Morgan, the big automatic still in his hand.

"The tire tracks?" Shepherd said.

"Too fresh, too much debris on the deck and dirt on the windows. The house was closed up," Morgan said. "Why, Shepherd? Scare me with a show of power?"

"The honcho figured it was a good idea. I told him no way it works."

"Jesus Christ," Krajic said, "what for's all the goddamn talk? There's two the fuck of us, we take the bastard."

Shepherd said, "You ready to die, Krajic? 'Cause one of us would for sure, maybe both of us. You see how he's on the wall where he got both of us and the windows in front of him, and no one gets behind him? Maybe he dies, but so does at least one of us, right, Morgan?"

"That seems probable. And I think I'd feel better if Krajic put that cannon somewhere."

Krajic's pale face went paler. Shepherd looked over at him and nodded. Krajic put the big automatic on a table beside him.

Shepherd said, "How come you been going around scaring the suckass and the muscle mind at Stoke-Higham, Charlie?"

"You mean you've been talking to Boyle and Chandos? Does that mean you take orders from them too?"

Shepherd leaned back on the couch, rested his head against the leather, and looked up at the peak of the A-frame high above. "Chandos, he's your standard rod-up-the-ass MP brass. Boyle's one of those bastards kiss up and shit down. He tried to strut the colonel on me, so I told Baliol to keep him off or he'd lose a good ass-kisser. Ralphie boy thought that was a riot, filled me in on Mr. Daly Boyle.

Seems he's a slum kid cruised through some two-bit Catholic college, sucked up so good that Harvard laid free law school on him.
He slid into a spot at a big company, got slick at golf and learned the
slime edges of big-corp law. When Baliol took over the company,
old Daly switched sides fast. Ralphie put him in some government
jobs for the contacts, made him junior legal eagle for his whole
outfit, and sent him up here because the doubtfuls in town are kind
of surly, and he figured he needed a first shirt with a whip."

Morgan had been in the CIA almost ten years when he learned
about John J. McCloy: the poor boy who rose to become the great
intelligence expert, and turned the richest foundation in the U.S.
into a piggy bank for the CIA. Responsible for the roundup of Japa-
nese-Americans on the West Coat in World War II, McCloy went on
to deny that Jews were dying in gas ovens. In charge in Germany
after the war, he freed thousands of ex-Nazis, especially Alfred
Krupp. He exonerated Krupp of war crimes and canceled the con-
fiscation of all Krupp property. McCloy devoted his life to being a
legal leg-man for the rich to protect their wealth and power from
the uncertainties of a democracy. McCloy and Boyle would have
recognized each other.

"You're keeping great company," Morgan said.

"Name of the game," Shepherd said, brought his gaze down to
look at Morgan. "So tell me straight. What's in all this for you,
Charlie? I mean, coming up and making waves?"

"I told you. I don't like Baliol or what he does to people."

"What people? You worried about the bushwhacker?"

"I don't know who that was, do you?"

"Let's say we're zeroing in, but nice try. If it's not the sniper,
what?"

"We've got laws and courts for two reasons, Shepherd. To bring
criminals to justice, and to bring justice to criminals. I don't know
what Baliol plans to do to whoever shot him, but I know what
he's doing to almost everyone up here. I know what he's done to
Barbara Schoenhausen."

Morgan heard the faint step on the deck, and saw a shadow from
the window beside the outside door flicker for an instant on the
floor. So did Roy Shepherd. Krajic heard and saw nothing. Shepherd sighed and shrugged to Morgan, spoke to Krajic, "Krajic, go
out and tell Grumman to drive the two of you back to base. And

don't try to be smart, Charlie over there knows how to keep it all on the line.''

Krajic was shocked. ''Why the fuck you tell him Grumman's gonna be out there?''

''He knows, Krajic, he knows. An' Grumman ain't *gonna* be out there, he *is* out there. Back to base, no tricks, okay?''

Krajic was confused, but he picked up his .45, looked at Morgan and carefully put it into his belt, and walked out the front door. Shepherd and Morgan both sat in silence until a car started, crunched through the forest duff to the blacktop road, and faded away back toward Gaul.

''You wouldn't have missed having a tail-end Charlie.''

''No way,'' Shepherd agreed.

''Who brought in the troops? Baliol? Some of his blue-collar goons?''

''The honcho cut the orders, those turtles was my treat. They come cheap, I use 'em sometimes for show.'' Shepherd's pale tunnel eyes looked toward the outside door as if seeing through it. ''Sorry assholes. Ain't they pitiful? They still believe, you know? The whole shit. They think they're for real. I mean, they believe in their own fucking lives! Can you buy that? They think it's all for real. They even believe how tough they are. That's all they got to make 'em feel big. Fucking pathetic.''

They both listened to the silence. A silence that was far from silent, full of the sounds of the forest from the calls of birds, the sudden movements of small animals, the occasional louder movement of something large, to the soft wind in the trees at the crest of the ridge.

''Why?'' Morgan said. ''You don't like Ralph Baliol any more than I do. You don't like what he is or what he does.''

Shepherd nodded almost absently, and then abruptly sat forward. ''This Schoenhausen lady, she mean all that much to you, Charlie?''

''I don't like to see her used or in danger.''

''What makes you think she could be in deep serious?''

''She's missing from her home. I think, one way or the other, she's up here with Baliol. Is she?''

''Let's put it like this, Charlie. If the lady's around here, it's because she wants to be around here. Okay?''

"You're all up here together, one happy gang looking for the villains?"

"Search and destroy all the way."

Morgan said. "When did Baliol hire you, Shepherd?"

"Couple of days before you showed up in Santa Barbara. Bodyguard and a little snooping. He figured the shooter got to show again, wanted his people watched too."

"And the villains are from up here?"

"That's how the honcho reads it. I just do the job."

"Do the job and take your pay? No questions?"

"Hey, you don't ask the questions, you don't hear the lies. You and me, we're the same people, Charlie. We just got hired on different sides. It's the only way they let us live. The shit jams up in the bowl, they send us to clean it out. We're the ones can put our arms in the shit and open it up. All they can do is make the shit."

"You could be right, but we *are* on different sides," Morgan said. He got up, the Czech pistol still in his hand but pointed down at the floor of the closed-up A-frame.

Shepherd said, "No reason we got to be, Charlie. This up here really ain't your shit. That's the plain facts."

"I came up here to find Barbara Schoenhausen, make sure she's safe. If I happen to get in Baliol's way, I guess that's the way it has to be. Now I think we'll walk out to the cars."

"Why not?"

Shepherd got up and walked ahead of Morgan out the front door. He'd shown no weapon, but Morgan knew he had one, probably more than one.

"You go out first," Morgan said.

Shepherd got into the big old Caddy with its steer horns, sat with both hands on the steering wheel. "What say I ask the lady to come to your room down at the inn, lay it out for you? You get the word, cut for home, and no one gets hurt."

"Baliol's that worried about me?"

"You want to talk to the lady or not?"

"I want to talk to her."

"Then that's what goes down."

20

Morgan lay on the bed in the warm room and waited for the knock to come. He watched the shifting pattern of sunlight on the ceiling the way he had in all the warm rooms and cold rooms in cities where the soft knock on the door could be triumph or betrayal. He was like someone far under the surface of the sea who watched the shimmer of the water above where the bottoms of boats passed distorted and undulant and waited for rescue. She would come.

There had been Morgans in the valleys and mountains of Wales of the last century who saw that when their valleys had been cut open and dug up to feed the factories of other people, they would be left with only ruined health and a ruined valley. One of these clear-eyed Morgans found his way first to the walls of New Spain— too late for any stolen gold—and then to the United States. In Cuba this Morgan learned, like his distant kinsman Sir Henry, the famed scourge of the Spanish Main, the ways of the sea. Later he moved to the open bays of Long Island, New York, to work on the fishing boats of a colder sea.

He worked hard and died young and left his son, Denys, a boat and an old house on an inlet in Sag Harbor. He left his grandson, Langford, a little knowledge of Spanish. Langford's mother sent him to college to learn to make his life anything with more security and less risk than a fishing boat captain's. She kept him off the boats, but about then the conflict in Vietnam escalated, and Langford was an eager young man who believed in his country. Most young men do. And these young men go to war because they believe, and because the other young men are going to war.

Lanford's belief in his country took him into the army, and his love of challenge and adventure took him into the special forces.

154

The special forces took him to Dak To in the central highlands of Vietnam to monitor an important infiltration route from the north. Over the next year he trained and worked with indigenous personnel deep in the jungles among the enemy in a program to use Vietnamese minority peoples to fight the war, the CIDG. With his Montagnard soldiers, Yards to the Americans, they killed many of the enemy, although it was difficult to tell friend from enemy, and too often they were the same man, woman, or child.

Eventually he went on a particularly difficult mission deep out-country in Laos to rescue a CIA field agent. They had to evade not only the troops of the enemy but their tribesmen allies too, because allies were a sometime thing to the tribesmen. It was Morgan who took charge and with the help of the CIA field agent got them all out unseen and unsuspected by the enemy, and without a single confrontation with the tribes. The CIA man was impressed, and six months later when Morgan received his half-million-dollar wound, an older civilian came to the hospital a few days before he was to be sent home. The civilian knew all about Morgan's father, mother, college leadership record, pre-law studies, Spanish, ROTC, enlistment, and Green Beret service. The civilian told Morgan he had the right stuff to be CIA. They needed men who could train others in the skills of counterinsurgency.

Still eager to serve, Morgan came home to do six months training in Virginia, then flew back to Vietnam. Morgan soon learned the CIA was a major player in Vietnam and that, in fact, he had been working for the Company his whole time in special forces. Vietnam was a war of infiltration, subterfuge, terrorism, and treachery, of undermining allies and forcing deep divisions within countries. It would be won by the side with the most singleminded purpose and the endurance to carry that purpose to the end. There were only two contestants who had those requirements in Vietnam—the old men in Hanoi who had been fighting foreign rule all their lives, and the masters behind the CIA and special forces who focused on the larger goal.

His new comrades told Morgan he was now a professional in the ultimate war. They told him this war would continue all over the world long after Vietnam had ended one way or the other. Morgan had been startled, no one in the army had ever suggested they might not win in Vietnam. His CIA leaders explained that was because in the CIA they knew they were in a longer struggle, that Vietnam was only a battle.

His first job was out-country in Laos with Air America to help supply our tribal allies in the war there. He learned that Air America didn't exist because the United States and the CIA weren't in Laos. He learned that the real interest of the tribal leaders was in having the means of getting their main source of income, opium, to market in a world turned upside-down by the U.S.–Vietnamese War. So after delivering a load of guns and supplies, Air America flew back the opium crop. In the black humor of soldiers, the unit was soon named Air Opium. Morgan didn't think this was all that funny.

"You worry about shit too damn much, Lang."

"Lighten up, for chrissake, and get the fucking job done. That's what we're here for."

"It's a damn good thing we *are* here or the whole world would go the fuck to hell in a handbasket."

They had a job to do that wasn't always done with pleasant methods and nice people. What counted was results, winning the ultimate war. The secret war and opium crop in Laos was one part of the mission, the Phoenix Program to destroy the Viet Cong through clandestine subversion and the assassinations of its leaders was another. As was the support of coups and other power plays in South Vietnam to make sure Vietnam had the right leaders, people as committed to American goals as the CIA itself.

As the war wound down Morgan was reassigned to the Latin American desk because of his fluent Spanish. In Montevideo he trained the military in counterinsurgency methods. In Mexico, he went underground to work with the Federal Security Directorate infiltrating exile and refugee organizations from Honduras, El Salvador, Guatemala, and Nicaragua. In Bolivia he worked on a coup to install a president—who turned out to be a dictator named Banzer. Then he went to Chile.

Salvador Allende, a populist Marxist who had been elected president of the more advanced nation of Chile, had begun to nationalize American business holdings in the country. This was unacceptable. But since the election had been at least as democratic as the United States's own, there wasn't a great deal that could be done in the open. President Richard Nixon called in the CIA, and Operation Centaur was put into motion. It was a rush mission, the president didn't want Allende to have any chance to change Chile. "Not one day, you all understand? Not one minute of peace to put in any programs, to change anything."

Morgan collected and coordinated the contributions and slush funds of the U.S. companies that did business in Chile, and put these millions to work against Allende. He went underground in Santiago to distribute a deluge of forged Chilean banknotes that would fuel a big inflation. His last job was to contact opposition groups the CIA could rally to overthrow Allende and give the popular support necessary to stabilize the country after Allende was eliminated. There had to be an uprising or a coup, the CIA didn't have time to wear the Marxists down with embargoes and other economic pressure. But a problem soon surfaced—there was no grassroots insurgency. There was no viable opposition except the military elite. The CIA had no choice. As Henry Kissinger said publicly, "I don't see why we need to stand by and watch a country go communist due to the irresponsibility of its own people." It had to be a coup, and it had to be the military.

With the murder of Salvador Allende, the coup succeeded. The iron fist of General Pinochet would rule for sixteen years, with the deaths or disappearances of thousands of Chileans by military arrest and repression. Chile was saved, and Morgan was sent on to other countries. He was undercover in Jamaica to destabilize the Manley government, worked with the army in El Salvador, Honduras, and Guatemala, training their elite regiments and national security agencies. Then came the Sandinista victory over the Somoza dynasty in Nicaragua.

Morgan went with a team to train a force to attack the Nicaraguan government, and spent the next few years with familiar allies —the cocaine and heroin dealers of Colombia, Mexico, and Panamá. Different drugs but the same deal. The Contras needed money, the drug lords had money. The Contras needed arms, the drug lords had the aircraft, the airfields, and the contacts. Morgan went to Colombia. He went to Panamá. When the war and U.S. embargo had weakened Nicaragua to the point of collapse, an election brought in a government more to the taste of Washington, and Morgan was assigned once more to Laos to destabilize another communist government.

He was back where he had started, and after twenty years the war that never ended came to an end for Morgan exactly where it had begun—in war-weary Laos. His career in service of his country came full circle, and a violent anger finally erupted inside him.

He knew that he had never been doing what they said he had been doing, what he had believed he was doing.

He knew that when one country talked of bringing democracy to another country, it meant support of the elite who had always ruled and who would keep conditions right for its benefactors with careful elections and violence. Nicaragua had not been a democracy, so the CIA had to free it. El Salvador, South Africa, Indonesia, and Colombia were democracies, there was no need to interfere in their freedom.

He knew he no longer wanted to work for a government or an organization that routinely lied to and fooled its own citizens.

He hated everything he saw around him. Capitalist, fascist, socialist, anarchist, it was all materialism and self-interest, swimming pools and champagne.

The world wasn't the simple innocence of his youth. It was men from Washington and men from Moscow, men from Damascus and Tel Aviv, and men from Colombia. A world that lived on the advantage to be gained and the dollars to be made from other people.

The world and its people were hopeless. He couldn't beat them so he might as well join them. Have his own swimming pool and champagne. There were always angles in the shadow world his country had put him into, and only suckers played an honest game.

His angle was one of the lesser Colombian gentlemen who had helped his bosses in Nicaragua and who knew the value of a CIA man who could help him become richer, safer, and a more important dream merchant without harming the CIA or his country. An agent close to a drug boss was of great value to the CIA, few questions were ever asked, so it was a simple matter for Morgan to take "compensation and rewards" from the Colombian gentleman, and skim from the CIA slush funds. He worked only for the one Colombian gentleman who was more than grateful for his help, and gave good service against all other drug lords, so pleased his CIA bosses. He was doing what he had done for years, except now he made a lot of money for himself.

He didn't push it too far, got out before he had outlived his usefulness or began to worry anyone. He left the country and settled down with his money. He chose Costa Rica because when it had learned how it had been used by the CIA and the drug cartels, it banned both.

In Costa Rica he was discreet, started his export-import business to justify both his lifestyle and his presence. He enjoyed life in his house on the mountain with its wide view of San José, his long hiking trips into the mountains and villages of the cloud forest, his running and his workouts, his gambling and his women.

Until Rachel Winrod sent for him to come to Santa Barbara.

Behind the drawn shades of the suite bedroom, Morgan lay on the large bed in the warmth of the somnolent September afternoon. He had hung up his suit and tie, put away his dress oxfords, and changed into jeans, a wool shirt, and his boots. His Akubra hat lay crown up on the bed beside him, ready for when he jumped up to answer her knock. He had been wearing the hat that first day in the anonymous cocktail lounge in Santa Barbara.

When the knock came Morgan got up, put his hat on, crossed the sitting room, and opened the door.

She came in without looking at him. "You wanted to talk."

Her eyes were hidden again behind the large, silver-rimmed sunglasses. She walked to the center of the room without any other greeting. She took off the dark glasses and sat on the gold upholstered love seat that faced the door. She felt the rich old fabric the way you would stroke a cat, and then raised her head and looked closely around the elegant sitting room.

"What a lovely room, Ford," she said. "What a lovely old hotel."

Morgan sat on the matching love seat, and faced her across the coffee table. "Your husband's worried about you."

"No, not really. He's worried about his wife. About his house and his children, his peace and his comfort. I'm not there for his and the children's needs. That leaves an empty role he doesn't want the trouble and bother of trying to fill himself. It's not his role."

The change in her Morgan had seen and felt in the Plow and Angel back at the San Ysidro Ranch in Montecito had gone further. Her hair was cut short in a simple swept-back style. She wore designer jeans, slim and tight, a mannish gray silk shirt opened to reveal deep cleavage, and soft black boots. All her jewelry was gone, even her wedding ring. She looked like her own daughter, and had a harsher edge.

"I've been worried about you," Morgan said. "I was worried you'd been kidnapped, were being held hostage or worse."

"That's why you came up here? To rescue me?" Her right hand turned the air around the finger of her left hand where her wedding ring had been. "I don't know what could have made you think anyone would want to kidnap me, Ford, and I never gave you a reason for coming after me."

"I gave myself a reason," Morgan said. "When you walked into that lounge the first time. Later, everything suggested you could have been abducted. You were involved with a man who was shot and whose associate was murdered. Who knows what you could have seen or known? After you ran away from me at San Ysidro Ranch, I found out that Baliol's hired hand Roy Shepherd was there and followed you out of the parking lot. Then you disappeared without a word, not even to your children who were so important you clung to a marriage you knew had gone sour. You vanished without even telling them or your housekeeper that she would have to take them to school and pick them up."

Her black eyes were as hidden as they had been behind the dark glasses. "I came up here because I wanted to, Ford. Alfred and the housekeeper can take care of the children for a few days as well as I can. Later, Alfred and I will talk."

The sitting room had a large marble fireplace framed by polished redwood from floor to ceiling. Morgan saw that a fire had already been laid in the ornate fireplace in preparation for the colder nights of September. He hadn't noticed that when he'd returned to wait for her in the warm room. A fire for the winter of Humboldt County. A wet winter, raw and cold, with heavy mists low on the redwoods at the crests of the mountains.

He said, "You're telling me you were lying in the San Ysidro bar? Baliol isn't the same mistake over again? Baliol was lying when he told me you two were finished? That you'd demanded too much from him, made it too hard, and he had Anne Neville who wouldn't demand too much? Those were all lies? Anne Neville was lying to help you both fool me? Fool everyone? All smoke to cover the two of you running off into glorious romantic passion up among the redwoods where Baliol just happens to be looking for the people who want to kill him?"

"You don't have the right to ask those questions."

"Is that why you walked out on me at San Ysidro Ranch when I wanted you to understand what had happened to my life and why you were becoming important to me? It was because you were lying, were going to run off with Baliol, give up everything and do whatever he wanted you to do? You know damn well he won't marry you. He won't even dump Anne Neville, for Christ's sake!"

Morgan could hear the low summer river running under the bridge. Even now, listening to his tirade and looking like her own daughter, the dignity of her face was smooth and unbroken. A dignity she had used as a mask for a long time, probably as long as she had worn her wedding ring.

"Is that it, Ford?"

"Who does have the right to say those things, ask you these questions?"

"No one."

"Your children have the right," Morgan said.

She stood. "I'm going to leave, Ford. I'm sorry if I somehow gave you the wrong message, I never meant to. I saw you liked me, yes, and it made me feel better when I wasn't feeling all that good and needed to feel better. About what was happening, and about my-self. I suppose I was thinking only about myself. That wasn't fair or honest, but you don't really want me. You don't know enough about me to want me. It's something else you want. I don't know what it is, and I don't think you know, but it's not me. You had nothing to come up here for."

"I thought you needed help. The woman I met in Santa Barbara needed help."

"Things changed."

"The Ralph Baliols don't change. Not even if they want to. And I'm not important to him. Why would he bother to lie to me?"

"Maybe because I asked him to. I also told him I thought you liked me and I didn't want to hurt you. Maybe he was just trying to make things less complicated. I have to thank you for finding me in the first place and forcing it all out into the open, but there was no reason for you to come after me."

"I'm glad I was useful."

She walked to the door. "I'll be going back to Santa Barbara soon. When I do I'll tell the children everything, and then I'll take them with me."

"You really think Alfred is going to let them or you go so easily?"

"He will now. I'm not his good wife anymore. I ran away in full public view, rocked the whole boat. Helga will insist he disown me. He cares about his possessions and his trophies, his position and his name, not me."

"The children are Schoenhausens."

"Then we'll have to take them."

"We?" Morgan watched her where she stood at the door. "I'm going to tell you a story, and you're going to listen. You owe me that. It's the story I wanted to tell you back there at the ranch. I'm going to tell you about myself, and about becoming what you hate and what that does to you."

She said nothing, but she didn't open the door to leave. He told her about the boy who had believed and gone to war, about all the years and events and faces that had happened to that boy, about everything he had thought alone in the bedroom while he waited for her knock. He talked, and felt like the old Yankee peddler, the snake-oil pitchman, the hustler working a crowd. He told her about the man who did what he was told to do for his country and the world. He told her about the anger, and then the indifference, and, finally, the second anger while he had been married to Rachel, the anger he had remembered in the bedroom of the Fernald Point house. He talked and he was the hustler, the pitchman, the Yankee peddler. But who was the mark? Her or himself?

As he talked she came back and sat down facing him again. Hands clasped in her lap, her whole attention fixed on his face like a congregation waiting for the word. He told her the CIA and the drug bosses were the same. The world was corrupt, so why not become corrupt? He told her that after twenty years he had become what he hated. Twenty years, because when you're young it takes a long time to lose your faith, to see you were never doing what you thought you were doing. Governments and systems do that to people, and people do as much and worse to themselves.

He told her, "But you can't solve your problem by becoming everything that gave you the problem, Barbara. I came to Santa Barbara because I had the sudden feeling that Rachel had been unfinished business. But it wasn't Rachel, it was me. I'm unfinished business, denying the past and going nowhere. Then I met you and there seemed to be a future again."

She was immobile on the gold Victorian loveseat. Her arms were crossed over her breasts under the silk shirt. Sometime during his story she had put her dark glasses back on, looked at him now from behind them. When he finally stopped talking, she sat waiting for him to continue. They both waited in the silence. Morgan was aware of the warmth in the sunny room. She reached across the coffee table to put her hand on his arm.

"I'm not that important, Ford. No one is. Not to you or to anyone except myself. You came to Santa Barbara and you helped me. You don't know how much you've done for me. Now you have to do more for yourself. We all think we need nothing more because we don't know what more there is or could be. But there is 'more' somewhere out there for everyone."

Morgan felt the soft pressure of her fingers on his arm. A pleading pressure. Go away, Morgan. Go away. He could see her hidden eyes clearly in his mind. They were sad eyes. He put his hand over hers. "I don't believe for a second you're up here with Baliol because you want to be."

She held his arm for another moment, her hand under his, then took it away and sat back on the loveseat. "Why am I up here?"

"I think you know something he can't let you tell."

"What could I know?"

"That Baliol and his hired gunman killed Fletcher Comrie and that man at Anne Neville's house."

"How could I know something like that? Even if it were true."

"Perhaps Baliol talks in his sleep. Perhaps you overheard them talking, or found some other evidence. Perhaps there's something else I don't know. But if I'm right, he can't leave you alone to tell anyone."

"I'm alone with you. I'm not telling you."

"He has some hold on you. A threat against your children or Alfred. Roy Shepherd is a loose cannon, he'll do whatever Baliol pays him to do."

"Why would he let me come here, Ford?"

"Sooner or later I'd find you. Sending you would be worth a try. I might go away."

"I'm telling you I came here on my own. I never gave you cause to doubt me."

"So I should go away?"

"Yes." She walked around the table and past him to the door and was gone.

Behind him, Morgan heard the door open and close. He waited in the warm room for a full minute before he got up and went out after her. She wasn't in sight. He walked along the corridor and down to the lobby. He stood inside the hotel doors as he watched her walk toward her blue 450SL at the far end of the parking lot from his rented BMW. He waited in the entrance until she was in the little Mercedes, then he ran to his BMW. In the Mercedes she had to come past him on her way to the exit. He followed her out of the parking lot. On Main Street she turned left toward the head-quarters of Stoke-Higham.

She didn't turn into Stoke-Higham but continued straight ahead along the same road where Roy Shepherd had led Morgan earlier. Morgan dropped back and she went on out of sight, not luring him the way Shepherd had. He sped up again as the road wound along the river. Ahead, he caught sight of the little blue Mercedes before the sharp turn at the bridge over the river, and almost ran into an ambulance that half blocked the road where it crossed the bridge. The Mercedes disappeared on the far side of the river, and Morgan saw that a car was off the road on this side of the bridge. Two ambulance attendants laid a stretcher basket on the road in front of Morgan. Other attendants were gathered around a woman on the ground.

Morgan rolled down his window to ask if he could help. The woman on the ground jumped up, and the four attendants pro-duced rifles. They all wore ski masks, and one rifle was an M–16. Without a word they opened the car door and pulled Morgan from the BMW. He struggled, broke loose once, but they were too many and too strong. They took his gun and prodded him to the ambu-lance. Three other masked men pulled him inside and pushed him to his knees on the floor. He kicked out, but they held him down and the doors closed. He felt a sudden cold against his skin and the sharp sting of a needle.

21

The outline of a room grew out of darkness like a Polaroid snap-shot, or the picture tube coming to life on an old television set. He saw a bureau with a framed mirror on top. A rectangular mirror, the corners of the frame rounded. An old washstand that had oak doors below a marble top. A straight wooden chair against a wall of vertical redwood boards. The oil painting of a rocky coastline. A single small window. Red-and-white-checked curtains at the window. Outside the window the world was thick and white and moving.

"You have to understand what it means. All they want is power and privilege. For thousands of years they've raped and murdered the earth, and everyone and everything on it."

A firm voice, slow and measured. Morgan had an irresistible urge to turn his head to look for the voice, smile at the voice, talk back to the firm voice. But that was what they wanted him to do. The interrogators. They always tried to make you think you were free, that the situation was normal and you could do what you wanted. Then they stopped you. With a violent blow or an electric shock. A burning match or a blowtorch to your feet. Some intense pain that made you scream. Each scream widening the break in your de-fenses until they slipped inside you and you told them who you really were and why you were really there and who else was there with you and who had sent you.

"They came here and they didn't change. They never change, it's their greatest source of strength. They brought their castles and their purpose with them. And they brought us, the rest of the world. The peasants and serfs, the willing yeomen and the eager slaves."

He knew where it was, the voice. Close and to his right. Some-where close behind him. It was difficult not to turn, but he lay and looked straight up at the low wooden ceiling, or to the left at the window that was only a thick, moving white. They weren't going to fool him into helping them. He wasn't going to think of normal things, of what he wanted to do. He focused on his purpose. He would think of his purpose.

"Ordinary people always came with more reluctance than eager-ness, often with sadness for what had been left behind. People who took care of each other. People who lived close to the land, with the animals and the trees, the days and the years. The ordinary people who connect to the earth. The barons connect only to each other."

What was his purpose? He couldn't remember his purpose. He had to have a purpose. Why else would he be here listening to the voice that tried to make him turn to look so the voice could slip in and find the answers inside him? An hypnotic voice that stroked him like a cat rubbing against his head.

"The ordinary people of the village below the castle. History doesn't say much about them. They conquer no lands, plunder no cities, burn no temples, erect no monuments to themselves. They won't destroy the world for the riches of today. They won't be part of the great events brought about by chiefs and shamans, rulers and soldiers. They will feed and clothe those soldiers and rulers, and be raped, pillaged, plundered, and slaughtered by those soldiers and for those great events. They don't want to serve and refuse to rule, and they will go on."

A slow, steady, soothing voice that washed over him but he would not turn and look. He would remember his purpose. But what was his purpose?

Morgan turned his head. An empty wooden chair stood beside him where he lay on some bed. An empty chair in an empty room.

A straight wooden chair beside the bed in a room that looked oddly familiar. He looked at the bureau, the washstand, the oil painting of some coast, the single small window with the red and white curtains. Redwood walls. It was like a room he had seen in an old photograph somewhere far away.

Morgan reached under his back for his little Czech Vz70. The pistol was gone. The holster was gone. He looked for the pistol under the pillow, on the empty chair. Under the bed. There was no pistol.

He sat up, swung his legs off the bed, and stood. Weak, he held onto the wall. The weakness passed and he went to the door. It was locked. He crossed to the single window. It was barred with nailed or screwed-on two-by-fours on the outside. There was a heavy white fog through the window, and the shadows of trees through the fog. He unlocked and raised the window. The cold fog drifted into the room, and the shadows of the trees were close enough to have branches. The sound that rose and fell was the sea. Waves breaking on rocks somewhere below in the fog.

Morgan sat on the bed. He remembered the masked people with guns, the ambulance, the sting of the hypodermic. He remembered there had been too many of them, and no time to reach for his Vz70 against his spine. He remembered Barbara Schoenhausen in the dark blue 450SL. He remembered a voice. A slow, measured voice. A voice that rose and fell in a long pulse as rhythmic as the surf on the rocks below. He remembered nothing between the sting in his arm and the voice. He wore the same jeans and wool shirt he had worn as he waited in the hotel room. His boots were on the floor, his Akubra hat properly on its crown on the bureau. Only the pistol and its holster were gone.

How long had he been in this room?

"One night and parts of two days."

She wore heavy wool pants that made her look like a logger, a red-and-black Rob Roy plaid shirt, and heavy laced boots. Her red hair had been brushed back like a man's, and she carried a tray with a bowl of soup steaming on it, a plate of sandwiches, and a teapot with a cup and saucer. She set the tray down on a chair.

"You were talking to yourself," Jenny Stoke said. "I guess isolation will do that."

"A knockout shot might have something to do with it. And I wasn't alone. There was a voice."

"My father. He wants you to understand."

"What am I supposed to understand?"

"Would you rather have a table? I can have one brought in."

"I'd rather eat somewhere else."

"Give them some time, they're worried about you."

"Your father, Mr. Stoke I presume, and who else?"

"Mr. Higham."

"Higham? You mean Baxter—"

"My father."

"Your father what?"

"Is Roger Higham. Roger the Third. Stoke is my married name. We're the poor Highams. The black sheep."

Morgan rememberd the way the chief of police in Gaul had said, *Jenny Stoke? You talked to her, did you?* The chief who didn't want to know who the extremists in Gaul were.

Morgan said, "It wasn't an accident you were in the tavern, you didn't just happen to sit beside me."

"You were from out of town and asking questions about trouble at the mill."

"The bellman."

She smiled. "It was a nice dinner."

"Tree huggers," Morgan said. "And rural guerillas?"

"More like environmental irregulars, activism instead of talk and protest marches. My father believes the time has come to do more. We all do."

"I don't know anything, Jenny. I'm not the enemy."

"I told them that. You're up here looking for a man and woman associated with Ralph Baliol. That's your only real interest in Stoke-Higham. They don't believe me. You're carrying a gun, you have those ears and the finger, you were asking questions about trouble at Stoke-Higham. You'll have to convince them yourself."

She went out, and the door closed and locked. Morgan listened to the surf through the fog. Was it morning fog or evening fog? Soup and sandwiches should be lunch. His stomach was queasy, but he was hungry. The soup was homemade lentil. The sandwiches were restaurant-made. They had the bellman at the hotel, the owner or manager of some restaurant, at least two relatives of the president of Stoke-Higham, and someone who could get an ambulance, a strong sedative, and always used alcohol before he gave a shot. A doctor. Professional people, solid citizens. With ski masks and at least one M–16 assault rifle.

The fog lifted before evening. Between the two-by-four bars of the window Morgan saw the fog bank lying offshore with the shadows of great rocks inside it and a surging, half-invisible gray-blue sea. Closer, between the fog and the window, a strip of blue ocean broke below on the beach of a small cove. The house was built on the edge of a cliff. A headland curved out to sea to the left, with straggling young redwoods on top in the drifting edges of the fog. Directly in front of the window a giant dome rock stood where the beach and sea met.

The door opened again behind Morgan, and a wiry man with a lean face weathered to the color of saddle leather stood in the room. He wore heavy corduroy trousers, hiking boots, another Rob Roy shirt, and a denim jacket. A revolver was thrust into his waistband. He leaned his back against the door and began to talk. It was the voice.

"They were ordinary men, the four who started Stoke-Higham, but they grew rich and built castles on the hills above the village and became the barons. Even Roger Higham, my great-grandfather. But he realized the truth in time. You can't join the barons without becoming a baron. If you want to be a baron, you have to lose yourself. If you don't erase even the memory of yourself, the barons will take back the castle."

At the window, Morgan saw the resemblance to Jenny Stoke in the old man's face scoured and burned by seventy years of wind and sun. "Roger Higham the Third," Morgan said. "Who was the second Roger Higham?"

The old man's eyes were intense, "I saw it early, Mr. Morgan, what you had to do to be a baron. It made me walk away from the castle. My father didn't see it. My brother didn't see it. No Higham except me saw it after the first Roger, so the barons came and took the castle away. My nephew Baxter never will see it. He'll die wondering why he lost the company."

Roger Higham III had an urgent need. Each word he spoke into the room was placed like a brick in a new bridge. A bridge between himself and the world. The words flowed out of him with an implacable logic. A logic that in the old man's mind could not be escaped, and that had made him act in a way Morgan and the world must understand.

Morgan said, "But not you, Mr. Higham. You know why it happened, and you decided to do something. I'll bet you know how to use climbing spikes, and that pistol in your belt looks a lot like a thirty-eight. You shot Ralph Baliol and Fletcher Comrie. You and Dan Derbyfield and maybe someone else from Gaul."

If Roger Higham III heard Morgan it did not stop the flow of words. Nothing would do that until he had built his bridge. "I walked into the redwoods, built this house. I lived in the forest, picked berries, farmed, fished, married, raised kids, and eventually walked around the world. East and west, north and south. Down to the tip of South America and back up the other coast. Took my time. Any side trip that struck my fancy. I learned a trade, roofing, and helped out in villages where help was needed." He came away from the door and close to where Morgan stood at the single window. "Only I was wrong. Wrong to walk away from the castle and let the barons take it back. Because they don't just take the castle, they destroy everything around the castle. The town, the trees, the land, the village, and eventually the world. They don't care about the world, only what they can take from it."

Morgan said, "So you decided to stop them. At least stop two of them. Ralph Baliol and Fletcher Comrie. Dead, they wouldn't rule anyone. But it won't really change anything. Baliol Investment will go right on, and all you'll accomplish is prison or death for you and everyone with you."

Roger Higham took the pistol from his belt and held it out flat on his hand. It was a small caliber revolver on a large frame, a .22–LR at most. A plinking gun for killing varmints in the woods. "We may be fools, Mr. Morgan, but we're not idiots. As far as I know I was never seen in Santa Barbara, or left any evidence, and the offending thirty-eight will never be found."

Roger Higham shoved the pistol back into his waistband. He walked to the door and knocked on it. When the door opened, he stepped aside for Morgan to leave first.

"Walk through to the deck."

The top of the giant dome rock towered directly in front of the open deck. The thick bank of fog still lay a hundred yards offshore. The headland was hazy in a drifting mist, and the sun shone only on the beach below and the deck itself. The six people on the deck watched Morgan as he sat on a redwood bench against the outside cabin wall. Only two of them smiled: Jenny Stoke and an older man in tweed and a sweater. He wore a tie, had the manner of a family doctor. The three in logger boots and wool shirts sat on the rail with rifles next to them.

Roger Higham leaned against the outside rail with his back to the fog and the sea. "This is called the Lost Coast, Mr. Morgan. From Point Gorda down to the Mendocino line there's no way in or out except foot trails and some dirt logging roads. No towns, and only a few houses damned hard to find even when you know where they are."

A younger man in a jacket without a tie said, "You came to Gaul asking questions. You could be working for Baliol Investment. You could be the one who killed Dan Derbyfield. You could be a government agent. We have to know why you're here, who you work for, what you know, and what made you come to Gaul, and we intend to find out one way or—"

Jenny Stoke said, "We're not the KGB, George. I expect Mr. Morgan has had enough experience with them. Can we act human? I told you, I think he's basically on our side."

"You've been looking me up," Morgan said to Jenny Stoke.

Roger Higham said, "George there is my son, Mr. Morgan. He's not like me. He decided to be a lawyer and work for Stoke-Higham; now he's decided being a lawyer isn't enough. That one in tweed is Doc Hordle. Jenny you know. You don't need to know anyone else." The old man looked up at trees above the house. "Have you heard of masterless men, Mr. Morgan? In the middle ages if you weren't a baron or didn't belong to a baron, you were a masterless man. Beyond the law, without status or rights. You didn't exist. They still think that way, the masters. But we have rights, and we want a future. George started us off the first time he heard the order to clearcut an acre. We formed the Save Trees, Save Jobs Committee. A lot of the town backs us because they know now that first you lose the company, then you lose the trees, then you lose the jobs, then you lose the town. When the trees are gone, the barons will sell everything, pack their gold, and go on to find another village to rape."

"When did you decide to start shooting people?" Morgan said.

"When they forced us to," George Higham said. He had more anger in his voice than his father, but not the complete, implacable conviction. "I told them they'd destroy the company and the town if they clearcut. Daly Boyle fired me. The old management knew the truth, but those who stayed on weren't about to risk their jobs, and those who left needed to find other jobs so didn't want to be branded radicals. The tree huggers backed us from the start, even came from out of town. That alienated the loggers and millhands, but when hours were doubled, wages lowered, and the clearcutting went on and on, they realized we all wanted the same thing."

The doctor, Hordle, said, "Save Trees, Save Jobs organized a boy-cott, got publicity, started environmental lawsuits, and went to the county, state, and federal governments. We marched, picketed, held public rallies, and publicized the lawsuits. We decided to try to buy Baliol out. When all that got us nowhere, some of us turned to more direct action—harassing operations, hammering nails into trees, destroying their tools, any sabotage to make Baliol Invest-ment see reason."

"Including murdering Ralph Baliol and Fletcher Comrie," Mor-gan said.

Roger Higham said, "Baliol was my decision and mine alone. I planned it, Dan Derbyfield and I went down to Santa Barbara to do it. My only regret is that we failed. With Ralph Baliol dead, Baliol Investment would think hard about selling a company that's been nothing but trouble."

Jenny said, "Roger never told us what he and Dan planned, but it's done and we're all together in this. Our job is to make Stoke-Higham too much trouble for Baliol Investment to keep."

Doc Hordle said, "We won't stand by and watch everyone lose by the financial manipulations of men without conscience."

"Conscience?" Morgan looked around. "I'd say Mr. Higham is calling the tune and you're all dancing. Murder and kidnapping have little to do with conscience."

"When you're opposing men without conscience," Roger Higham said, "conscience is a luxury you can't afford. And no one has been murdered."

"Fletcher Comrie didn't commit suicide, Mr. Higham."

Jenny Stoke said, "Who was this Fletcher Comrie, Ford? None of us knows anything about him."

"The man who made it possible for Ralph Baliol to buy Stoke-Higham," Morgan said. "He turned on the junk-bond fountain."

"Then we have to thank whoever did kill him," Roger Higham said. "The list of suspects must be long."

"And you're at the top of the list. A matchbook from a place called Taffy's was dropped in Fletcher Comrie's house when he was killed. If you people didn't kill Comrie, who dropped the match-book?"

"No one from here," Roger Higham said. "We—"

Heavy footsteps approached the deck at a fast walk. The man who appeared and hurried up the steps was a rawboned giant in his sixties or older. He carried a hunting rifle that looked like a toy gun in his hands, and spoke low to George Higham. The younger Higham nodded, and the giant went into the house. George Higham motioned for them to gather around him. They conferred as Morgan watched and waited.

It was Jenny who finally turned to Morgan. "Tell us about the man and woman you came up here to find?"

"The woman is Barbara Schoenhausen. She had an affair with Ralph Baliol. She disappeared from Santa Barbara a few days ago without a word or a note. I decided Baliol had come up to Gaul to chase who had shot him, and could have kidnapped her because she was some threat to him. The man in the Cadillac with the steer skull on the hood is Roy Shepherd, a bodyguard hired by Baliol to protect him and probably to do a lot more. He would have done any kidnapping for Baliol, and would be holding her. That's why I was looking for him."

"And why you talked to Uncle Baxter and Daly Boyle? You wanted to find those people, not us?"

"I was pretty sure someone up here had shot Ralph Baliol. They could be holding Barbara Schoenhausen. So I asked the chief about them. He said he didn't know anyone who would harm a fly."

"Have you found this Shepherd and Barbara?"

"I found Roy Shepherd right after Chief Walker picked me up. Or Shepherd found me. Probably because Baliol wanted to know exactly what I was doing. That was yesterday, or was it the day before?"

"Yesterday," Doctor Hordle said.

George Higham said, "What did you learn from Shepherd?"

"He admitted Barbara Schoenhausen was here in Gaul, said he would send her to talk to me. He did. She came to my room at the Mill Inn and told me she was up here because she wanted to be, but I don't believe her."

"Does that mean Ralph Baliol's in Gaul?" Roger Higham said.

"It would seem so."

Jenny said, "The woman driving the Mercedes you were following was Barbara Schoenhausen?"

"Yes."

"You think Roy Shepherd is here to look for Roger?"

"For all of you."

"Baliol hired him to find us and turn us over to the police?"

"That would be one option," Morgan said.

Roger Higham looked at the others. "Baliol wouldn't want me to talk to the police, the newspapers, or anyone else. They might listen, and that would cost him money. He didn't hire this Cadillac cowboy to help the police."

George Higham went into the entry hall of the big old house. When he returned he carried an M–16 rifle.

"Take him back to the room."

As Morgan was locked in the small bedroom again he heard two large four-wheel-drive vehicles pull away from the Lost Coast toward the east and the distant highway.

22

Long after dark Morgan heard the vehicles return. On the narrow bed in the locked room he listened to the doors slam and the fog-muted footsteps move toward the house, climb the steps to the deck, and enter through the front door. Then he heard many voices off in the living room. Eventually, the footsteps of a single person came along the hall, the door opened, and Jenny Stoke stood in the doorway.

"They want to talk to you again. And it's time for some dinner."

In the dining room, seven men and two women sat at a long table. Three of them were Doc Hordle, Roger Higham, and Jenny. George Higham and the giant who had come to whisper in George's ear on the deck backed through the kitchen door carrying bowls of food steaming in the cold night. Morgan knew none of the others. There was bread, a meat stew, bowls of boiled potatoes, cabbage, carrots, broccoli, and beans, and a mammoth bowl of salad. A meal for both loggers and tree huggers.

Roger Higham bent to his food at the long table, said, "Tell us again about this man Ralph Baliol hired, Morgan. Everything you know."

Morgan looked at the serious faces around the table as they all waited for him to speak. "He's been here looking for you. That's where you went. Your sentries spotted him, you went out to see what he was doing, and you're worried."

"A Cadillac has a hard time in this kind of country," George Higham said.

"We're worried," Jenny said. "Tell us about him."

Morgan detailed the history of Roy Shepherd as it had been given to him by the CIA man, Hughes Bremner. "A loose cannon is what I heard, and formidable is what I saw."

"From the way you describe him, Mr. Morgan," Roger Higham said, "a move to another location would be a good idea."

"I'd say it was."

"How did he find us all the way out here?" someone asked.

"I doubt that was much problem," Morgan said. "Gaul is a small town, most of you know each other. The chief knows who you are, even if he won't admit it. I'd bet Baxter Higham does, and Daly Boyle and Carson probably know at least who some of you are— Mr. Higham, George, Jenny, and maybe the doctor. What Boyle knows, Ralph Baliol and Shepherd know. This is Mr. Higham's house. Shepherd can put two and two together, and he may even know who shot Baliol by now."

Roger Higham said, "How would he know that? No one saw me anywhere near Baliol or his estate, I left no evidence except the bullets, and the gun is gone."

"You left a dead partner."

"Without any identification, we both made sure we carried none."

"They identified him the day after they made the possible connection between Gaul and Stoke-Higham and the shootings. They called the chief up here, and I expect the chief could work out who the other most likely suspects were and who was out of town at the right time."

Roger Higham nodded, as much to himself as to the others. "He's right, of course. Everyone will have to leave here, find a safer place to meet. Baliol wants me, and he doesn't want what is happening up here to get into the headlines. If his mercenary gets his hands on me I won't reach the police. I'll have an 'accident.' Something no one can prove but everyone will understand."

George Higham said, "Then we'll stop Baliol and his hired—"

"Yes, we will," Roger Higham said. "But first you all get out of here. We don't want him finding anyone else."

When the others had gone, Morgan and Roger Higham sat on the night deck above the sea with the fog hanging at the edge of the bluff and the giant rock a hunchbacked shadow in front of them.

The house behind them was silent, empty of everyone but Jenny Stoke. The surf below was muffled by fog. Above the fog, the stars were thick across the black sky.

"What about me?" Morgan said.

"Jenny will drive you back to town tomorrow," Roger Higham said. "We're sorry, but we had to make sure about you. Of course, from what Jenny told us about you, we could use your help."

"What makes you think I'd help you?"

"Jenny says you're on our side, and I think she's right."

"Perhaps I am, perhaps not, but you need more than my help. You're not violent people. Look what happened in Santa Barbara. Real violence takes devotion and practice. A lot of practice."

As if to emphasize the point, the all but soundless shadow of a night-hunting owl passed heavily in front of the deck, the strong rush of its wings felt more than heard. Both Morgan and Roger Higham seemed to wait for the sudden squeal of the small victim, but it never came. The owl had found no prey this time. The only sounds that came were Jenny moving around inside the house behind them, and some animal far too large for an owl to dream of violence moving among the trees.

"You remember the California Outlaws, Morgan?" Roger Higham said.

"Something to do with the Southern Pacific Railroad."

"Yes, the old SP. They were building west after the Civil War and reached the San Joaquin Valley in the late eighteen seventies. Their concept of land rights was to take all the intervening land on the way to the sea by any means, no matter who might be on that land. Indian land, farms, ranches, the homes of settlers, it made no difference. The government helped them in every way. The land was condemned, the former owners forced to accept the pittance from the railroad. If by some chance condemnation didn't get the job done, the railroad swindled, lied, cheated, or sent for gunmen. Anything the company wanted to do and did was considered legal, including the massacre of seven settlers at Mussel Slough in eighteen eighty.

"The San Joaquin Valley settlers finally banded together, and the California Outlaws were formed for the single purpose of attacking the octopus of the railroad. They'd stop a train, go straight for the company safe and only the safe. They never robbed the passengers

or touched the U.S. mail, never harmed anyone except railroad
guards, and only then if they offered armed resistance. With the
help of almost all local residents, the Outlaws battled the railroad
for years. In the end, the lawyers, legislators, U.S. marshals, sher-
iffs, railroad gunmen, Wells Fargo guards, and Pinkertons jailed or
killed most of them, usually the latter since there was a bounty. The
survivors went into hiding. Christopher Evans, their main leader, is
still affectionately known down in the San Joaquin Valley as the
Old Chief.''

"And," Morgan said, "the Southern Pacific Railroad is still thriv-
ing. It was as futile as the Weatherman underground in the sixties
and seventies.''

"I think that could be called impertinence, Morgan. Who are you
to judge the ultimate effect of commitment and faith? Those Outlaws could have been what finally brought some control to the
railroad barons. The Weathermen reached *some* minds, maybe one
was the crucial mind for social justice. If you assume there's no
hope of change, you guarantee no change. Sometimes violence is
all they leave you. If you make power bleed, you may wake up the
powerless." Roger Higham looked up at the stars above the fog. "Or
maybe it's only that there comes a time when you have to do something more than hope for a change of heart where there isn't any
heart.''

Morgan saw the lights of a jet crossing beneath the stars. He felt
like the African native who knew nothing of where the jet he saw
passing above him came from or where it was going. The native
could understand flight, had probably even seen aircraft up close,
but the worlds the one up there passed between he knew nothing
about and could not have understood if he did. Locked by time and
space into his own world. We all become locked inside the world of
our own truths.

Morgan said, "A lot of what's happening to the loggers and millhands and the townspeople here is their own fault. They believed
they and the company were equals, they believed they both wanted
the same thing.''

"I know," Roger Higham agreed. "That's the real American
myth. Individual opportunity and self-creation. It's how we understand and define ourselves. A myth believed long enough creates its
own facts, its own reality. A false reality created by those who run

the actual world for their benefit, not ours. But we're a self-aware species, we can grow and learn."

"Is that your myth?"

Morgan saw the old man smile in the dark. Roger Higham had tried to murder a man, would try again if he felt it necessary, but on the deck of his cabin with the fog and the redwoods he was at peace. No more and no less than the trees around him and the rocks and the sound of the surf that were all simply there and required no explanation.

"I sit out here a great deal in the evening, Morgan. I watch the sunset over that domed rock. It can be spectacular on this coast: red and orange and purple and gold. Then it's dark. The stars appear, and I often look up and try to find one of the brilliant stars that probably mean supernovas. There are twenty to twenty-five supernovas a year, astronomers tell us. Five billion to only a few million of our years ago all those stars supernovaed and died. All over the universe, and maybe other universes too. Massive stars exploding and disappearing, and their planets disappearing with them. Vanishing all across the cosmos year after year. What does that make us? Microbes? Cancer cells in the cosmic matter? On a cosmic scale we're invisible dust motes with no purpose or effect. We came into existence on this planet like rust on a ball of iron, and we'll vanish without a trace when the ball dies with its star."

"Then why bother about a few redwoods, owls, and jobs?"

The glitter of Roger Higham's eyes captured light that wasn't there. "Of course, the logical question. I've thought about that too. The way we're going today, our meaning and eventual fate isn't important, we'll never last that long. Less time than the dinosaurs. Then I realized that was the point. On the cosmic scale we're less than zero, a blip on the universal radar screen, here and gone. But for *us*, a billion or so years is eternity, and who knows what we can become if we survive until the end? On the cosmic scale, the lords of rule and grab seem right, but on the human scale they're wrong. We might all just as well commit suicide as grab for today if we look at the cosmic scale, and that's really not a bad alternative to exploitation and destruction. But look at us on the human scale, and then a billion years is forever and worth fighting for."

Roger Higham talked, and the coast of night and fog seemed to Morgan to be on the edge of the universe. The far lands of the Vikings, Ultima Thule of the Romans.

Morgan was asleep when the door opened. Awake in an instant, he groaned and rolled over as if in his sleep until he could see the door. Jenny Stoke stood in the doorway wearing a pale blue robe and nightgown.

"You've been in too many places where someone in your room at night meant serious danger, Ford."

"If I'm that obvious now," Morgan said, "it's a good thing I'm not still in those places."

"You ran into an expert at feigning sleep. Come out by the fire."

Morgan got into his jeans and wool shirt, put on the heavier outer shirt they'd lent him. In the living room she sat on a cushioned redwood couch that faced the fire. The flames of a new log licked up the chimney, and she sat with her arms folded across her chest the way Barbara Schoenhausen had as he'd told his story in the room at the Mill Inn yesterday. Morgan sat on the floor with his back against a chair and held his hands to the flames.

"Are you going to turn Roger in?" Jenny asked.

"No."

She stretched her legs toward the heat. Her feet were in low sheepskin boots. Her nightgown was a deep navy blue that made her short red hair richer.

She said, "Are you going to stop him trying again?"

"Should I?"

"Will it do any good? Killing Ralph Baliol?"

"I don't think so, but you never really know."

She tucked her feet under the dark gown, then leaned forward not so much toward the fire as toward the movement of the flames up the black flue.

"He's a patriarch," she said. "He doesn't know that. He would never want to be a patriarch. He's Roger Higham, free of everything that corrupts human potential as part of the natural universe, one with all humanity and nature."

"You sound angry at him."

"He walked away from the mansion, the power, the influence, and the country. He stood on his convictions of right and wrong, 'wouldn't be a master any more than he would be a slave.'" The sound of the flames, like the breathing of the chimney itself, enclosed and dominated the night. "But he didn't walk away from being a patriarch." She nodded toward a long row of framed photo-graphs on the mantel over the fireplace. Photos of at least three different women and many children. "Patriarchs need women around them. That's what a patriarch does: governs women and children and everything else. Roger would say he takes care of his women, but in reality they take care of him, and he expects them to do that. And a patriarch needs children to instruct. They're no problem because the women raise and take care of them. He had George and his two sisters with his first wife. My mother had four of us. His last wife had five; he was getting older, needed more validation. She divorced him, the children live with her. Roger spent a lot of time with all of us—out in the woods, on the ocean, teaching us—but all the time we were growing up he came and went as he pleased. He sent money when he worked, and the women did the rest. I doubt it crossed his mind that the women could want anything else."

Morgan watched the blue tips of the flames at the exact point the flame vanished up the flue. "Does being a patriarch have some-thing to do with him wanting to kill Ralph Baliol?"

"He's old and without a woman. Except me, and I'm only a daughter who doesn't live with him. He needs to act, thunder like Zeus. Do something powerful and bold to save the town and the trees."

"But you're doing it with him."

"He's my father. I won't live with him. I'm not part of him any-more. But he is my father, and there are expectations."

"Somehow that doesn't sound like you."

She uncoiled from the couch, took the poker, and stirred the logs until the flames licked higher. "I guess no one's totally immune to public opinion." The play of the flames above the logs seemed to mesmerize her. "He also could be right. At times violence is all that's left. It solves nothing, but it could define the problem. The violent understand only violence."

"There's always another way, Jenny."

"I'm not sure there is."

"It takes time to change what everyone accepts as reality."

"Reality? You mean the Golden Rule of the Baliols: the ones who have the gold make the rules."

Morgan noticed her eyes where she stood over the fire. They were an odd blue, almost green against the dark navy blue of her nightgown. He hadn't looked particularly at her eyes or her face. She wasn't a woman who made you feel the immediate impact of some unforgettable feature, of a dazzling figure or an inescapable presence. Only her thick red hair, cut short in a careless indifference, and herself. You saw her. All of her together. The face and figure and presence, solid and contained within herself and part of all that was around her.

"It's the rule we all grow up with," Morgan said.

"I suppose it is. And if only the one with the gold rules, then if you want to be important gold is all that counts." She hung the poker on the stand, tucked herself back on the couch. "My husband's name was Murray. He worked for the MacKenzies on their big Seaforth Ranch over in the delta at the south end of Humboldt Bay. The first MacKenzie arrived in the county about the time Stoke-Higham started up. He set up a cattle ranch to feed the miners over in Trinity. The Seaforth has been in the MacKenzie family ever since, and Murray went to work for them out of high school. He was good with animals, especially horses, worked his way up to foreman by the time he was thirty. But what he'd really wanted to do was breed and train quarter horses.

"We'd been married about five years, he was nearing forty, when he got the chance. A breeder he knew needed a trainer but couldn't pay a lot. We didn't especially need money. I had a good job, and we had no children. I thought it was all set, and he was excited until Seaforth Ranch decided to make him manager of one of their smaller satellite spreads with a big raise, our own house, the prospects of being manager of Seaforth someday and maybe a vice-president of the corporation. It was the first major fight we ever had. I told him to take the job with the breeder. How much money he made wasn't important. He couldn't do it. He'd worked and battled for money all his life, and he couldn't turn down the money even to do what he wanted to do. He wouldn't be an idiot or a sucker."

The flames had subsided again to small eruptions of yellow and blue over a thick bed of white-hot coals, the intense heat enclosing them in an envelope of heat against the night wind outside.

"Murry still works for Seaforth. He's assistant to the overall manager. He'll never stop working for money whether he needs it or not. He knew what I thought and started staying away from me, sneaking in from all-night sessions with his male friends or his women. I pretended to be asleep, and after a year or so I left him and he sued for divorce so the town thought he'd left me."

"You let him?"

"Anyone I cared about would know the truth."

She would not let others make decisions for her. Or make decisions for others. She got up once more. With the fire down, the room had grown chill, cold air from the fog and the night sea flowing in through the walls and doors. She put on another log, poked it until the flames sucked up the flue once more, and came back to the couch with her legs tucked sideways under the robe and gown.

"Green Beret, CIA, businessman in Costa Rica. You don't act like a Green Beret or an ex-CIA man, and you don't look like a businessman in Costa Rica, someone who exports and imports Mayan artifacts."

"What do I look like?"

"Someone close to drowning."

The new log had caught, the sound of the flames sucking up the flue filled the quiet room. "You want to hear my life story? All of it?"

"Did you tell it to Barbara Schoenhausen?"

"Yes."

"Then I think I'll pass."

She got up from the couch, leaned down, and kissed him. When he reached up for her, she stepped out of reach. "It's easy to invent answers you want to hear. The woman I saw leave your room yesterday afternoon has a lot of anger in her. Now you better get some sleep. We have an early meeting of the committee in town tomorrow morning, I'll drive you back to your hotel."

23

By dawn on the Lost Coast the fog had turned to a hard gray rain that dripped from the redwoods all along the logging road. The road dissolved into mud under the wheels of Jenny Stoke's Jeep Cherokee, but they finally came out onto the freeway and made better time north to Gaul. Jenny left Morgan at the Mill Inn and went on to her house on the other side of the river where she had a meeting of the full Save Trees, Save Jobs Committee.

Morgan showered, shaved, and dressed in warm navy-blue cords and the heavy shirt they had loaned him, then called Ralph Baliol at Stoke-Higham. A nervous and harried operator informed him no one was taking calls this morning, but she had been instructed to take messages if he would speak slowly.

"Tell Mr. Baliol I want to talk to him and to Barbara Schoenhausen." He had to spell Schoenhausen. "Tell Baliol I know she's here, and it's me or the police. Make that really clear. You understand?"

The operator caught the threat in his voice and gave a nervous laugh as she hung up. The echo of the laugh became sirens and many voices talking and moving down on the main street in front of the inn.

Morgan went to the windows. The rain clouds lay low on the forests and slopes that surrounded the town, drifted through the tops of the redwoods. Below, a crowd filled the main street and walked toward the far end of town and the Stoke-Higham mill. Two highway patrol cars crawled past, their sirens warning in short bursts as they escorted a paramedic truck through the crowd. Three men climbed onto the paramedic truck and rode ahead with it. Morgan recognized two of them: Doc Hordle and George Higham.

Morgan was putting on his boots when the knock came at the

184

door. Jenny Stoke stood out in the corridor. She looked past him at the pair of gold loveseats and the whole empty room. She made no move to come in.

"There's been an accident at the mill."

In the rain on the main street, Morgan and Jenny walked among the murmuring people at the rear of the crowd that moved ahead with a reluctant apprehension.

Jenny said, "They say three men are dead."

"How?"

"I don't know yet. Half the town's down there already."

"Any of your people?"

"I don't know that either."

In the rain, the redwood logs were half submerged in the log pond like ancient beasts about to crawl out of the mist onto the land. On the cloud-drifted slopes of the mountains encircling the town, ghostly shadows moved among the trees like great hairy mammoths waiting to descend. Or perhaps the blighted gray landscape was more a nightmare of the future, a devastated land of self-destruction where nameless birds sang alien songs.

"When did it happen, Jenny?"

"All I know is that it was discovered about an hour ago. George and I were in the meeting when we got word."

"Where's your father?"

"On his way, if he isn't there already."

They moved ahead faster as the silent people parted to let them through. A special passage given not to him, the stranger, but to Jenny. If the whole town wasn't behind the militants, they all knew who the militants were and gave them both respect and at least tacit cooperation. Roger Higham could be the fuse needed to turn tragedy into a sudden and nasty riot.

Jenny read his mind. "Roger won't make it any worse, Ford. If he risked someone it would only be himself."

When they reached the entrance to the mill the crowd filled the entire street, and four police officers formed a semicircle in front of the gates. Roger Higham stood at the front of the crowd facing the police. George Higham, Doc Hordle, and some of those Morgan remembered from dinner last night stood with him. The police had no weapons in their hands. There was no shouting, pushing, or shoving. Only the ominous mass of waiting people.

Inside the gates a small group of millhands from the current shift stood behind a foreman who talked with Stoke-Higham's security chief, Robert Chandos. To the right Baxter Higham, Daly Boyle, and Ralph Baliol watched from the shelter of the administration building doorway. In a dark blue pin-stripe suit and a homburg, Baliol sat on a chair brought from inside in deference to his rank or his barely healed wounds. In the parking area in front of the building, Mancuso sat in Baliol's limousine and Roy Shepherd leaned half-hidden against a parked panel truck in the shadows.

Farther back still, two police cars and the paramedic truck with its rear doors open waited in front of the debarker building. At the debarker itself Chief Walker, the assistant chief, and one more patrolman walked around examining the building and the ground. The entire Gaul police force, Morgan guessed.

In the steady rain the whole tableau could have been a reconstructed model in a history museum—industrial accident, late-twentieth-century United States of America.

When Jenny and Morgan reached the front of the crowd Jenny pulled her half-brother aside.

"What happened?"

"They found three bodies inside the debarker," George Higham said. "It was running when the morning shift arrived, but jammed an hour or so ago. They shut it down, went in to clear it, and found the bodies."

"Oh my God."

"Have they identified them?" Morgan asked.

Doc Hordle's voice shook. "In a redwood mill, Morgan, the debarker is a huge revolving drum. The logs enter from the pond, are rotated together with high-pressure water jets until all the bark is removed and the stripped logs are fed out to the conveyer that will take them into the sawmill building. When the debarker jams, the mill workers have to stop the machine, lock it, and go inside with chain saws to cut away the log jam."

The doctor paused to watch the police and the paramedics push a gurney with a body bag out of the debarker building and roll it to the paramedic truck. When the body had disappeared into the truck, he turned back to Morgan. "The debarker must have jammed sometime on the night shift. They went in to clear it and somehow the machine started up again. I can't remember it ever happening before."

Morgan imagined the screams of the men trapped alone inside the massive drum where no one could have heard them over the thunder of the rotating logs and high-powered water jets. He imagined the giant machine grinding trapped men and massive logs against each other, and what the bodies looked like when the machine finally stopped.

Jenny said, "They won't know for sure who the men were until they can match up dental and medical records, or the families realize their men are missing."

In their minds the people in the crowd were trying to locate husbands and brothers and sons. Too many would not be sure just where one or the other was today. And even if they were sure, they would be thinking of those who didn't know and wondering which of their friends was being carried out. Morgan remembered his Welsh grandfather's tales of mine disasters when entire villages stood at the pithead to watch the lifts come up with blackened men on the early stages and then empty level after empty level.

All they could do, the hundreds of faces in the gray rain, was stand outside the gates and wait until someone told them who and what and why.

The rain that still fell through the early afternoon mist had lightened. The paramedic truck had loaded the three body bags and begun its trip to the morgue. As the truck drove away, its lights revolving but the siren not yet wailing, the crowd walked with it until only a last few remained outside the mill gates.

Inside the gates Chief Walker and Roger Higham talked with security chief Chandos.

"What are you going to tell us happened, Chandos?" Roger Higham asked.

"I'm not going to tell you anything," Chandos said. "You don't work for the company, you don't have relatives that do."

"Everyone in Gaul has a relative who works for the company."

"Get out of here, Higham. You're trespassing."

"How about my nephew Baxter? He works for the company."

"Maybe not for too damn long."

The chief said, "What are you going to tell *me*, Chandos?"

The security chief wasn't too concerned with a smalltown police chief in a town where the company paid the bills and financed the police force. "You've made your investigation, Walker. You know it was an accident, and when the company knows exactly what caused it we'll issue a statement. But from what I can see, the three men got careless, forgot to lock the machine. Maybe they'd been drinking."

Chief Walker looked at the foreman. "What do you say, Gus?"

The foreman shook his head. "We don't drink on the job. Everyone in the mill knows that'd be damn dangerous."

Chandos said, "Maybe, but we've suspected drinking on the job lately. Maybe some of the old employees aren't happy. Maybe—"

Daly Boyle appeared beside Chandos, patted his burly shoulder. "That's fine, Bob, I'll take it from here."

The security man stepped back. Ralph Baliol stood behind Boyle in the rain. He spoke to Chief Walker and watched Morgan over Boyle's shoulder. "I suggest we all look into possible sabotage too, chief."

"That would be murder," the chief said.

"That's what it would be."

"Are you accusing anyone, Mr. Baliol?"

"Murder and attempted murder have already been committed by someone in this town. I've heard of strangers coming here and asking a lot of questions about what wouldn't seem to concern them. I have to wonder who or what might be behind those strangers."

Morgan said, "Conspiracy? Tear down our way of life and all that?"

"I thought I told you to stay away from Stoke-Higham, Morgan," Daly Boyle said.

Morgan watched Baliol. "Behind the times, aren't you? We don't have evil foreign ideas anymore, or outside agitators leading our good, loyal workers astray. Or do you figure if that lie worked before it should still work?"

Ralph Baliol said nothing, and Daly Boyle knew his role when the boss was silent. "Shouldn't you clear all these people from company property, chief?" Boyle said. "I think I'd say the show was over."

"I'll send them all home, Mr. Boyle, and then I'll notify the sheriff and the Cal division of OSHA. They'll want to help you investigate," Chief Walker said. "And I wouldn't call what happened here a show, Mr. Boyle."

Roger Higham said, "That's exactly what Mr. Boyle would call it. An irritating sideshow. An unfortunate interruption in production. Not in public, of course. There he'll smile and assure everyone what a responsible company the new Baliol Investments–owned Stoke-Higham is, but back in the board room it's only more annoying delays, costs, and interference."

"I would think," Daly Boyle said to the chief, "our noble Mr. Higham would be more concerned with the welfare of the town after the tragedy than with making fanciful speculations."

"The town is as concerned as I am to know what caused the tragedy," Roger Higham said. "And don't talk about strangers. This town doesn't need outside agitators to explode."

"Is that some kind of threat, Higham?"

"I wish I could say it was, but you need more support to make threats than I have. You never know though, this could be the mistake that turns the whole town to my side."

"Because three men were careless?" Boyle pointed at Chief Walker. "And that really did sound like a threat, Walker."

"Everyone on the shift was an experienced man," the foreman said. "They wouldn't have been careless around the debarker, unless they were tired and working too fast. More likely something went wrong with the machine."

Roger Higham said, "If you knew your employees and their families, Boyle, you'd know who's missing and what they would and wouldn't have done. A few years ago, Baxter over there would have known."

"That's why Mr. Baliol and I are running the company and he's not."

"It could be why three men died too. Baxter at least knows how to run a lumber mill safely and you don't."

"That is very close to slander, Mr. Higham."

"Sue me," Roger Higham said. "You're already in trouble with the EPA and the Endangered Species Act, not to mention state *and* federal fish and wildlife people. If it turns out that this horror was caused by cutbacks and overwork, too much overtime, ignored safety precautions, a reduction in supervisors, poor or nonexistent maintenance, just plain careless plant operation, or any and all of those, as I suspect it will, you'll have OSHA all over you and I hope a lot more than that."

"Not if it was sabotage," Daly Boyle said. "I've heard of people who might want to shut us down, Higham."

"Arrest someone. Have a trial. Let the whole country know what's going on here."

Over the river behind the mill the clouds were lifting from the valley, and the mist was rising like smoke blowing from the trees on the slopes of the mountains.

Ralph Baliol said, "These people have been asked to leave company property, Walker. I suggest you enforce the law and escort them off. The foreman too, his shift was over long ago."

"I know how to enforce the law," the chief said. "These people are part of an investigation. I have three deaths in my town."

"You may know how to enforce, but you haven't been doing a lot of it lately. I'm not sure your heart is really on the side of law and order. As far as Stoke-Higham and Baliol Investments are concerned anyway."

"You know, Mr. Baliol, you may be right. About enforcing the law, I mean. I hear Stoke-Higham crews have been cutting in that old-growth redwood grove over on Eagle Creek. You know, the grove Judge Arthur up in Eureka put you all under injunction not to cut unless both state and federal wildlife officials gave you the go-ahead. That would put Stoke-Higham in violation of both state and federal law, and I'd have to enforce that law."

Daly Boyle said, "Eagle Creek isn't in your jurisdiction."

"Stoke-Higham is. The sheriff might want me to hold you for Judge Arthur, or even shut down the plant until the matter's settled. I'm pretty sure the feds would."

"We're in court tomorrow afternoon in Eureka," Boyle said. "And we don't need government approval to log our own lands."

Ralph Baliol put his hand on Boyle's shoulder, but his attention remained on Chief Walker. "If any of our crews have broken the injunction, chief, I'll be shocked. I'm going out there first thing in the morning to check on the situation personally. Now, I think we've had enough tragedy for one day. Will you join me at the club for a drink, chief?"

"I'll pass."

"Suit yourself."

Ralph Baliol walked away toward the administration building

with Boyle and Chandos following him. Both Baxter Higham and Roy Shepherd had disappeared. Chandos went on into the building, and Baliol and Daly Boyle climbed into Baliol's limousine. Mancuso drove the limo out through the gates and along the empty main street toward the river. The big black car stopped only two blocks away in front of a two-story building.

A weak sun emerged as the last clouds blew away over the forest and mountains, and on the street outside the gates Jenny, George Higham, Doc Hordle, some others of the Save Trees, Save Jobs Committee, and the foreman talked with Roger Higham beside his ancient Jeep. Roger was doing most of the talking.

Jenny came to Morgan. "My car's at the inn. Feel like a drink?"

"What are your father and the others talking about?"

"The accident and the cutting at Eagle Creek. They think they've identified the three dead men. Roger wants George and the doctor to visit all the families."

"Not him?"

"He doesn't feel he knows the families that well. And he wants to get together with the rest of us to plan something about Eagle Creek."

"Plan what about Eagle Creek?"

"A demonstration, I think. Perhaps a protest out at the site. How about that drink? Want to join Baliol at the company club?"

"Can you get us in?"

"As a matter of fact, I can."

The Stoke-Higham club was an imitation of late nineteenth-century eastern seaboard men's clubs, which were in turn imitations of eighteenth- and nineteenth-century London clubs. The tiny entrance foyer was protected by an attendant inside a cage who scrutinized all who tried to enter, and hung an ancient metal tag on a hook to indicate their presence in the club.

"Roger was given a lifetime membership by my grandfather at birth," Jenny said. "He enjoys coming once or twice a year to tweak their noses, especially cousin Baxter. Privileges include the family. Women used to be restricted to the dining room through a separate ladies' entrance, but the club was dragged into the present the last few years before Baliol came."

They went through a large reading room where two older men

sat alone with drinks and the newspapers. Everything was dark
wood and dusty maroon upholstery. In a dining room to the right
tables for two and four were set for dinner with silver bowls and
cruets, stiff white linen, and gold-trimmed bone china. It was
empty, older waiters in company-colored uniforms doing nothing.
A small writing room was off to the left, the bar lounge straight
ahead. The writing room was empty, only two tables were occupied
in the lounge, and the long mahogany bar was deserted until Morgan and Jenny sat down.

"Baliol gives memberships now in a big country club he likes
near Eureka. It has a golf course, and a lot of executives from other
companies."

The bartender polished glasses without making a move toward
Jenny and Morgan.

"Hello, Walter," Jenny said. "How about two Red Tails?"

The bartender studied the shine on his glasses and glanced
toward the two occupied tables. Ralph Baliol, Daly Boyle, and Baxter Higham sat at one. The four at the other table were all strangers
to Morgan. No one gave any indication of seeing Jenny, Morgan, or
the bartender, who carefully finished his glasses before he bent to
open a cabinet under the bar and take out two Red Tail ales. One of
the great successes of the lords of the manor was how their servants
and retainers became more protective of their rights and privileges
than the barons themselves.

"Thank you, Walter," Jenny said.

"Your father coming in?"

"Have no fear, Walter, your pampered powers-that-be over there
will not be upset by Roger today."

They were half through their Red Tails when Ralph Baliol noticed
them at the bar and signaled the bartender.

"Mr. Baliol wants to talk to you," the bartender said. He didn't
offer to carry their drinks to the table, didn't expect they would be
there that long. Neither did Daly Boyle.

"What are you doing in here, Morgan?" Boyle said.

"He's with me," Jenny said.

Baxter Higham said, "Roger has a lifetime membership."

"The old man with the big mouth at the mill," Daly Boyle explained to Baliol. "He's her father. She's got a big mouth too."

Ralph Baliol nodded to Morgan. "It looks like you found your
level. Over-age hippies and born losers. I'm really surprised, I

thought you were smarter than to get mixed up with killers and other criminals."

"Speaking of killers," Morgan said, "you know that Roy Shepherd has an M–16 assault rifle in his car?"

Baliol turned to Daly Boyle, "Why do we permit non-employees to have memberships in this club, Daly?"

"It's a tradition started by my great-great-grandfather, Mr. Baliol," Baxter Higham said. "Any executive could purchase a life membership for his sons."

"Cancel it."

"Legally, we would have to close the club."

"Then close it."

No one had offered Morgan or Jenny a chair. Morgan pulled two from the nearest empty table, gave one to Jenny, and sat down himself. "Didn't you get my message this morning, Baliol?"

"Message?"

Daly Boyle leaned close to Baliol and whispered in his ear. Baliol's eyebrows went up. "Barbara Schoenhausen again? Didn't I warn you about her, Morgan? The lady is a ballbreaker, you really want to stay away from her. Sorry, Miss Higham, but you *are* in a men's club."

"I've actually heard of balls. And it's Ms. Stoke."

Morgan said, "Do I get to talk to her, or do I get the police?"

"Go back to Santa Barbara and talk to her all you want," Baliol said. "What is that to me? Go anywhere you please, as long as it's out of my business."

"You're trying to tell me she isn't in Gaul?"

"I'm telling you I don't know or care where she is."

Baxter Higham looked at the clock above the bar and stood up. He spoke low to Daly Boyle. The only words Morgan could catch were *injunction* and *Eagle Creek.* Baxter nodded to Jenny, gave a stiff acknowledgment to Morgan, and left through the large sitting room.

Jenny said, "You're still planning to go to Eagle Creek tomorrow, Mr. Baliol?"

"Not that it's your business, but that's exactly what I intend to do first thing in the morning. After that, I'll waste an afternoon in Eureka answering your injunction."

"When you break the law you have to expect the law to stop you."

Daly Boyle banged the table. "We're cutting our trees on *our* property! The only law we're breaking is a law specifically designed to prevent Mr. Baliol and his company from exercising their full and proper ownership rights. That is a gross abuse of power by the government. They should be *protecting* our property rights, enhancing our efforts to make money."

"Then you won't mind going to court and stating that," Jenny said. "And if you're doing nothing wrong, you don't need to have your crews out there covering up any evidence, do you?"

Ralph Baliol laughed his loud, fake laugh. "How can all you Highams be so different? Baxter the mouse is as quiet as one, and you and your father are as loud as your spotted owls. And that last statement is close to slander again. You're keeping bad company too, Mrs. Stoke."

Morgan said, "Roy Shepherd is what I would call keeping bad company."

"I didn't hire him as a tennis partner."

"What did you hire him for?"

"Business. My business."

"Business that involves Barbara Schoenhausen? And don't tell me again she's not up here with you. I've seen and—"

Baliol stood up. "I'm not going to tell you one damn thing more. What you want or don't want is of utterly no importance to me." He called to the bartender. "Walter! When these two finish their drinks I want them out of the club. Daly."

Baliol strode out of the lounge with Daly Boyle behind him.

24

Morgan sat with Jenny Stoke in his BMW in the parking lot of the Mill Inn. Her Jeep Cherokee was parked beside the BMW.

"What are your father and the others really planning to do at that Eagle Creek grove tomorrow, Jenny?"

"A demonstration, maybe some sabotage if it's obvious trees have been cut."

Morgan shook his head. "I don't think so. You were pumping Baliol in that club. You were making sure he was going to be at Eagle Creek tomorrow morning. That's what your father and the others are doing right now, aren't they? Planning some attack against Ralph Baliol at the grove or on the way to or from it. Probably an 'accident' of your own."

The September sunlight angled in long, bright shafts through the fresh, rain-cleared air and blue sky east of the bridge. Across the river, close against the peaks of the mountains and the dark green of the redwoods, the other half of Gaul was still under drifting clouds.

"All right, yes. The accident at the mill and the cutting at the Eagle Creek grove were the last straw. Roger says we can't wait, and most of them agree with him. When Dan Derbyfield was killed Roger pulled back, but now he says there's no other way. Talk, demonstrations, and sabotage aren't going to get Ralph Baliol out. Power is all that matters to him. Stoke-Higham belongs to him, the redwoods belong to him, and no one is going to beat him and take it away from him."

"It's wrong, and it won't work."

"I know it's wrong. I'm not sure it won't work. George has done a lot of investigating, he's talked to a lot of Wall Street people.

Stoke-Higham isn't the kind of safe business Baliol Investment is used to, and the problems with environmental activists, endangered species, state and federal regulations, the workforce, and the town are driving them up the wall. Without Baliol, we think they'd sell to the employees or anyone else in a minute."

"Maybe, but believe me, Ralph Baliol has no intention of letting anyone kill him in an accident or any other way."

A column of smoke rose into the low clouds blowing across the distance on the other side of the river and rapidly grew thicker. Chief Walker's unmarked car passed at high speed and echoed, metallic, across the bridge. Sirens began on the far side of the river.

"It could be Stoke-Higham's information center," Jenny said. "The town's feeling pretty violent about the accident."

"Listen to me, Jenny," Morgan said. "Baliol doesn't tell his enemies anything, and he was far too conveniently definite about going to Eagle Creek first thing in the morning. He even provided the road to Eureka as the route in case there's more than one road. I'd say he *wanted* you to know exactly when and where he could easily be targeted. He wants you to take the information to Roger and the others."

She watched the column of smoke. "I can't talk to Roger anymore. Maybe not even to George. It could be too late for anyone to talk to anyone." She looked back at Morgan. "Except maybe an outsider."

"Then I better talk to Roger and George."

"I'll take you there."

"Just tell me where they are. You should go and talk to Chief Walker. If someone's burning Stoke-Higham property, he'll want to talk to Roger and the others too."

"You couldn't find them without me." She got out, leaned back in through the open door. "I don't think they'd listen to the chief now anyway."

After the rain a dazzling orange evening sun set behind the mountains. In the forest where Jenny and Morgan climbed in silence it was already dark enough to hide the heavy redwood trunks, until they emerged on an open ridge with the last glow of light still in the sky and swallows flying in and out of the dark. The trail turned down into a narrow canyon shaped like a wedge with the small end to the right and the wide end opening into a broad river valley. At the narrow end, a lighted cabin was built against a steep, wooded slope. Down the slope behind it a creek flowed placid and shallow among exposed rocks.

"Where are we?"

"It's a fishing cabin that belongs to Dan Derbyfield's brother-in-law. He lives up in Oregon. He hasn't used the place for years, and no one around here even knows who Dan's sister married."

A woman sat on the small porch with a hunting rifle across her lap. She nodded to Jenny. "Who's that with you?"

"Ford Morgan."

"Roger said nothing about expecting Morgan."

"He has to talk to all of you. It's important."

Roger Higham came out of the cabin. "It's all right, Deborah. Where will he be, Jenny? Eureka or Eagle Creek?"

"The Eagle Creek grove."

"Good."

"Good for Ralph Baliol," Morgan said.

Roger Higham turned into the light of the cabin. Jenny and Morgan followed. George Higham, three other men, and two more women sat at a long table cleaning rifles and George's M–16.

Roger Higham took an empty chair at the table. "What does 'good for Ralph Baliol' mean, Morgan?"

"He thinks it's a trap," Jenny said.

"I know it's a trap. Whichever place you choose to attack, someone's going to be waiting. The sheriff's deputies, the highway patrol, the FBI."

"What brings you to that conclusion?"

"Baliol knew why she was at the club, made sure to tell her exactly what he'd be doing tomorrow and where. He was much too open and revealing for him. Whether it's his own idea or Roy Shepherd's I don't know, but he's setting a trap."

"All right, he's expecting us, and he has the police on alert. We'll have to use that against him."

Morgan sat on the edge of the long table. "You won't be able to think up anything Roy Shepherd or the sheriff haven't anticipated. You won't be able to execute anything well enough to fool them even if you could think it up. You'll go to jail, if you don't get killed. *Prison. Death.* Those aren't words on TV news or late-night reruns.

They've already killed one of you. It's not a game to Baliol, and Shepherd's a professional."

"It's not a game with us either," Roger Higham said. "And this is our country, not his."

"Okay, then I guess I'll be going. I've got my own business to finish."

"I wish we could let you," Roger Higham said. "But you might try to save us from ourselves."

A late-night moon was halfway down the sky at the open end of the creek canyon. Tied comfortably to a redwood chaise on the dark porch, Morgan had been alone with a single guard since Roger Higham and the others who had gathered at the cabin went to prepare their 'accident' for Ralph Baliol. The silent guard dozed in a chair on the porch. Morgan watched the moon above the ragged outlines of the redwoods. He had stopped testing the ropes hours ago. The redwood guerillas were all loggers, hunters, and fishermen. They knew how to tie knots.

And Morgan had no particular desire to escape. If he couldn't talk them out of attacking Ralph Baliol, there was no way he could stop them without betraying them, and he wouldn't do that anymore than Jenny Stoke would. He knew he was, in the final analysis, on their side, if he didn't think they had much hope. An "accident" to Ralph Baliol would not disturb Morgan's convictions nor his conscience. He had seen and caused too many deaths that would always disturb him: enemies who had not been his enemies, friends who had been used to reach enemies, people neither friend nor enemy whose deaths had been necessary for the success of the mission. But Ralph Baliol's death wouldn't disturb him. He lay back and let his muscles relax, closed his eyes, and when he looked again the moon was all the way down the far side of the sky and Roger Higham sat in the other chair.

Behind him inside the cabin Morgan heard the sporadic voices of many people too nervous and excited to sleep. Morning wasn't far off, and he was wide awake now. Roger Higham was awake too, seemed to watch the inch-by-inch movement of the moon down the sky.

"Have it all set up?" Morgan said.

"There are so many bad places on our roads. Eroded slopes, hair-pin turns, sharp curves, rockfalls, cliffs, steep drops. We never could get the companies and the county to make the roads safer. We lose some people every year, usually strangers. It never takes much. People look the wrong way for a second and, bang, off the road they go. Rocks slide, trees fall, a loaded truck skids."

The old man's face caught the reflection of moonlight from the moving creek. Roger Higham had no need to sleep, and no real need to talk. He had reached that inner tranquility where he had no needs except to sit calm and alone in the night. Tomorrow would come. Few of us totally escape the time and place we live in. But Roger Higham was that rare individual whose thoughts and conclusions were mostly his own, instead of those of the society he had been born into.

"You ever live in Los Angeles, Morgan?"

"Yes."

"It's the modern city. Once it had urban villages. Like black South Central. Segregated, deprived, exploited, but a village with a life of its own. There aren't any villages now. The barons have no need of villages."

"I was trained in insurgency and counterinsurgency," Morgan said. "I know what they'll do. I could help."

"It wouldn't be right to involve you. It's our war and our battle-ground."

"You'll make them think you've set it up at one place and failed because they were ready for you. Then you hit them at another place. Maybe do it three times. I'm pretty good at running a diver-sion or a decoy."

The moon was down, the night as dark as the hour before dawn in Vietnam and a war that could not be won. No war could be won. Battles but not wars. Winning wasn't the purpose of wars. The purpose of wars was to fight them and go on fighting them. That was how a warrior king became and remained a warrior king. Power and advantage *within* the kingdom was the purpose of wars. Wars always ended where they began and always had to be fought again. Wars were to keep the barons in their castles, the elite on their estates, the colonels in their headquarters, and the chiefs in their regalia.

"I'd like to help," Morgan said.

The first gray of dawn slowly revealed the moving surface of the creek and the outlines of the tall redwoods. They sat on the cabin porch and watched light spread across the forest and the distant river at the wide end of the canyon to reveal the sweep of the trees, the wide expanse of the sky, and the distant river.

Roger Higham said, "It's our war, Morgan."

"Well now, colonel, that ain't strictly true." The new voice came from where it was still dark at the edge of the porch nearest Roger Higham. "And don't you even think about moving that hand anywhere near your belt, okay?"

At the corner of the cabin, Roy Shepherd held his M–16 aimed at Roger Higham, and smiled his smile. He gave an arm signal and his two men, Krajic and Grumman, came from the trees at a trot and crossed the porch into the cabin, their weapons at ready. Shepherd walked around the porch and up the two steps. He took Roger Higham's .22–LR pistol from under his belt and sat on the rail with his cowboy boots and the M–16 dangling.

"Your whole army's off the line, colonel. It's R and R from here on for the troops." He looked toward Morgan on the redwood chaise. "That you they got all tied up tight as a colonel's ass over there, Charlie?"

Morgan said, "A preemptive strike for Baliol, Shepherd? That won't work, you know. Nothing's been done yet."

"Not hardly for the honcho, Charlie. This is strictly freelance."

The broad, pockmarked Krajic came to the cabin door with his arms full of rifles and shotguns. He nodded to Shepherd, and went back inside.

"That wraps it, colonel. We got your cabin secured and your sentries tied up tight as you got Charlie over there. We figure to hold your weapons and babysit you a while so you don't go do nothing stupid like trying to waste the big honcho with the sheriff and the CHP waiting for you. I tell you true, colonel, this morning you got lucky. If you'd tried to hit old Ralph anytime, anywhere, you were all gonna be crispy critters. We had you boxed all ways tighter than a general's asshole."

"Your concern is touching," Roger Higham said.

Morgan said, "What made you change your mind, Shepherd?"

"The love of a good woman, Charlie. That was it, right, *mama san*?"

Barbara Schoenhausen stepped from the shadows of the trees in the same designer jeans she'd worn to Morgan's hotel room three days ago, the same low black boots, a heavy gray wool shirt, and a man's leather windbreaker too large for her.

25

On a rock at the edge of the creek, Barbara looked down at the flow of water over the clear rocks. Her black hair caught the pale light of the morning sun.

"Roy was there when Ralph laughed at me."

Across the creek a wary doe had come to the edge to drink. Barbara looked at the doe the way you look at the interior of a bus station as you go in. Something you know you should do but don't really care about. Your mind, everything inside you, is focused elsewhere. On what isn't there.

"After you found out about Ralph and me, and we talked the first time in that bar, I confronted Ralph at the hospital. I said you knew about us, it would all come out, and I wanted to know what he was going to do. He tried to placate me, insisted there was no problem, we could go on as we were, there was plenty of time to make a final decision. He had so much on his mind. There was the attack on him to handle. He loved me, he wanted to be with me, he couldn't go on without me. He soothed, soothed, soothed. Petting the poor weak woman. Reasoning with the overemotional woman. Guiding the childlike woman. Lying to the unimportant, disposable woman."

The anger of her voice startled the doe across the creek. It leaped away among the towering redwoods, a shadow fleeing into the darker shadows. "His only real concern was to *hide* our relationship! I demanded to know what future we had. Should I divorce Alfred? When would we get married? Did he want to continue our relationship without marriage? I would accept that if it were us and only us. I expect I said more, quite a lot more, including that I wasn't going to put up with other women, and especially not his son's girlfriend. He listened to it all, and when I finished, he laughed. He said he wouldn't be pressured or limited in what he did, and if I insisted on forcing the issue we'd better call it quits. He had Anne Neville, she knew a good thing when she had one. We'd had fun, no one had been hurt. He was sorry it was over, but that was my choice not his. If I changed my mind later, he could always handle Anne Neville."

The sound of the doe's flight through the trees was there long after it disappeared. Small stones and clods of dirt continued to drop into the creek where the doe had stood, sending ripples across the slow-moving surface that would be swift and violent by winter. A winter that would be as cold as the fury in her voice.

"I tried to tell you about him in that bar," Morgan said.

The black eyes looked at Morgan. "Women in love are so blind, aren't they? So foolish."

"I'm sorry, Barbara. That was stupid of me."

"Yes, it was." She looked away again, breathed slowly, and let the rigid muscles of her face relax. "Roy was there. He heard it all. When I walked out of that room and down to my car, he came after me. Inside I was a sea of rage, and I realized as he caught my arm, stopped me, that he was feeling the same rage. He gripped me so hard without realizing it that his hand bruised my arm. I knew that if I gave the word he would go back and kill Ralph."

Up the slope at a corner of the cabin porch that was visible from the creek, Roy Shepherd sat on the rail, the M–16 still dangling muzzle down. He was looking down to where they talked. There were trees between, he couldn't see them clearly, but he looked straight toward them alert and waiting, the M–16 as much a part of him as his legs in their battered boots. Ready to do whatever he had to do. Morgan remembered when he had been like that. Sure of what he had to do and unconcerned with reasons.

"I knew at once that he could and would kill Ralph. Without hesitation. It frightened me. I tried to pull away. He dropped his hand, and his eyes were hurt. I felt instant guilt, and in the next instant an excitement I'd never known. An excitement I'd never even thought about, or thought possible, but recognized at once. It was the naked hurt in his eyes, and the violent, murderous, naked anger before that. An excitement not about him, but about me. A sense of perfect rightness, perfect harmony. I was completely comfortable, even peaceful. I was happy. I smiled and he smiled. He said we would have a drink and talk. I said we'd have more than a drink and more than talk." Up the slope through the trees, Roy Shepherd was gone from the corner of the porch. "He was staying in a condo Ralph owns in Summerland. I called Alfred, said I had to stay the night with a woman friend who was in trouble. He was upset that the children would have to be taken to school by Elly, our house-keeper, but that was all. Roy and I must have talked most of the night. About our lives, our views, how we felt about life. About what we wanted and how we wanted to live. We saw each other every moment we could after that first night, and when he had to come up here for Ralph, I came with him. I didn't think about it for a second. I knew what I wanted to do."

"Why didn't you tell me about Roy at the ranch? At least at the Mill Inn?"

"Ralph didn't know about us. If he found out, we knew he'd fire Roy or worse, and we needed Ralph's money. Or Roy thought we did. But we decided the money wasn't worth letting Ralph hurt any of these people."

"The children?"

"Alfred will agree children belong with their mother. Old Helga will be delighted. Alfred will find a proper woman. He's not a bad man. He has some sense of others."

"Do you know what you're getting into, Barbara? What Roy Shepherd is?"

"I know what he is and who he is. I know everything about him."

Since the late middle ages the Shepherds were hardworking yeo-men in the vicinity of the English village of Epping less than two days' ride from London. By the middle of the seventeenth century these same Shepherds were hardworking tenant farmers in various rural areas of the southern American colonies.

By the beginning of the twentieth century John Wesley Shep-herd had put down roots in rural northern Arkansas, owned his own farm, managed to feed his large family, be a deacon of the local church, and pay the mortgage to the bank. All that blew away with the Dust Bowl and Great Depression of the thirties. The wind took the land, the bank took the farm, and William Jennings Shepherd took his wife, his two sons, old John Wesley, and his model-T Ford to California.

William Jennings and his caravan wandered from the Imperial Valley to the San Fernando Valley to the San Joaquin Valley. John Wesley died, the first two sons vanished in Los Angeles, and the Model-T broke down near Bakersfield. By the time Roy Rogers Shepherd was born William Jennings and his wife were employed by a large agribusiness between Bakersfield and Fresno. Roy grew into a jovial boy who made his older and younger sisters laugh, and did more than his share of the work around William Jennings's house. He went to work on the farm at twelve when the picking season was on. At fourteen he worked after school and all day on Saturday at a Kentucky Fried Chicken not far from Interstate 5. At fifteen he assaulted his first man.

The man was the manager of housing for the agribusiness, and was being unpleasant about needed repairs to the Shepherd house and a rent increase. After he had shouted and threatened William Jennings, and ordered Mrs. Shepherd to shut up and get the hell out of the room, Roy knocked him through the door that happened to be closed and completed a savage beating out in the hard dirt of the front yard among the chickens and rusted car hulks.

William Jennings beat Roy, apologized to the manager, agreed to pay the rent increase without the repairs if the company would please not fire him. The company let William Jennings, who was a good worker, keep his job, but they prosecuted Roy, and he was sent to juvenile hall. Being a strong and determined boy, he learned a great deal there without suffering much harm, and at sixteen committed his first robbery.

What happened was that Roy had only a few months left to serve when his mother visited him with the news that William Jennings had lost his job after all, and they had to move out of the company house. It seemed the agribusiness owners had decided to mechanize their operations and were laying off workers over fifty in favor of younger men who would be more easily trained on the equipment. Some of the girls could soon be hired in the packing plant, but William Jennings would have to find a new job and his own housing.

The problem was cash flow. William Jennings didn't have any cash, and the company had no obligation since he was a day worker and always had been. Roy escaped from juvenile hall, which wasn't hard, and held up a liquor store on his way home to help William Jennings get a new house for the family and tide them over until he found work. The sheriff was waiting for Roy when he arrived; he hadn't learned enough in the hall. Sent to a more severe juvenile institution for incorrigible cases, he got into no further trouble, was released for good behavior at nineteen.

While Roy was in juvenile hall, William Jennings finally found a job at a produce warehouse in Fresno. He rented a house for the family. The job was mostly pushing a broom, but it was the first permanent job William Jennings had had since he lost the farm in Arkansas, and he was so grateful he went to church three times as often and became a lay preacher.

Roy got a job driving a truck for the wholesaler, and at twenty married a girl he'd met in juvenile hall and who had followed him to Fresno. She was a dancer but took a job as a waitress when no one in Fresno wanted an underage dancer who wouldn't take her clothes off, at least in public. At twenty-one Roy decided driving a truck for a wholesaler in Fresno didn't appeal to him as life's work, and the dancer wanted to dance. He'd seen enough of farming, and unskilled factory work wasn't something to do for forty years. Without investment money or a special skill, what was left in Fresno was fast food, low-paid service, custodial sweeping, or pick and shovel. Skill would take time to get, so the solution was money.

Roy and the dancer pooled the only skill they'd learned so far and robbed a department store. They missed the payroll, and the police missed them. Even without the payroll, the haul was substantial, and so was the heat. When they fled for help to William Jennings, he denounced their evil ways and refused to hide them. But he didn't turn them in either because he was afraid the authorities might come down on him. They fled again, and the dancer's family and friends in Bakersfield hid them.

After a few months the pressure got to be too confining, and they both knew if they hung around Fresno or Bakersfield they would sooner or later make a mistake. Something had to be done before they went crazy or ended up in the real slammer. Roy chose the time-honored way for poor young men to hide out from the law and maybe get a skill at the same time. He joined the army. The dancer took an equally well-established path for young girls with ambition. She went to San Francisco to find a man with more money and in a better position to help a dancer.

The parting was relaxed and amicable, the divorce was easy and long distance, but the army proved to be as confining to Roy as hiding out from the law, and he was soon in trouble with the brass. After many restrictions to base and more than a little company punishment he was on the verge of the stockade when an old sergeant who'd been through World War Two and Korea took him to the PX and over many beers explained the army, the world, and what happened to outlaws who didn't learn to work either or both. The sergeant also explained there were always angles. Roy had no intention of letting the army or the world tell him what to do, but he also had no special love for the joint or the stockade, and took the wisdom of the old sergeant to heart.

There was no possibility Roy and the army would ever live happily together, but for a time he managed to find some of the sergeant's angles. He persuaded the battalion warrant officer who supplied pot and booze on the base that his operation would be more efficient if he had a rep in each company, took the job in his company for himself. That got him in good with the low brass up to the captain, and he pulled an assignment to the army's security police school. When he completed the school he was transferred to the military police.

He fitted in better with the MPs, the angles were more extensive, and he accumulated a sizable bankroll for a rainy day before the unit was loaded into a C–147 and sent out to Vietnam. As in all war zones, the angles for profit were even wider and deeper in Saigon, and when there was real military police action to perform he was better than most. The colonel decided he was a hell of a good soldier, until the inevitable collision finally came over a woman.

She was a Vietnamese widow whose husband had been forced into the ARVN and killed thirty miles from Saigon with the annihilation of his entire patrol by a Viet Cong unit they never saw. Roy felt even closer to her than he had to the dancer, made a home in two small rooms in the big house of her family who had been French-educated and rich until her father denounced the French, joined the Viet Minh, and was killed fighting in the north years before. Roy admired the old hardhead, but it had been hard on the women. When three drunken marines tried to rape the woman,

Roy shot one and beat two unconscious. They sent him to the stockade in Long Binh for a year. When he got out he told the colonel he wanted to marry the woman and stay in Vietnam. The colonel sent him away to an MP section attached to the Twenty-fifth Infantry Division in the iron triangle and there they put him down into the Viet Cong tunnels with a flashlight. That was enough army for Roy.

He hitched the thirty-odd miles back to Saigon. He moved in with the woman in a part of the city that was a no-man's land between the Saigon regime and the Viet Cong. He learned the angles of playing both sides, then the woman was shot down by a berserk American MP who had gone out of his mind down in the delta. Roy went to find the killer, but they had shipped him to a mental hospital in the U.S. Roy broke up his HQ in front of the colonel, and they returned him to Long Binh.

The colonel, who still thought Roy was a hell of a soldier, came to talk to him. The colonel spoke of the difficulties for young men in foreign countries under wartime conditions, and especially in a country populated by an alien race. Of the needs of young men too often mistaken for love, which led them into bad situations that could not survive out of wartime conditions among their own people at home. Of the duties of brave young men as soldiers and patriots, of what they owed their friends and families at home, not to mention their country.

The colonel was eloquent and, when he finished, smiled and told Roy he would work to get him released soon and sent back to his unit with no further problems. They would all forget the past and go on into the glorious future together. Roy told the colonel that when he got out of the LBJ Ranch he would desert and probably join, or at least work with, Victor Charlie, whom he had nothing against and who, when he thought about it, probably had a hell of a lot more right to be fighting in and for Vietnam than the U.S. Army did. Besides, if you really thought about it, the blackmarket both sides used was probably a more honest and moral alternative, and certainly more lucrative, than either army. The colonel nodded and left, and Roy was soon shipped back to the States, given a bad conduct discharge for the good of the service, and told to get lost.

No one had come looking for him during his army years, so he assumed the authorities had no evidence about the robbery in

Fresno, but he avoided Northern California anyway and went to Los Angeles. He did contact the dancer who had kept him apprised of her successful progress with man and dance while he was in the service. The dancer had married the man with money and contacts, but had now outgrown him and came immediately to L.A. and moved in with Roy. They had a good six months while Roy explored areas of employment.

His skills consisted of stoop labor and other farm work, truck and tractor driving, fast-food service, various military police duties, and armed robbery. The fast-food experience tided him over until he located a position as a guard at a motion picture studio. Unfortunately, they learned of his bad conduct discharge and dismissed him. He drove a produce truck for a few months, then was promoted to supervisor and given a desk at the produce warehouse. Roy soon found he did not like to give orders any more than he liked to take them. The produce company also learned of his bad conduct discharge and needed to protect *their* pristine image. The dancer kissed him and said she had found a richer and better-connected man in the film industry, was going to divorce the husband in San Francisco, and marry once more.

It would leave Roy with no income at all, but that was his problem, not hers. He was delighted for her, took her out for a farewell celebration, told her to look him up any time she needed him, and wished her well. Then he set about solving his problem. In any job much above entry level the bad conduct discharge would always show up, and he had no stomach for becoming a colonel anyway. On the other hand, there was no future to life at entry level. Tractor, truck, time clock, and desk were still not for him. He was twenty-five when he committed his third robbery, and shot his first man, civilian or soldier, outside Vietnam.

The target was a factory outlet store near Barstow just after closing time. The clerk was only wounded, and Roy got away, but only barely. The haul wasn't all that good, he had to lie low for months, and was soon broke once more. There was nothing to do but try again. His fourth robbery and his last on record. He went for a large liquor store where he knew there would be plenty of cash. The money was there, but so were the cameras and a quick-shooting guard. Roy winged the guard and escaped, but was hit himself and easily caught through the doctor he went to, his images on the surveillance cameras, and the photo taken for his badge at the motion picture studio.

They would have put him away for twenty years plus, except the dancer made her new husband send a high-priced lawyer to defend him. The lawyer got the bad conduct discharge excluded, explained away the juvenile record with a heart-rending picture of the plight of a boy going to work in the fields at twelve, bribed the Barstow clerk from robbery number three, and defended him as a first offender. Roy got five to ten. He started in Soledad, was a model inmate and got transferred to the California Men's Colony after two years, and was paroled in four.

He went back to L.A., hooked up briefly with the dancer who was in Beverly Hills by then with husband number four. After two weeks she told him her future was to play the game in the grid, and he didn't fit into that future. She kissed him goodbye once more, sadly but permanently, and Roy was alone with a record, a bad conduct discharge, and only two skills that had any chance of leading to the happiness we all have the right to pursue: police work and armed robbery. It was time for serious pondering.

He drove out into the desert, sat under a saguaro, and listened to the voice of that old sergeant explain the army, the world, and what happened to outlaws who didn't learn to work the angles with either or both. "If you're a real hardcase, boy, they'll get you in the end for sure, but use your head 'n' you can do it your way 'n' still last pretty damn long."

Using his head, Roy realized if he hoped to live pretty damn long, robbery was a poor option. The days of the highwayman and bank robber were gone. Pretty Boy Floyds had never had much chance, and had none at all in an electronic age. On the other hand, no one, public or private, was going to hire or license an ex-con with a bad conduct discharge. And the voice of the old sergeant returned: "There's always angles, boy."

What he needed was a chink in the grid, a crack in the system. He found it in the twilight zone that has existed in all attempts to organize human life so far. Those who acquire want to keep, and need someone to guard what they acquire. Those who acquire on the edge of legality also need guards, and these people usually wish to continue to acquire so need persuasion as well as safety. Roy already had a resume and an employment agency—his record, civilian and military, and his contacts in the joint. He hung out his shingle, so to speak, in the right places, and was on his way to what he figured would be a good life, if maybe shorter than guys with a bigger edge and better hand than he'd been dealt, but, then, you pretty much got to play her as she lays, right, Charlie?

26

🦑

"Have gun, no questions asked?" Morgan said. "A little assault, a little murder?"

"He's murdered no one. He is what he is."

"And what about you? I thought you were a career woman, a wife, and a mother. A woman in a bad marriage, but with children she wanted to raise and work she wanted to do. Have I missed something?"

Morgan had seen at once when she had stepped from the dawn shadows that her face was thinner, the bones bare and more prominent. She wore no makeup, had looked older but no less beautiful to Morgan. Now he realized she looked older and younger at the same time. The youth of coming to peace with herself. Someone who has emerged from a painful passage into a better time, has left the pain behind but not the experience of the pain.

"We adapt to what we were born into, Ford. We don't know it, or that we've done it. I had a marriage I was unhappy in. My solutions were to go back to college, do volunteer work, fall in love with another man and have an affair. A romantic fling with a man very much like my husband. All the standard responses in the same familiar world."

Up the slope through the trees, voices sounded from the cabin. Anxious voices, excited. No one appeared on the porch or around the cabin. Morgan looked up the slope, but whatever was going on came from the front of the cabin, toward the forest and the trail that led over the ridge back to the road in the redwood grove on the other side. Some of the voices faded toward the ridge, and others continued to talk at the front of the cabin. One voice sounded like

Jenny Stoke, and she was upset. Barbara Schoenhausen didn't seem to hear any of the commotion.

"After I left Roy that morning to go home, I was in a daze. I'd forgotten to buy plastic glasses for the children. Alfred hates glasses being broken, even our everyday ones, and children break glasses. So I stopped at Robinson's. The china department is near the housewares. I was trying to understand what I was about to do with Roy, and wandered into the china department. They had a display of Royal Doulton patterns. One of them was Carlyle. I saw it and I wanted it. I imagined the plates and cups and bowls on our table at a dinner party with our best crystal and silver, how wonderful they would look, how happy I would feel to have the Carlyle. That was when I realized how we dupe ourselves. I realized it wasn't a matter of running away, but of changing who and what had power over me."

"And that means Shepherd?" Morgan said. "Why?"

She sat on the rock totally unaware of the cabin up the slope. "In sixteenth-century France there was a man named Martin Guerre. He was an imposter who served in the army with the real Martin Guerre, then went to his village and impersonated him. He must have been a genius. He remembered every detail the real Guerre had talked about so well he fooled the entire village, including Guerre's wife. At least until they went to bed. Her marriage to the real Martin Guerre had been arranged, there was no love or attraction; he had been afraid of her needs, resented that she had any needs beyond serving him as she was supposed to. The imposter wasn't afraid of her or her needs. With the imposter she felt like a person. No one knows for sure what the imposter had intended— probably to get all he could and vanish before the real Guerre came home. When he tried to sell Guerre's share of the land, the village became suspicious and denounced him. At his trial, the only one who swore he was the real Martin Guerre was the wife, who was the only one who knew for sure he wasn't. She wanted him; together they were real. But the husband returned, the imposter was sentenced to hang, and she was trapped. If she stood by the man she wanted, she was doomed. He knew that, and he protected her. She was a person to him. He saved her and went down alone."

"You think Shepherd would go down alone?"

"Yes, but I don't think I would let him."

"He's an outlaw, Barbara. A killer."

"Oh, he's killed people, so have you. So have all of us in our modern world, one way or another. He works for people who hire him, but he lives with himself. He's killed people who would have killed him or the person he was guarding. He lives how he must."

"He murdered Dan Derbyfield and Fletcher Comrie."

"Dan Derbyfield tried to shoot him. He reacted. But he didn't kill Comrie, Ralph did. When they went to Comrie's house Ralph said he was going to scare Comrie with Roy's M–16. But Ralph stood him against a wall and shot him down in cold blood. Roy was enraged, he almost killed Ralph on the spot for tricking him, for risking Roy's neck. But Ralph said he had it all worked out, the police would believe it was the same people who'd shot him, no one would ever suspect him or Roy."

"Ralph had the matchbook cover from Gaul?"

She nodded. "Mancuso found it in the bushes at the mansion after Ralph was shot. When Ralph regained consciousness in the hospital Mancuso gave it to him. Then you told Ralph about Comrie's manipulations. He hadn't known, and he was enraged. Ralph killed Comrie for cheating him, adding millions to his takeover costs. But mostly for making a fool of him. He left the matchbook cover to put the blame on the people up here. He thought that was a brilliant stroke."

"Shepherd better tell the police right now."

"How can he talk to the police? They'd never believe him, and anyway, he was there with Ralph. He's not going to prison again."

The tone of her voice added that she wouldn't let Roy go to prison again even if he were willing himself. Morgan looked up the slope to the empty corner of the cabin porch where Roy Shepherd had sat.

"What will he do?" he said.

"Whatever it is we'll do it together."

"A cowboy in a white Cadillac?"

"Why not? He wants me, and he's honest. If you can't play their game anymore, and they won't let you play yours, a cowboy in a white Cadillac might be the best deal in town."

Up the slope the voices grew louder. Too many voices for only Roy Shepherd and his two men. Agitated voices all around the cabin. Two people came down toward them through the trees. One was Jenny Stoke. The other was Roy Shepherd. Jenny Stoke reached the creek and them. "Roger's gone. He got out of the cabin and away over the ridge. He took one of the pickups."

Roy Shepherd said, "If the old guy's planning what I think he is, Charlie, he's in number-ten deep serious. If any of you try to go after him, you're right in the shit with him. Old Ralph's got the troops and the firepower. If it's my call, I let the old guy fly his own pattern."

"We have to stop him, Ford," Jenny said.

Shepherd shrugged. "You all want to charge into a red LZ, that's your problem. I tried, *mama san*. Now it's time to roll the poncho and fly away."

Jenny Stoke said, "He'll try to attack Baliol himself, Ford. It's suicide."

"Maybe that's what the old guy's got in mind," Shepherd said. "You send yourself up in smoke on the temple steps, sometimes you make 'em take a look at you. Maybe it's worth it." He held his hand out to Morgan. "It's been real, Charlie. You win some, you lose some, right?"

He and Barbara Schoenhausen walked up through the trees to the cabin. Roy looked at his watch and called back. "You really want to stop the old guy, Charlie, the troops should be on the road out of that Eagle Creek grove in thirty minutes. They expect to be hit along the trail. But everything's smoke and mirrors, you read me? The woods're gonna be full of Indians, and what you see ain't gonna be what you get."

Jenny Stoke's Cherokee bounced and lurched over the steep curves and ruts of the logging road. Morgan rode beside her, Doc Hordle in the back. The two pickups were ahead and the second Jeep behind them. The four vehicles drove up and over the divide between the creek and the river to where the main county highway followed the river through the valley toward Eureka and the sea. Doc Hordle pointed below where the two-lane blacktop angled sharply around a huge outcropping. The road had been blasted into a shelf of the mountain with a lethal drop into the river on the far side.

"That was where we were going to let them think we'd tried to fake a truck accident that would push Baliol off the road," the doctor said. "We'd miss, let some of us get caught to make it look real."

The two Jeeps and two pickups stopped among the trees above the wicked curve with the hundred-foot drop to the river. George Higham and two others got out carrying binoculars and ran to the edge of the dirt road to scan the slope below. Those without binoculars shaded their eyes against the morning sun penetrating through the trees in long shafts of pale light.

"Anyone see him?"

"Concentrate on close to the road."

"Look over there," Doc Hordle pointed. "Just before the curve."

A California Highway Patrol car waited hidden from the highway among the trees.

"There'll be another one on the far side of the big rock," Jenny said. "They know the best spots for an accident too."

Below on the road, a plain black Buick sedan drove past and out of sight around the giant outcropping. After a small gap, a Ford Taurus painted the light blue and red of Stoke-Higham followed, and twenty yards behind it the black limousine passed and went on out of sight. After another short gap there was a second Stoke-Higham vehicle and then a longer gap to one more simple black Buick. A highway patrol helicopter swung lazily across the road and looped back and out of sight. It could have been routinely monitoring the traffic, but it wasn't.

"Smoke and mirrors," Morgan said. "That's what Shepherd was telling us. Daly Boyle's in the limousine, deputies are in the Stoke-Higham cars and the Buicks. The HP chopper is watching everything ahead. Roger won't have a chance."

The second site, where Roger Higham had planned the real attack was fifteen miles away by the highway but less than half that on the logging road. The drive was rough and jarring, and the oldest Jeep broke down. Its occupants scrambled into the backs of the two pickups. They went on as fast as they could, and had to hope Baliol's convoy would move still more slowly while it tried to lure the attack it expected. It was a silent journey as they bucked and bounced over the rutted road. George Higham in the lead pickup finally pulled off and parked.

The two other vehicles parked beside him on a slope a few hundred yards above where the river passed through a narrow gorge formed by high cliffs on the far side, and flowed fast and deep. There was no sign of the convoy, but the helicopter hovered in the distance. There were no cliffs here on this side of the river to create a fatal drop, but the road ran close to the edge of the dark water. The slope down to the highway was littered with fallen trees and logs, with an irregular pile of old logs less than fifty feet above the highway that wasn't as haphazard as it seemed.

"If you look closely," George Higham said, "those uprights are doing more than lean on the stack. If you pull two away, the rest'll go like a row of dominoes and the whole stack will roll down on the limousine, sweep it into the deepest part of the river, and there'd be no way to prove it wasn't a freak accident. That was the plan, anyway, but Roger can't do that alone. He—"

"There!" Morgan pointed. "In that stand of trees close to the road."

Far below, Roger Higham stood among the trees at the edge of the highway. Morgan strained to see through the forest, but all he could make out was the distant figure as motionless as one of the tree trunks. A shadow among the shadows, and even across the distance Morgan sensed a change. A force larger than life stood among those trees. Morgan had seen too many men in states of desperation and exaltation. Infiltrating Viet Cong soldiers who died to the last man to accomplish their mission. Buddhist monks sitting in the street without a sound in flaming immolation to make the world listen. The rebel priest in Latin America who put himself between his villagers and the soldiers.

George Higham started down through the slope with the others behind him.

Jenny called out, "Dad!"

"Roger!"

The shattering noise of the helicopter exploded over the tree tops and drowned their voices as the first black Buick drove into the narrow gorge below and on past Roger Higham.

The first Stoke-Higham company car appeared.

Then the limousine.

Roger Higham stepped out of the trees, raised an old World War Two carbine he had been holding hidden along his leg. A Korean War model with the larger magazine. He shot out the front tires of the limousine. The long black car lurched, skidded, smashed into the guardrail, and screamed to a stop a foot from the edge of the river. The old man ran toward it, firing from the hip. Bullets ripped into the metal, glass shattered, but the limousine ground into reverse and fishtailed backwards, the flattened front tires shredding in smoking shards. Roger Higham ran after it, still firing.

The Stoke-Higham sedan ahead of the limousine braked and slewed sideways across the highway. While it was still moving, the outside rear door flung open, and Ralph Baliol jumped out with a long-barreled pistol in his hand. He dropped to one knee, held the gun in both hands, and shot Roger Higham twice in the back. As the old man stumbled forward and fell to his knees, Ralph Baliol shot a third time.

27

Highway patrolmen held back the traffic from both directions. The sound of the swift river was a low pulse in the narrow canyon, and far up the highway the siren on the paramedic's van growled slowly toward them as it made its way through the backed-up cars. The sheriff and his deputies controlled the empty stretch of highway where the bullet-scarred limousine steamed from its shattered radiator and Roger Higham still lay in the roadway.

George Higham, Doc Hordle, Morgan, and the six other men who had come running down the hill sat in the dirt at the edge of the highway like Viet Cong prisoners in a rice-paddy ditch. The sheriff himself stood over them with two armed deputies behind him. He held the modified 9–mm army-issue Beretta with the long barrel he had taken from Ralph Baliol. Out on the highway, Jenny Stoke and two more deputies looked down at the body of Roger Higham. Jenny was crying.

George Higham said, "He murdered my father, sheriff. In cold blood. As simple as that."

"The man was armed and trying to kill me," Ralph Baliol said. "Was I supposed to wait until he did?"

Up the road Mancuso, Robert Chandos, and a shaken and bloody Daly Boyle, wearing Ralph Baliol's blue suit and homburg, waited beside the steaming limousine for the arrival of a tow truck.

"You think all three shots were necessary?" Morgan said.

Baliol turned on him. "Did you count your shots in the heat of every battle? I shot until he fell. What else would you do if someone was trying to kill you? He was shooting at my car, he was shooting at my employees. How did anyone know what he'd do next?"

"Hell, you knew the deputies in the other cars were seconds away."

"He was armed and shooting at the car he thought I was in. If he'd turned and seen me even a second before the police arrived, I could have been killed."

"All right," the sheriff said. "You'll all have your say at the inquest." He nodded to Ralph Baliol. "I'm not saying it wouldn't have been better if you'd waited for my men to handle it, Mr. Baliol; I think maybe you should have, but I can understand how you felt. I'd have been scared he'd turn and see me too. I—"

Morgan said, "Then why not stay in the car, sheriff?"

"I was the closest to Higham, the first one out of a car, and he was still shooting at my people," Baliol insisted.

The sheriff said, "We sometimes do funny things when someone's trying to kill us. Someone already tried to murder Mr. Baliol down in Santa Barbara, and did murder an associate of his. He came to us a few days ago and told us he was sure the murderer was up here and was going to try again. We set up the trap. The murderer did try again and got shot. I'm sorry he died, but you could say that was a risk he took when he picked up a carbine and started shooting. There'll be a full investigation, inquest, even a grand jury, but Mr. Baliol's life had been threatened, and as far as I'm concerned it's self-defense and nothing else."

The paramedics had finally broken through the line of cars and irate drivers, and up the road they put Roger Higham into a body bag. They carried the bag to the ambulance and closed the doors. Jenny Stoke stood alone in the sunlight on the morning highway.

"You saw what you expected to see, sheriff," George Higham said. "What you wanted to see."

Anger was hard in the sheriff's voice. "What we expected to see, Higham, was more than one man with a gun, and it looks to me like we should have. You were all up on that logging road like you knew something was going to happen right at this spot. In my book, that means a grand jury should take a look at all of you. For now, we'll take you in, get your statements, and then you can all go home. You'll get your day in court, and so will Mr. Baliol."

"My father's dead," George Higham said, "and we can bury him? That's how it happens now?"

"And consider yourselves lucky you're not going to prison, or being buried with him," the sheriff said.

* * *

The coroner would not release the body of Roger Higham until the next day at the earliest, but all Gaul gathered that afternoon at the pale-blue-and-red-trimmed church on Main Street east of the river for a memorial service to Roger Higham and the three men who had died in the debarker. The grisly fate of the three had been officially declared accidental, without explanation of how the debarker had started again but assurances from the company that everything was being done to find the cause of the tragic malfunction. Roger Higham's death had been officially pronounced justifiable homicide, pending an inquest.

Baxter Higham attended the service in the old church built by his and Roger's family. He gave one of the eulogies to a vast silence. Robert Chandos stood at the back of the packed church to watch the mourners as they entered. Ralph Baliol and Daly Boyle did not attend. When the service ended, the crowd moved in a mass up the street and stood at the gates of the mill. The police and the sheriff were called. Chief Walker stationed his officers outside the gates, but did nothing more. It was the sheriff's deputies who fanned out to disperse the crowd. No one resisted or protested. No one hurried either. They walked home at their own pace in their own silence.

Later that evening Morgan and the members of the hard core of the Save Trees, Save Jobs Committee gathered at Jenny Stoke's small house. It was a two-bedroom board-and-batten cottage on the other side of the river from the mill. The mountains and the redwoods came down to the edge of the backyard, and across the river and highway the eastern mountains were dark purple in the fading evening sun. Jenny sat on her small deck on a high-backed redwood bench beside Morgan.

"What will you do now, Jenny?"

"Bury Roger, go back to work, and go on doing what I've been doing. I need to work to live. We all need to save the trees and the land. What are you going to do now?"

"Go back to Santa Barbara, I suppose." On the bench he leaned his head back and looked up at the same sky he and Roger Higham had stared up into down on the Lost Coast, but the stars weren't out yet. "And then to Costa Rica."

"You don't sound convinced."

"Convinced that I'm going back to Costa Rica?"

"Convinced that you're ready to go back."

Morgan looked for the first star but couldn't find it yet. "You don't think I've given up. You don't think I'm going to forget about Barbara Schoenhausen. You think I should give up and forget her."

"I think you should give up and forget her. I don't think you can. Not yet."

"When will I?"

"I have no idea, Ford."

They listened to the song of the night: the river, the swallows in and out of the dusk, the squeak of bats, the light wind in the branches of the redwoods. To the voices inside the small house where the others talked and drank and ate sandwiches. Urgent voices. In Costa Rica there was nothing urgent except Lareina. Or whoever was to come after Lareina, and the woman after that.

"I think maybe I'd like to stay here and work with you," Morgan said.

"At my job or for the trees?"

"The trees. I wouldn't make a very good PR person. I have quite a bit of money. I think I could get more from other people and perhaps help buy the company back."

"How much money is 'quite a bit?' "

"Too much."

"We can always use too much money."

All but the last faint line of pale gold above the western mountains had gone. Night darkened in the river valley. Her profile was a darker shadow where she sat quiet on the bench. She seemed to wait for Morgan to say more. When he didn't, she turned to look at him and he saw the white of her teeth in the darkness.

"We better go inside. I'm hungry, and we could both use a beer."

Morgan talked with them until it was past midnight. They spoke a lot about Roger Higham. Stories and memories. Hopes and frustrations. He had been one of the nonviolent who turned to violence to oppose the violent. They talked of the future where there would be ancient redwoods and clean rivers and jobs for everyone. A future where a man like Roger Higham would not want to shoot another man, where there would be no reason.

When the talking ended Morgan walked alone across the bridge to the inn.

*   *   *

Morgan had breakfast with the committee people. The coroner had released Roger Higham's body, and when they left for the funeral parlor he did not go with them. He was, after all, an outsider, an observer, who didn't feel he had earned the right to be there.

He returned to his suite at the Mill Inn to pack and check out. Jenny and the others would be busy for days with the arrangements for the multiple funeral. It would be the biggest Gaul had ever seen. Morgan was taking one last look around when the telephone rang.

Chief Walker said, "There's a man here who needs to talk to you."

"Who?"

"A Sergeant Koons from the Santa Barbara sheriff's office."

Morgan left his bags in the lobby and walked up Main Street to the redwood columns of police headquarters. Koons rose and shook his hand. Chief Walker waved Morgan to the third chair in the office.

"Did you find Barbara Schoenhausen?" Koons asked.

"I found her. She came to Gaul on her own, and she came with Roy Shepherd. No abduction, no hostage."

"I guess that takes care of one question, then. Where is Shepherd?"

"As far as I know he left town. He quit working for Ralph Baliol, and probably saved a blood bath up here. Except I'd guess both of those were more her idea than his."

"Blood bath?"

Chief Walker explained, "A group we have here wanted to force Baliol Investments to sell Stoke-Higham, and they may have been considering violence. So Ralph Baliol, the sheriff, and the highway patrol set a trap. Roy Shepherd warned the group. The way things have turned out, Morgan is probably right. I'd say we have considerable to thank Mrs. Schoenhausen and Shepherd for in Gaul."

"We don't have much to thank Shepherd for in Santa Barbara," Koons said. "You know where he's gone, Morgan?"

Morgan shook his head. "What's the second reason you're looking for him?"

"We finally identified Shepherd as the guy you saw outside Anne

Neville's place that day. Didn't you recognize him when you found him?''

"I told you, with the shadows and his hat pulled low, I never had a good look at him. How did you identify him?''

"A little luck. The day before the guy was killed—his name was Daniel Derbyfield, by the way—two people saw an old Cadillac convertible with a cow skull on the hood parked in the area. In Montecito they get suspicious about cars that don't look like they belong in Montecito, so they called our office. A deputy couldn't find the car, but one of the people gave him the license number. He ran it through Sacramento, got the I.D., but found nothing unusual or suspicious and forgot about it. That's how those call-ins usually wind up. He didn't think about it again until morning roll call two days ago when I spoke about the case, and mentioned the address. It rang a bell. The tag number gave us Shepherd's name, we got his record and photo. The photo matched your description, we showed it in the neighborhood, got three positive makes.''

Morgan said, "Derbyfield was one of the two who went down there to kill Ralph Baliol. He was armed—''

"You can't kill people because you think maybe they're going to shoot someone, Morgan.''

"Derbyfield shot first, sergeant. I was there.''

Koons looked at him curiously. "We still have to arrest him and let the lawyers and the courts figure it out, you know that. I told Baliol the same. He could be in trouble himself for hiring Shepherd.''

"When did you talk to Ralph Baliol?''

"An hour ago. Right before he left town.'' Koons looked out the office window. A corner of the mill pond was visible, two giant redwood logs floating in it, and across the river the forested slopes that climbed out of sight. "What Shepherd did or didn't do to Derbyfield doesn't matter that much anyway. He's got bigger trouble.''

"Bigger?''

"Fletcher Comrie wasn't killed by anyone from Gaul, and that matchbook wasn't left by mistake. Roy Shepherd planted it after he killed Comrie.''

Morgan said, "Shepherd says it was Ralph Baliol who killed Comrie, sergeant. He—''

"Shepherd?'' Koons said. "You talked to him about Fletcher

Comrie? When? Where? What did he say? He *admits* he was there when Comrie was killed?"

"He says Mancuso found the matchcover, gave it to Baliol. Baliol was enraged over the stock manipulation Comrie had used on him, so he took Shepherd with him to Comrie's house to confront Comrie. Shepherd thought they were going there to scare the hell out of Comrie and get the money. But Baliol took Shepherd's M–16 and cut Comrie down in cold blood. Executed him."

"Come on, Morgan, what the hell else would Shepherd say?" Koons shook his head. "You remember that scrap of paper we found in Comrie's living room with his address on it? Turns out it's Baliol's assistant's handwriting. Gerald Kirsch. Roy Shepherd said he wanted to talk to Comrie about the shooting of Baliol, Kirsch wrote the address down for him. We checked. The sheet of paper's from Kirsch's desk pad all right, and Kirsch, Baliol, and the chauffeur Mancuso all saw Roy Shepherd put the address in his pocket. He got careless and dropped it at Comrie's place when he killed him. So we *know* Roy Shepherd was there. There isn't a shred of evidence Baliol was there, or anyone else."

"How would Shepherd have gotten the matchbook cover?"

"Higham or Derbyfield must have dropped it when Baliol was shot. Shepherd found it on the estate while Baliol was in the hospital. Probably kept it to himself so the job would go on longer. Baliol thinks Shepherd spotted Comrie as an easy mark for some strong-arm scam or a robbery, but Comrie was a tough little nut, resisted, and Shepherd shot him. The M–16 will prove it when we pick Shepherd up."

"Baliol has the motive to kill Comrie."

"The stock manipulation? He says he knew all about that, it was part of their private dealings. He says he told you that in the hospital."

"What's Shepherd's motive?"

"With his record? Robbery. Burglary. Extortion. He saw a millionaire, he tried to score, and it backfired. Guys like Shepherd, it's got to happen sooner or later."

Koons went out into the main headquarters room to set the wheels of justice on their inevitable course. Morgan watched Chief Walker swivel in his chair to look out at the river, and he knew what had to be. Whatever Roy Shepherd said would make no difference. Could make no difference. Roy Shepherd—ex-convict, bad-conduct soldier, thief, killer, criminal, and outlaw. Ralph Baliol —rich, powerful, respected. No prosecutor, no judge, no jury would believe Shepherd. Not without overriding evidence, and not for sure even then, and there were only two people who could know the truth. Morgan himself would be a strong witness against Roy Shepherd. *Did Mr. Baliol tell you he and Mr. Comrie had a business arrangement involving the stock manipulations? Yes, but I didn't believe him. Mrs. Wallman, would you say that Mr. Morgan dislikes Mr. Baliol intensely? For God's sake, Ford hates Ralph. And is it true that Mr. Morgan had a romantic interest in a former mistress of Mr. Baliol who herself has an interest in protecting Roy Shepherd? That's what I hear, yes. Mr. Morgan, did you or did you not see Roy Shepherd on the scene when Daniel Derbyfield was murdered? Well, I'm not sure—* The M–16 was Shepherd's. Mancuso would lie. Gerald Kirsch would lie. Kirsch had written the address down, but he would have given it to Ralph Baliol. Baliol had dropped it as they left Comrie's house that morning. Ralph Baliol never let much stand in his way, and left little to chance.

The chief swiveled in his chair. "Ralph Baliol killed this Comrie?"

"That's what Roy Shepherd says."

"And you believe him."

"I believe him."

"Just in case the matchbook cover didn't work, Baliol had a backup frame on Roy Shepherd."

"Cover front, rear and both flanks," Morgan said.

"And he murdered Roger Higham?"

"I'd say that too," Morgan said. "The sheriff and the courts won't."

The chief swiveled back and forth and contemplated his fingernails. "Sooner or later they'll get the town to replace me. They have the money and the power, and they'll find the reasons. Right now the town is against Baliol and the new management, but towns are people, and people have strong needs and weak memories when it comes to their security, a smooth life and all the comforts." The chief seemed to listen to the river outside his windows. "He was in 'Nam? This Roy Shepherd?"

Morgan nodded. "He didn't like it."

"I didn't like it too much myself. We live in a cynical society, Morgan. That's why we got into 'Nam in the first place, and why we couldn't beat them in the end. To fight people successfully you have to understand them. We had no way to understand them, so we never had a chance. I don't think this town or the redwoods have much chance either."

"But we can try."

"We can try," the chief agreed. "What do you do now?"

"Go back to Santa Barbara. I left a friend there."

"Well, drive carefully."

Morgan walked back to the inn. He checked out and loaded his bags and pistol into the rented BMW. He drove out of Gaul and turned south toward San Francisco and Santa Barbara.

28

From San Francisco, Morgan turned east on I–580, the connecting freeway that took him inland to I–5, then on to Highway 152 and U.S. 99, and finally to Fresno. He checked into a motel that had a bar and a restaurant, and looked up William Jennings Shepherd. There were few Shepherds listed among the Armenian names, and only one possible listing: Reverend W. Jennings Shepherd.

The address turned out to be in a shabby warehouse section. A small, rundown church that had once been proudly Methodist. The faded but still visible lettering on a wooden signboard announced its past glory above a crude new handmade sign: Jesus Loves You Gospel Meeting. The church was dark. Morgan walked around behind the church and saw light in a weatherworn house directly in back. A sign on a porch post announced the residence of Reverend W. Jennings Shepherd, "Everyone welcome." There was no doorbell. Morgan knocked.

A thin man with the broad face of a bulldog opened the door. He wore a loose pair of wool trousers held up by faded gray suspenders over an undershirt, and looked like he should have been behind a plow back in the rolling fields of southern England a century ago. When he saw Morgan he took a suit jacket from a coat rack inside the door and struggled into it. His large hands looked like pieces of leather that didn't belong to the rest of him.

"How can I help you, my friend?"

"Reverend Shepherd?"

"That I am. Step inside, Mr.—?"

"Langford Morgan."

"Mr. Morgan, step right on inside."

Morgan went into a small living room as neat as a showroom,

with old-fashioned antimacassars on the backs of every threadbare armchair and the single worn couch. A Victorian English parlor used only for guests—the local vicar, the lady of the manor, a visiting bishop—and in Fresno he, Langford Morgan, was a guest. As he took a seat on one of the armchairs a woman appeared from another room and looked at him with open resentment. Morgan knew without a word being said she was one of the Reverend Shepherd's daughters, Roy's sister. The resemblance was too strong to miss. She looked sourly from Morgan to her father.

"You want me to bring something?"

"Would you like some coffee, Mr. Morgan?" the Reverend William Jennings Shepherd inquired. "Beer? Water?"

"We got no beer," the woman said. "You done drank it and didn't go buy no more."

"I don't want anything, thank you," Morgan said.

The woman disappeared without another word. The reverend sat facing Morgan. "We all commit small sins, forget to buy more beer when we drink the last can. Is some small sin your problem, Mr. Morgan?"

"Roy is my problem, reverend."

"Roy?" The broad, sunken face was empty for a moment, and then reddened and darkened. "If you're any friend of my son's, you're not welcome here."

"I'm someone who wants to find him."

"Then you're at the last place in the world you ought to be. I will never allow him to come here until he cleans the filth from his heart and returns to God. Are you a cop?"

"No."

"Who else would want to find Roy Shepherd?"

"He has a woman with him. I need to find her."

"If she's a decent woman, I'm sorry for her. If not, she's found her level. My son is a thief, a murderer, a liar, an adulterer, a coward who abandoned his duty, and a godless defiler of all that is sacred and ordained."

"He never comes here?"

"Since they threw him out of the service of his country, he has come here once. He was being hunted by the authorities. I told him to repent, find Jesus, and submit to his punishment. He chose the path of evil instead. We have not spoken since, and I don't expect us to ever speak again in this world."

"Isn't that a little lacking in Christian kindness and charity, reverend?"

His thin shoulders grew rigid. With his broad face of bones and hollows he looked like some carved gargoyle on a medieval cathedral. A gargoyle about to pounce or take flight, a knot of rage somewhere hard inside. He sat that way for almost a minute, then abruptly sat back and his large leather hands shaped the air of the small room into a circle in front of him. His voice became an echo of a life in which no one had been kind.

"You haven't found the Lord, have you, Mr. Morgan? It isn't any kindness to indulge evil. Yes, my son is evil. He has no work for his hands, no loyalty to honor, no tradition to respect, and no God to guide him. I'd like to say he was ruined by that Satan of a female he married when he was still a boy, but I can't do that. He was evil long before her."

William Jennings Shepherd studied the hollow of air within the circle of his hands the way a Druid priest would have studied the sun rising over the altar stone of his sacred circle. "It is hard to imagine, but Roy Shepherd was born evil. Satan lives in us, Mr. Morgan, and Satan found him. All my other children are humble in the love of Jesus. Roy had the same chance, the same guidelines and rules. He was raised in the Lord and abandoned Him when he turned his arrogant and blasphemous back on the place given to him on this Earth. Jesus knows us better than we know ourselves. He has given us this world, and its natural laws, and our place within them. This whole country is sick. Women make love with women, men with men. There is no discipline in our lives. No respect for our elders, no honor of our leaders, no trust in God or what He has perfected on Earth."

The emaciated old man continued to look through the circle of his leather hands. He stared through the hands into some private distance. What he saw, Morgan didn't know, but whatever it was it wasn't in the small living room. In the night outside, the high voices of some women giggled as they passed. The Reverend Shepherd showed no reaction to the giggles or even consciousness of them, neither heard nor cared about the laughter of women in the night.

"Reverend Shepherd? Do you know where Roy lives? Where I can find him?"

William Jennings Shepherd slowly turned to stare at Morgan. He shook his head as if from a great distance, and returned to the vision inside the circle of his worn hands, as rigid in the chair as any stone gargoyle.

Morgan left. Outside, he walked to his rented BMW. It was a clear night in Northern California. Cool and quiet under a sky of distant stars hazy through the thin smog of the inland city.

In the morning, Morgan ran his ten miles through the streets of Fresno, had a slow breakfast in the motel restaurant, and watched the migrant workers picking in a field across the highway. Bent to the dirt, they moved slowly down the rows that reached out of sight.

After a fourth cup of coffee he checked out and drove the long way back to Santa Barbara. This was north again to Highway 152 and then west all the way to Highway 1, the coast highway through Carmel and Big Sur and south to rejoin 101 at San Luis Obispo.

The two-lane road at the edge of the continent is cut into the face of the mountains. Driving south, rocky slopes rise close to the left, and sheer cliffs plunge straight down to meet the sea on the right. There are few towns after Carmel and before San Luis, and the drops that appear to fall away into nothing force constant attention to the road. But there is an exhilaration in the wild beauty, in the white surf on the rocks below, and the suspension of time and the familiar.

As he drove Morgan's attention shifted from the road to the spectacular cliffs and the surf far below and back to the road, and he thought about Roger Higham and Roy Shepherd and Barbara Schoenhausen and the Reverend W. Jennings Shepherd and himself, Langford Morgan. He didn't know if all of them, from the narrow exaltation of Roger Higham going to his suicide, to the self-proclaimed reverend of the shabby and unknown splinter church, was tragic or comic. If he, Morgan, was tragic or comic. He drove on through the coast mountains and out past San Simeon with its tragi-comic monument to genius and delusion, and somewhere north of San Luis he decided that the answer depended on whether you thought with the mind or the heart.

He stopped for lunch overlooking the sea at Pismo Beach, and when he finally reached Santa Barbara he stopped at the sheriff's headquarters across from the county jail. It was evening visiting hours, the jail parking lot was full and the sheriff's parking lot nearly empty. The sheriff's office workers were on their way home, leaving only the night-shift deputies and a few detectives. Sergeant Koons was still there.

"Did you find Roy Shepherd?" Morgan asked.

"We will. Sooner or later."

"What happens to Barbara Schoenhausen when you do?"

Koons sat back in his chair. "That depends a lot on her. Look, take some advice, Morgan. Take it slow and let it rest. Pick up the pieces later."

"When you find them, will you let me know?"

"I'll think about it."

The coast highway route, and the stop to talk to Koons, had been enough to make it past 6:00 P.M. when he reached the cottage at San Ysidro Ranch. The bar was full and the cottage empty. He left his bags in the living room and went to the bar. Lareina would not be there. Neither would Rachel or Ralph Baliol or Roy Shepherd or Barbara Schoenhausen. But there were enough people enjoying their ease and privileges for Morgan to sit unnoticed with his rum cooler.

He hadn't eaten since lunch in Pismo Beach, and two coolers were enough to soothe his mind if not his heart. He ordered a third and went out to the entrance to use the telephone. He called Roy Shepherd's business number in Los Angeles, the number CIA man Hughes Bremner had said was only a message drop. Morgan wasn't sure whether he intended to leave a message or was simply groping for any way to reach Shepherd and Barbara Schoenhausen before Koons did.

A careful voice answered. "Roy Shepherd's office. Who can I say is calling, please?"

The careful voice and a click on the line told Morgan he was too late. The police were already at the mail and phone drop, and they were monitoring Roy Shepherd's phone. He hung up and went back to his table. The rum cooler was waiting for him. Sergeant Koons had wasted no time, and Morgan felt that the net was closing around him as much as around Roy Shepherd.

He drank half his rum cooler and went back to the telephone. This time his call was local. The brief silence at the other end was as much a part of Alfred Schoenhausen as his stiff voice and his accent. "Mr. Morgan? I would rather you did not tie up this phone."

Morgan heard the pain and the hope in Schoenhausen's voice. "Are you expecting a call from your wife? Did she call earlier? Where from? Did she say—"

"I do not know if I have a wife, Mr. Morgan. She did not call earlier, she was here. With the man. I am not expecting her to call, I am hoping she will call."

"They were there? What did they say they were—"

"If you wish to talk to me, Mr. Morgan, come to the house."

Schoenhausen hung up.

In Hope Ranch, behind its gates that stood open in the early night, the imitation English country manor had light upstairs and in two downstairs windows. The driveway was dark and deserted, and the front door with the elegant leaded glass was closed. No one answered Morgan's rings but the door was unlocked.

The polished pale wood of the entry hall glowed in darkness. Light from an open doorway on the left reflected from the fan-shaped transom and high windows. The delicate maple stairs up to the second floor curved in and out of shadow. Morgan's footsteps echoed from the parquet floor as he walked to the open doorway. It was the family room where he had talked to Alfred Schoenhausen earlier.

"Come in, Mr. Morgan. I could have missed her call had I left the room."

Schoenhausen sat in his large leather armchair. A bottle of Glenlivet scotch whiskey stood on the table beside his chair. The old-fashioned glass in his hand was half-full of the deep amber whiskey and ice. "We Germans never developed a fine whiskey or great brandy. Only beer and white wine. My ancestors were always traveling abroad for the finer things, importing scotch whiskey and cognac for their cellars."

Schoenhausen held out a second glass of the single malt. Morgan took it. There were no other chairs for adults, and the heavy couch faced the television set the same as the armchair. Morgan sat on the floor with his back against the television cabinet where he could see Schoenhausen.

"When were they here?"

Schoenhausen looked toward an old grandfather clock in the far corner. "Two, perhaps three hours ago. She talked for a long time to the children. The man waited here with me. It was unpleasant."

"She talked to the children? She didn't take them?"

"No."

"Did she try to take them? Did you stop her?"

"She spoke to them and then she left without them."

"That means they know the police are after Roy Shepherd."

"He is the man you spoke of earlier, this Roy Shepherd? The man who might have kidnapped my wife for Ralph Baliol? But who did not have to kidnap her, did he? She went with him of her own free will, as you Americans say." He drank the fine whiskey and closed his eyes to savor the smooth texture, the deep smoke of the flavor. He couldn't change the curve and set of his life even now. A reflex, the savoring of the good whiskey, unaware of what he was doing. "He is a criminal. Crude and illiterate. Uncouth, loud, and ill-mannered. What can he ever be beyond what he is? A man without past or future. Without order. An outlaw, Mr. Morgan."

Schoenhausen emptied his glass. Morgan drank. A wonderful whiskey, heat without a trace of flame that could burn inside. In the complete silence of the large house they could have been two ghosts, insubstantial wraiths with no connection to the solid world of time and space outside the walls and windows.

"Do you think she will call, Mr. Morgan?"

"No."

Schoenhausen turned his glass of whiskey around and around in his hands. Morgan became aware of the faint whining of a child's voice, and the quieter, softer sound of an adult voice being calm and soothing. One of the children and the housekeeper somewhere upstairs.

"What did she tell you when you spoke with her earlier, Mr. Morgan? About my family and myself? About our marriage?"

"I don't think that's for me to talk about."

Water ran in a sink upstairs. Morgan heard the clink of a glass. A glass of water for a sleepless child.

"If you hadn't called me, Mr. Morgan, I would have called you."

"Why?"

"Because when my wife left, I asked her why she had found it necessary to find another man, to leave the life she had with me? Why the first man, Baliol, and why now this man? She said I must talk to you, that your stories were the same. What did she mean? Have you left a wife for another woman, Mr. Morgan?"

Morgan wasn't sure what Barbara Schoenhausen had meant, except it would not be about his marriages. "I don't know what she meant, but the way she talked about your marriage has a lot to do with the way you talk about her. When you talk about her to other people, you call her your wife, never Barbara. When she said her story and mine were the same, you interpreted her words in the same way you interpret her leaving. Narrow and literal, without nuances. She left you for another man, so I must have left a wife for another woman."

"Does what she has done require any interpretation?" Schoenhausen said. "She left her marriage for another man. What is there to interpret?"

"When we talked she said that when your children were born you simply assumed the boy would be Alfred Erich Helmuth, and the girl would be Helga to honor your mother. It was what the Schoenhausens did. No beards for Schoenhausens, no tilting at windmills. No improper clothes for a Schoenhausen wife. The clothes you bought her were like the clothes your family sent her for Christmas and her birthdays: good quality, reserved, proper for a wife and mother. Not clothes she would have chosen for herself if she'd ever thought about it."

The glass stopped its constant circles in Schoenhausen's hands. "Clothes? She spoke of clothes? What are clothes?" The glass began its endless journey again. "A first son is named to honor his father and closest male relatives, it is always so. My mother suffered much to preserve the family. The names in my family have a status, a thousand years of history. Did she want to name our son 'Duane' or 'Mambo'? Our daughter 'Laverne' or 'Traci'?"

"Did you talk to her about it?"

"Of course I did! We discussed it thoroughly. Some things must be done in a family. There would be more children. I wanted another son."

"She could name the next son?"

"We would have discussed it!" He waved his arm, splashed whiskey. "Windmills? Beards? Long hair? That is all Helmuth. Why would she think so much of Helmuth? Helmuth failed his duty, abandoned his place. In the end, he was nothing."

"I think she saw in Helmuth what she would want to see in herself, and hoped to see in you."

"What is that?"

"An individual."

Alfred Schoenhausen stopped turning the whiskey glass in his hands. He opened his mouth but he didn't speak, and sat looking past Morgan.

Morgan said, "She also told me my ex-wife was alone with herself, with who she is and what she wants. She said the same of you. She said you came here, became a citizen, made money, married, fathered children, but that none of that was really you. Your wife was American, your children were American, but you weren't American. You're *an* American, but you're not American. You don't live here. You live with Bismarck, Goethe, Kleist, and Barbarrosa. Mrs. Alfred Schoenhausen, your wife, was in your mind sometimes, but Barbara Allison never was."

Morgan waited for Schoenhausen to speak, move, do something. Schoenhausen did nothing. The glass remained motionless in his hands. He remained motionless in the big leather armchair. His chair. Upstairs a child was crying, and the gentle voice of the housekeeper began to sing. A German song. Schoenhausen turned his head to listen. He nodded his head in time with the ancient lullaby. He continued to listen until the song and the crying stopped in the silent house. Then he nodded abruptly, and took a long drink of the fine whiskey.

"I will take them back with me. To Germany."

"She could still call."

"She will not."

"They're her children too. She might not want them to go to Germany."

The glass began its circling again. "My wife is dead, Mr. Morgan."

"Dead?"

"As dead as my brother whom she admired so much."

"Are you going to turn the mirrors to the wall?"

But Alfred Schoenhausen wasn't listening. He was wrapped in anger, an anger that had come to his rescue. "I will leave this country where they allow criminals to wander the streets. A country without history or duty. The Schoenhausens are part of history and they know their duty. They know who and what they are and always will be. They will go on forever."

"In the castle."

"Yes, in the castle." He stood up. "I will show you out, Mr. Morgan. I thank you for coming. It has helped me to know what I must do." Upstairs a child was crying again. "Goodnight, Mr. Morgan. I must go to my children."

"They said nothing about where they were going? Barbara and Roy Shepherd?"

"Somewhere out of the country is what seemed to be on the criminal's mind. Somewhere he knew 'where the sun shines all day on rivers and mountains and there ain't no cops,' I believe is the phrase he used. They had some unfinished business, and then they had to 'deedy mow to the big rock candy mountains.' Is that some kind of actual language, Mr. Morgan?" Schoenhausen's anger and pain had finally overflowed into a bitter scorn for the uncouth Roy Shepherd.

"Di di mau, to leave quickly," Morgan said. "It's from Vietnam."

And he went quickly out to his car.

29

The small pedestrian door beside the electronic gates of Ralph Baliol's Montecito estate stood open in the night. The blacktop driveway, a silver gray by the light of an early moon, curved silent ahead through the dark and ragged second-growth trees and heavy brush.

As he walked up the drive Morgan listened the way he had listened as he walked behind the shadow of the point man on Daniel Boone operations into Cambodia over twenty years ago. The innocent and eager years. The naive and idealist years. The stupid damn fool years. The blind years and the cynical years.

The enormous bulk of the Italian *palazzo* came into view like a massive darker shadow in the moonlight. The only human light was high and far to the right in three windows of the servants' wing. Everything else was black. Morgan moved up the long curve of the drive past the terraces and on into the shadow of the hulking building. He had spent too much of his life moving through blackness. So much human folly was done at night, so much human betrayal occurred in the night shadows where only the few knew what had happened, and what more would happen as a result.

He reached the deeper dark between the *palazzo* and the long garage with its rows of open doors. The limousine and the Ferrari were both there. Gerald Kirsch's Toyota was gone, and Massimo Mancuso lay face down on the driveway in a shaft of moonlight at the rear corner of the mansion. In his chauffeur's uniform, he was sprawled in blood. His pistol was beside his outflung hand.

Morgan kneeled to feel the fallen man's wrist and throat. He was still warm, but there was no pulse. Morgan stood, took out his little Czech Vz70, and moved softly ahead around the dark building. The fence around the pool stretched away toward the wall of trees behind the mansion. The french doors were open. Faint light came from one pair of ground floor windows through heavy drawn drapes. Ralph Baliol's den.

Inside the darkened house, Morgan stepped quietly along the hall toward the line of light under the den door. The door opened, and Roy Shepherd came out to stand in front of Morgan with his M–16.

"She said it had to be you, Charlie. Come on in and join the party."

A wide strip of blood-soaked cloth was bound high and tight around Shepherd's left arm. Morgan slid his pistol back into its holster. Shepherd lowered the M–16, waited for Morgan to walk past him into the den, and followed him in.

Ralph Baliol sat behind his big mahogany desk. A stubby Colt revolver lay on the desk, out of his reach among scattered papers. Some of the papers had fallen to the floor. No one paid any attention to them. Baliol's face was contorted in a bizarre replica of the snarls of the animal heads mounted on his walls between his racks of guns. There was a fury in his face where he sat in the desk chair, both hands carefully flat on the legs of his pale chino trousers. A casual blue sport shirt open on his chest hair and bandages, and a khaki hunting vest. At-home clothes, worn by a man relaxed and secure behind his walls and alarms.

Barbara Schoenhausen sat in an armchair with a silenced army-issue Beretta automatic held in both hands on the lap of her dirty jeans. It would be Shepherd's automatic. The one he'd used to shoot Dan Derbyfield outside Anne Neville's house what seemed like weeks ago.

Barbara looked at Morgan. "You must have talked to Alfred?"

"Half an hour ago," Morgan said.

"How is he holding up?"

"He says his wife is dead."

She nodded. "That's what he needs to feel. It'll help him, make it easier for him to find an acceptable explanation."

Her short ebony hair was tangled and unwashed. The shine was gone, and the grooming. She wore the same designer jeans, stained and dirty now, and a grimy and wrinkled blue workshirt. Clothes worn for days, slept in at night, and worn again all day the next day. The oversize leather windbreaker over everything else, and dirty running shoes at least a size too large.

"He says he's going back to Germany," Morgan said.

"The children too?"

"That's what I understood."

She sat in the chair, the big pistol pointing at the floor. Roy Shepherd had said and done nothing since he and Morgan had come into the den, but there was a shared pain in his eyes above the armor of the perpetual smile he showed to the world, and a sadness and resignation that reached out to comfort her without words. His grease-stained trousers and workshirt were a size too small. Clothes bought in secondhand stores along with his worn work boots. He looked like a thousand factory hands who lived in their work clothes. Only the smile and the cowboy hat remained of the Cadillac cowboy.

"Where else could they go?" Morgan said. "Who else do they have to go with?"

"Perhaps he'll be a better father than he has been, back there where he belongs. At least it's going to be an adventure for them."

"You'll give them up? Like that?"

"I don't really think we can take them with us now."

Ralph Baliol looked toward her too, but what was in his eyes wasn't sad and it wasn't shared. It was the awareness of a trapped animal thinking only of finding a route and opportunity of escape. Baliol had realized she was not going back to Schoenhausen. He had misjudged her. She wasn't what he had been so sure she was, or if she had been she no longer was, and he could not be sure he knew anymore what she would do.

Baliol said, "If you'd told me you'd walk out on your husband, give up your children, I'd never have broken it off between us, Barbara. It's not too late."

"You're not worth giving up a pet rat for."

"And the two-bit hired cowboy is?"

Roy Shepherd said, "Stuff that in your nose, Charlie."

"He's a psychopath, Barbara," Baliol said. "A killer and a loser. He doesn't have a chance. Not a prayer. They're going to send him away forever if they don't gas him. Then where the hell are you?"

"They got to catch me first, honcho," Shepherd said, "and that's not gonna do you a whole lot of good right this minute, you know what I mean? I mean, here we are and there you are. The honcho with all the big lies."

Morgan saw a vague fear rise to meet the fury boiling inside

Ralph Baliol. An increased, violent rage at the contempt in Shepherd's voice, and a fear he would never really believe in. He was Ralph Baliol. He was better and stronger and the rage, the belief and necessity that he could never feel fear, might make the pistol on his desk seem closer than it was.

"He won't do you any good dead, Shepherd," Morgan said.

"He ain't gonna do me much good alive, Charlie. We got a real full general over there, you know that. The generals they never do anyone any good except themselves. Not even the poor sons of bitches all gung-ho to go down for 'em like old Mancuso out there."

"What happened to Mancuso?"

Shepherd gestured with his free arm, the one with the strip of bandage. "We were making a fast approach to talk to that son of a bitch over there, and the poor bastard came at us out of the dead zone around the corner of the fucking house. He came full-gear and blasting; I took a ten-cent piece, didn't have time to hold a meeting. The whole *bushido* shit, Charlie, you know? For lord, honor, and duty."

Morgan said. "Self-defense, the same as Dan Derbyfield. Mancuso didn't have the right to shoot you even if you were trespassing."

"That's pushing it pretty hard, Charlie. Anyway, we still got the nice little frame my cute-ass ex-honcho in the big exec chair cooked up."

"I cooked up nothing, Shepherd."

"We can beat Baliol's lies," Morgan said. "I'll testify. Barbara can testify. We'll find evidence he was there. Chief Walker doesn't believe him, and Koons is a good cop. We can beat—"

"Aw, fuck it, Charlie. With my record? You're not a bad old grunt, but life's too fucking short to sit in a goddamn cage. I mean, man, with my record I'd rot inside just for being with the bastard when he wasted his buddy. No way I'm ever going back inside. All those half-a-brain chickenshit yardbirds in the joint think they're colonels, or generals, or Zulu chiefs."

"Think of Barbara, for Christ's sake."

"He is thinking of me, Ford. I knew it wasn't going to be easy, a free ride over the rainbow. I didn't know it would get to be so hard so soon, but thanks to Ralph that's the way it's coming out. I have a lot to learn, and not a lot of time to learn it, and I can't do it alone."

"You an' me all the way, right, *mama san?*" Shepherd grinned.

There was a sense of touching across the distance between them. Morgan watched them, but Ralph Baliol continued to watch the M–16 Shepherd held loosely in one hand. If he heard anything that was being said, he gave no indication, too busy calculating how fast he could reach his pistol on the desk against the time needed for Shepherd to get both hands on the assault rifle, raise and fire. It occupied his whole attention, his whole mind and self.

Shepherd snorted in disgust. "Look at the asshole, Charlie. They never stop figuring the goddamn angles and the odds. You ever notice that?"

Morgan said, "If you knew that, why didn't you suspect a trick when he wanted you to lend him that M–16? When he used it to kill Comrie?"

"Never said I was smart. The man was paying me, I did the job."

Baliol said, "You know, Shepherd, it's not exactly smart to be here at all. For you or the lady. I doubt that Morgan came alone. Isn't that right, Morgan? Tell them the sheriff is outside right now."

"Jesus," Shepherd said. "Tricks!" He's trying fucking goddamn tricks. He don't even know when he's not foolin' anyone anymore. See, Charlie? Hell, you can't spend your whole fucking life looking for all the tricks they try to pull on you, now can you?"

Barbara Schoenhausen said, "Not a very smart trick, that one, Ralph. Ford didn't come here to save you. He's not on your side. He doesn't really know what side he's on, but he knows it's not yours."

"I came to stop you before it was too late," Morgan said. "Baliol's right, Shepherd hasn't got a chance. If he doesn't give himself up right now, he's doomed. They'll hunt him down, and you too if you stay with him."

"You came here for *me*, Ford. For your illusion of you and me and happy ever after. Your last chance to hide. All I am is your final longing to have everything be the way they told you it was. They told us both how it was supposed to be, but they were lying. They never believed it themselves. The lies are for us, not for them." She looked up and across the desk at Ralph Baliol. "His lies."

She raised the big automatic in both hands, neither smiling nor scowling, and shot Ralph Baliol four times where he sat in the high-backed chair behind the big mahogany-and-leather desk. Blood spurted from his chest and throat. He screamed once, and his eyes turned up and went blank. The chair crashed into the windows behind the desk. Smashed glass flew into the night and across the room. The echoes of the four short, sharp explosions of the silenced pistol reverberated like the crack of a whip as his body slumped grotesque against the arms of the chair, and dripped blood onto the Navaho rug under his desk.

The sharp echoes faded into silence in the room. Roy Shepherd said, "You made a true believer out of him, lady of mine, but you didn't have to. I'd have handled him."

"It wasn't for you, Charlie, it was for me."

"Then that's okay."

Shepherd never looked at Ralph Baliol again. He crossed to the door and listened. There was no sound in the house. He went out. His light footsteps carried back from the hall and then from the concrete outside in the moonlight. He moved around the house in the night. Reconnoitering the jungle and the enemy. In the den Barbara Schoenhausen still stared at the body of Ralph Baliol slumped in his desk chair.

"What does it accomplish?" Morgan said.

"Don't make the mistake of thinking only results are important, Ford."

When Roy Shepherd returned he held the M–16 and looked from her to Morgan and back to her.

She said, "He won't help them, Roy."

"Whatever you say, *mama san.* It's time to *di di mau* out of here."

Morgan said, "Good luck. To both of you."

Shepherd smiled. "We sure gonna need it, Charlie. Me and *mama san* there, we're a gypsy operation from here on in."

"If anyone asks," Barbara Schoenhausen said, "tell them I went exploring."

Her face was flushed. Her black eyes shone with excitement. Roy took her hand and they walked out the door unhurried and together. Sooner or later, wherever they went and whatever they did, someone would find them, they knew that. Later would be better, but not better enough to be nervous over, to hurry according to the time frame of other people. A walk in the sun, and their footsteps echoed along the hall and out and away until Morgan could no longer hear them.

He listened for a long time alone in the room with Ralph Baliol's body. There was no sound of a car starting. They would, of course, have a different car. Neither her dark blue 450SL, nor the battered old white Caddy with the flamboyant horns that was Roy Shepherd's pride and joy. You give to get, Charlie, and nothing lasts forever.

Morgan finally went to Ralph Baliol in the chair and looked for a pulse or any other sign of life. There was none. He sat down again, alone with the racks of guns, the mounted heads, and the bloody body. No one came, and nothing moved out in the night except the silver path of the moon as it passed across the sky. Whatever the cook and maids were doing in the servants' wing, they had either not heard the small, silenced shots, or hadn't been concerned enough to investigate. He didn't call the sheriff, or anyone else. The servants or the gardeners or Gerald Kirsch would find Ralph Baliol in the morning.

Lareina sat on the deck of the San Ysidro Ranch cottage with a rum cooler she had made herself, the makings inside on the kitchen counter. Her cocktail dress was as silver as the moonlight against her light brown hair. Morgan made a cooler for himself, and went out to sit beside her.

"Beverly Hills?" he said. "The dress?"

"Of course, *yanqui*. You think I am wait here for you with the candle in the window? You like the dress? It cost you very much money."

"I couldn't think of a better way to spend money."

"So? We can go to New York? Or maybe we go home."

An unusual chill filled the September night air. Morgan drank, aware of Lareina and the tight silver dress but his mind still with Barbara Schoenhausen somewhere out there. A hundred miles away by now, perhaps a thousand in the miracle of the jet age. He saw the exhilaration on her face, the excitement. Her children would miss her, they would be sad and angry, but they would survive and grow up. Children are less fragile than we sometimes think. They would be fine, would have their adventure, would go exploring, would learn that nothing was certain or unchangeable.

"Tonight I let two murderers escape without calling the police. A woman I thought I was in love with, and a man not all that much different from me. I want them to have a chance to run and hide and never be found. But they'll be found, of course. In Mexico or

Europe or Vietnam or wherever they go, and they'll be killed. But for now they're free and even happy."

"Who was murdered?"

"A man named Ralph Baliol. A man—"

"The man you did not like."

"Yes."

"And the woman?"

"Barbara Schoenhausen. The woman I went up north to look for. You know all about who she is too, Reina?"

"Of course. I have talked to Rachel, she has told me."

"*She* shot Baliol, Reina. In cold blood. When I met her the only word I could think to put on her was *soft*. She was so soft. She still is soft."

"Soft is a male word, my *yanqui*. Soft is a male idea of a woman. What you want, your fantasy. Perhaps she is soft, this Barbara of yours, but female soft, not male. A woman does not call another woman soft, or if she does it does not mean the same thing a man means."

Morgan swore, "Damn it, Reina, she's soft. And he's an outlaw. A thief and a killer. He's irrational and doomed and he'll take her down with him."

"Male words, poor Ford. Male values in a male world. For a woman, soft can mean very strong. When it is important inside, *yanqui*, we women do not care about male values."

She reached to touch his leg, comforting, and stood up. She took his glass and went into the cottage, her tight silver dress catching the moonlight as it moved like skin. He wondered where Barbara Schoenhausen was by now, where they were? Mexico? Or on some jet flying through a new day high above a new continent. A continent of the mind he had wanted to fly to with her. A world of their own where the last twenty-plus years would have been miraculously wiped clean. Male fantasy, or just fantasy?

Lareina handed him a fresh rum cooler. She touched his face with her hand cold from the glass. She kept the hand there for some time while her eyes searched his face and she smiled. Then she sat again beside him, the moonlight reflecting from both her dress and her glass.

"She shot Baliol four times," Morgan said. "Blew him apart. When they left she was exhilarated. Her face was flushed like a teenager's. So was his. When I sit here and see them in my mind, what I hear is 'Free at last, Great God Almighty, free at last.' "

Lareina looked up at the night sky. She frowned. "That much *libertad*, I think, is not so good."

"Not good? Why not good?"

"I want my father to have always his *finca*. I want the husband I will marry some day to have a *finca* of his own so I will have always my *finca*.''

She drained her drink long and slow, enjoying it in the night. As she moved in the chair the silver dress flashed like another shaft of light from the moon that had dropped lower in the sky. She looked into her empty glass as if trying to decide whether she wanted another drink or not.

Morgan said, "Roy Shepherd is only another Ralph Baliol in a different guise. The reverse of the coin. The minor key. The descant to Baliol's tune."

"You do not get it, my poor Ford. The man does not matter. It is the choice that matters. Her choice, *sí, yanqui?* That she has made the choice." She bent and kissed his forehead. "Now I make the choice. I go to bed. Tomorrow, I think, I go back to Costa Rica."

Morgan sat alone on the cold deck. Across the horizon the shadowy trees and the dark rooftops sloped down to the sea and the lights of the oil platforms out in the channel. He drank, and Barbara Schoenhausen walked through his mind the way she had come into the cocktail lounge that first day, soft and controlled and vulnerable, and as she had left Ralph Baliol's den only hours ago, flushed with excitement and her Cadillac cowboy at her side. Between the images he saw his house on the hill in Costa Rica with the lights of San José spread below. It was a dark hill above an empty city.

As both Barbara Schoenhausens walked out of his mind, that dark hill in Costa Rica and the memory of anger went with them. The memory of a violent anger, and on the deck overlooking the shadowy trees, the lights of the oil rigs far out on the ocean, and the distant glow of Santa Barbara itself, he knew that the unfinished business he'd sensed as he drank the *guaro* around the campfire in the Cordillera had not been with Rachel but with his forgotten anger.

Morgan looked at his watch. Not yet midnight.

He went in to the telephone in the dark living room and dialed Jenny Stoke's number in Gaul. "Did I wake you?"

"Of course you woke me. What's wrong, Ford?"

"Nothing's wrong. Nothing at all. In fact, everything is probably a lot better. Ralph Baliol's dead."

He heard her breathing at the other end of the line in the small house above the river in the other half of Gaul. "I guess that is good news."

Morgan said. "Would ten million dollars help to buy the company back?"

"It would help get their attention. Seed money for a loan. Or it would buy a lot of nails, ink, and legislators. Is that all you have?"

"Fifteen then. I was planning to save some for us. Security."

"There isn't any security."

"I'll be up tomorrow."

"You can tell me your life story."

"It's not important anymore," Langford Morgan said.